Too Beautiful For You

Too Beautiful
For You

Rod Liddle

C

Century · London

Published by Century in 2003

1 3 5 7 9 10 8 6 4 2

Copyright © Rod Liddle 2003

Author has asserted his right under the Copyright, Designs and Patents Act, 1988 to be identified as the author of this work.

This novel is a work of fiction. Names and characters are the product of the author's imagination and any resemblance to actual persons, living or dead, is entirely coincidental

The author and publisher have made all reasonable efforts to contact copyright holders for permission and apologise for any omissions or errors in the form of credits given. Corrections may be made to future printings.

First published in the United Kingdom in 2003 by Century
The Random House Group Limited
20 Vauxhall Bridge Road, London SW1V 2SA

Random House Australia (Pty) Limited
20 Alfred Street, Milsons Point, Sydney,
New South Wales 2061, Australia

Random House New Zealand Limited
18 Poland Road, Glenfield
Auckland 10, New Zealand

Random House South Africa (Pty) Limited
Endulini, 5a Jubilee Road, Parktown 2193, South Africa

The Random House Group Limited Reg. No. 954009

www.randomhouse.co.uk

A CIP catalogue record for this book is available from the British Library

Papers used by Random House are natural, recyclable products made from wood grown in sustainable forests. The manufacturing processes conform to the environmental regulations of the country of origin

ISBN 1 8441 3378 8

Typeset by SX Composing DTP, Rayleigh, Essex
Printed and bound in Great Britain by
Mackays of Chatham plc, Chatham, Kent

To Rachel, Tyler and the Wild dog

Contents

The Window

Marian sits, hunched with loathing, over her computer terminal as the clock on the wall hits thirteen. Most of the rest of her colleagues – those working today – are out; in pubs and wine bars and dinky sandwich stations, venting grievances over glasses of New World Chardonnay and warm goat's cheese salads. Marian would very much like to be out with them; her stomach is rumbling and she has deep, festering grievances to be divulged along with the best of them. But instead, she must sit and wait for a workman to come and mend one of the large windows in the middle of the office, the ancient metal frame of which will not close properly and which has been wedged into place with a copy of the 1997 *International Who's Who*, as a makeshift, temporary measure.

This waiting is a task with no official demarcation and everybody – save for maybe one or two of the middle managers – possesses the intellectual capacity to do it. But Bavins, who on her first day here she mistook for an escaped mental patient, a deeply troubled soul who had, perhaps, wandered inside in search of refuge but who was, in fact, everybody's boss, nervily asked if Marian would mind doing it and left before she could demur.

So she sits there, her stomach grumbling with anger, the Anger of the Just, as the loudspeaker reports the deaths of 165 people in Zurich, where a plane has just crashed into some flats. Hearing this news, and noticing the palpable excitement amongst her colleagues, she wonders when it was that the anger took hold and made the rest of the world, outside this building, seem smaller and of markedly less consequence. She hears people gibbering about Osama and al-Qaeda and she tries to think of the awful fireball approaching and the panic and the noise and the pyrolytic reek of burning aviation fuel and those microseconds of blind terror and all she can concentrate on is the window repairman with his bag of tools and triplicate dockets to sign.

When she first started work here she was eager to be a part of everything and, although people told her to watch out, it's a poisonous atmosphere, like Mercury, and full of pettiness, rancour and contumely, she dived in with delight. Now, when she arrives for work each morning and leaves the sluggish lift at the eighth floor, she sometimes loses her footing on the bile and gall which seep out from every office doorway.

Eight floors down, Dempsey hunches over his computer terminal and considers which would be the best way of killing himself. By best, he means a method which would allow at least seven people to stop him, including his girlfriend, his former girlfriend, Lucy. Last night he arrived home at, what, three, four? After being told again that it was all over between them – a long, tearful session which ended in him being sick in the driveway of his own home and later crying for long anguished hours on his wife's shoulder. So he looks pretty wrecked now and a numbness has descended and despite all those poor people killed in the Garuda jumbo, which is what really should be concerning him

— that and the fact that those nutters seem to have done it again, and what will happen *now*? — all he can think of is new and preferably decisive ways to persuade Lucy that this thing between them, whatever it is, can, you know, work.

Or at least be prolonged.

And sort of killing himself is what he comes up with, feeling as raw and woebegone and hungover and unshaven as he does at this moment and seeing pictures of charred remains being separated from blackened concrete, up there on the television monitor, that cold Swiss morning.

You think it would be a big deal, killing himself for Lucy? It would be no great sacrifice really, he thinks, full of self-disgust and self pity, tapping the keys on his computer to bring up the revised casualty figures and the latest apocalyptic speculations. He has been, for some years now, expedient in a professional sense. His job, despite the impressive (but meaningless) grade, is an island bypassed by all the currents of work – and indeed precisely designed to be such. His stock, before he started seeing Lucy, was pretty low. But Lucy acted as a sort of surrogate promotion; you could see it in the eyes of their colleagues when they were spotted out together . . . people began almost to take him seriously again. Or semi-seriously, at least. The man who's fucking Lucy Dow! But now Lucy has stopped seeing him eleven times in the last two months, each time more definitely than the time before, and Dempsey can't take it any more, he has used up every ounce of persuasiveness, every trick in the book, to keep them together and he is looking ragged and defeated and absurd. Killing himself, hell, he thinks, it would be a mercy.

★

Everybody takes Marian seriously, it is part of the democratic nature of the place that secretaries must be afforded respect equal to – what are they called these days? – line managers. So when editorial decisions are taken people ask her for her opinion and everybody goes silent whilst she explains and then it's yup, thanks for your help, Marian, I think that's a valuable contribution. In a very real sense. She was surprised and thrilled by this at first. Nowadays, though, it's different. Nowadays she says uh, sorry, I'm really not up to speed on that particular issue or some other equally lame excuse because she hates the quality of the silence as they listen to her thoughts and the nodding heads and the encouraging smiles and the yup, thanks for your help, Marian.

But at first she was thrilled, she was eager to be a part of everything these people did and was astonished they opened their world so quickly for her. There was a vibrant social life to the office and Marian yearned to be a part of that, too; something all too easily accomplished, as it turned out.

Marian picks up the phone and dials Building Services. 'Hello. Yes. You're meant to be sending somebody to fix one of our windows. Room 8106. Yes, a *window*. I rang this morning. Twice.'

After a moment or two a woman's voice asks for a reference number. Marian finds it on her memo pad and reads it down the line trying to convey, in the simple recitation of numerals and letters, a sense of unrestrained hatred. And there is a pause again and the woman's voice says the engineer should have been with you ages ago, he was dispatched one and a half hours previously. Marian keeps her voice low and level and with an aftertaste of prussic acid. There's nobody here, nobody to fix the window, send somebody else. Now.

Marian wonders if the engineer is lost in this city of a building, with its slums and suburbs and dark alleyways. Take a wrong turning and you find yourself adrift in one of the service or technology ghettos, a labyrinth of tiny rooms and walled-off corridors, stuffed with mysterious devices, flickering dials and vast computer terminals; or maybe you end up on a whole floor which has been gutted to create a vast open plan office and you stand there wondering if you're in the same building as the one you know. On night shifts Marian will sometimes wander off down these wide, shabby arterial corridors, with their dismal, framed photographs of celebrities grinning back from the grave. She invariably becomes lost and disoriented and absurdly anxious, agoraphobic in the huge building.

The woman tells her she will re-contact the engineer and put him right. Marian hangs up. Around her, people are jabbering excitedly about the jumbo jet and speculating about the Al-Qaeda denial and then talking about the dead, all those poor dead people, and are any of them British? – and Marian has only her window to worry about, which makes her feel petty and expendable. She did not always feel like this. Once she had harboured hopes of a promotion, of a job where her colleagues listened to her because if they didn't she'd bawl them out and make them feel terrible, not because it is a democratic office where all views count and must be heard, even those of the fucking secretary.

But promotion now is unlikely, if not untenable; partly because her drive has gone and partly because of

Julian's personal involvement with her and the consequent possibilities of conflict of interest.

She wanders over to the faulty window and looks out across the blowsy haze of west London. She sees a jet approaching Heathrow almost level, it seems, with her line of vision and she wonders if it will bank and turn and head for the building and that maybe this is the day, Osama or not, when all planes plough into crowded city centres and, really, just how bad a thing would that be? One of the young producers, a sweet girl with a semi-bob, still in a post-Benenden thrall with the world, touches her on the shoulder.

'Maid Marian . . . I'm off for lunch. Can I bring you back a sandwich or anything?'

Marian turns away from the window. 'No, thanks, Cassie. I'm going out too, as soon as this useless bastard turns up to fix the window. If there's anyone left to go out with.'

'Fuck; isn't he here yet?' She looks at the window. 'Well, I think Julian's in Needles with Chloe and some of the others,' she adds, either with grotesque naïveté or out of spite. Marian fixes her pretty levelly.

'No kidding? Well I'll do my best to avoid Needles, then,' she says, and turns away, busying herself with a work schedule document lying previously untouched in her in-tray.

Cassie half smiles and walks back to her screen, slightly affronted, and abstractedly scans the latest news wires. She thinks Marian is a difficult nut to crack and doesn't quite know how to act with the woman, whether you should mention Julian or not at all – their fling, or whatever it was, never made, you know, official.

The first thing Marian did when she arrived at the

building was look for a flat in the same part of London as everybody else, a sort of skewed triangle centred on Crouch End. But she couldn't afford it, the flats she was shown were just like that place they kept Terry Waite all those years, so she headed south and down-market and now has a one bed in Bermondsey, a good flat with views down over the Blue and the river, with the City a haze in the middle distance. The first time Julian visited her there, after a leaving party for an embittered drunk who'd finally accepted early retirement, they fucked against the sash window in her front room, illuminated by the fierce glare from the beautiful football ground four hundred yards away. She worried the window would burst and gripped hold of the curtains and wrapped her legs around Julian's waist in this wonderful drunk-fuck she has never since recaptured. People had watched them leave together that evening; there were dropped jaws and raised eyebrows. It was brazen and conspicuous and, she thought, a thrill.

He hardly ever visits Bermondsey now.

Dempsey, meanwhile, is so pissed he can hardly stand. He found half a bottle of Stolichnaya in his drawer and drank it as the casualty estimates rose and rose and then dropped and finally settled at 211. He drank so that he could face Lucy again and having drunk pushed his way into her cubicle, the tears beginning to form even before he slurred his first words.

'Talk to me, Lucy. At least talk to me . . .'

Lucy swivels around, appalled. 'For Christ's sake Martin, get *out* of here. This is so humiliating.'

And, in fact, it *is* quite humiliating. An open-plan office of perhaps one hundred and fifty people, the reporters quartered in little lean-to cubicles with their backs to the main newsdesk. What Martin and Lucy's colleagues will see, indeed *are* seeing, is a middle-aged man on his knees, on his *knees*, behind some moppety girl tap-tap-tapping away on her computer, apparently (although clearly, in reality, not) oblivious to his presence.

'Please, Lucy,' he whines, 'let me buy you lunch. Just *lunch*. Just let me talk to you . . .'

She spins around on her chair. 'Have you *seen* what's happened?'

He looks at the monitor. Those poor Swiss people, that cold morning.

'Have you seen?' she repeats. Her long blonde hair swings across her face when she gets angry, those big fuck-off grey eyes wide and deep and cold. She is too beautiful for him, he wonders how it ever could have happened between them. No matter how profound we believe our relationships to be, he thinks, the balance of power will always reside with the truly beautiful.

She is looking at him now.

'I'm trying to work. People are laughing at us, Martin; they are laughing. It has become ludicrous. Let me work, please. Go back to your wife.'

Oh dear, and he starts crying properly now and she's hot with shame and embarrassment. What on earth possessed me, she thinks, please let this stop now.

There has been an audible lessening of computer activity in the surrounding area as Martin and Lucy's colleagues strain to hear this compelling conversation a little better.

She stares fixedly at the screen and wonders if maybe she should go for lunch with him just to stop this appalling scene, but then she sees the same thing happening again and she cannot bear the thought. She closes her eyes and looks down at the worn grey corporate carpet. Her voice, when she speaks, is in glorious on-screen mode, an icy RP garnished with extract of Surrey. 'It's not going to happen, Martin, just face it. You've had your fun: now fuck off.'

And this does the trick, sort of. He rises noiselessly, wiping his face with the back of his hand, turns and leaves the cubicle. Lucy swivels back to her screen and tries to concentrate on the dead Swiss people and the burning buildings, but an all-too familiar voice sounds from behind her.

'I've had it, Lucy. I can't live. I will be dead the next time you see me.'

The melodrama, the selfishness, sickens her. She's watching, on the TV, a mini-story about this family of five, four of them killed on the plane, the only survivor a boy of seven waiting at the airport. She sees the incomprehension on his face, the gulf between under-standing what has happened and an appreciation of how things will be for him from now on; she sees the scared uncle and aunt huddle around him and already the terrifying grief counsellors making their ominous, emollient approach.

Without turning this time, Lucy replies: 'Well, Martin. That would be a tremendous loss to the world.'

He has had his fun, she's dead right about that. As he staggers back to his larger, but not much larger, office, he remembers all those nights of returning to his wife at four in the morning, undressing silently in the corner from boxer shorts and sometimes trousers still damp with semen (Lucy prohibited full penetrative sexual intercourse; it was a sort of unspoken promise for when he finally left his wife), the smell and taste of her still on his fingers and clambering into bed almost bent double with guilt and excitement. And lying there, unable to sleep as his wife rolled over and held on to him, making him feel despicable and desperately wanted. All that stuff was certainly fun and he wants it back, he can't face the rest of his life without the vividness of those emotions.

Just outside his door he collides with a producer tearing back frantically to the newsroom. He's young, with carefully trimmed short brown hair, spectacles setting off his light-grey suit. His skin is flawless. In his rush he doesn't, at first, notice Dempsey's dishevelled, tear-stained demeanour.

'It's not Osama! Pilot error, they're saying, it's just come through . . .'

Dempsey looks at him as though he were mad. 'What's pilot error?'

The young man's face suddenly transforms into a glistening sneer and, patting Dempsey on the arm, he says: 'Nothing, Martin, don't worry about it,' and runs off towards one of the studios.

Dempsey collapses through his door and reaches for the Stolichnaya; it's empty. He sits down behind the computer screen and wonders when the derision began, when it first became known that Dempsey was to be treated with amused contempt, and who was it gave the order. The things Lucy liked about him at first – his age, his wife and children, his initial insouciance – now all count against him in this crumbling building full of eager young things.

He remembers the plane. Aaah, yes. Pilot error.

But, pilot error; really?

The flight, bound for Denpasar, couldn't even clear Zurich. Designed for petite, wiry Indonesians, the poor plane instead found itself stuffed full of well-fed, complacent Swiss holidaymakers. In the scorching heat of Nusa Dua or Sanur they could gorge themselves on Wiener Schnitzel in wooden restaurants sprayed white with fake snow, whilst tiny Balinese waiters clad in absurd lederhosen plied them all with Gewürztraminer and Riesling. Pilot error; really? The plane, he can hear it now, groaning with the weight as it careered down the runway, gasping for breath as it lurched upwards and then, looking back at its passengers already clamouring for drinks and snacks, suffering two embolisms. The first causing the Swiss holidaymakers to become strangely silent and flecked with sweat, but not yet understanding; the second massive and fatal, sending the Boeing 747 careening into three blocks of exquisitely manicured, rent-controlled flats. *You can't have everything.*

He thinks about the plane and then he thinks about throwing himself from the roof. What's wrong with that? Four seconds of soaring terror, his arms out-stretched like Superman, or Christ, and then perhaps a microsecond of unimaginable pain. A microsecond, that's all. Surely he can live with that? And then, after that, nothing; absolutely nothing. We all go into the dark, eventually, don't we?

He taps a short message to Lucy via e-mail – the very medium which, as it happened, fomented their relationship. He taps, 'I loved you' – and then logs out of the system. Best use he's made of the past tense for years.

It's two-thirty and most of the office is back from lunch now except, Marian notes, Julian and Chloe, who are presumably still ensconced in the corner booth of Needles wine bar. This is how affairs begin, Marian remembers, usually before the people having them realise they've started. A quick semi-professional lunch drifts on and on and before you know it you're being banged senseless and what, really, can you do except hang on for dear life? Marian likes, or liked, Chloe – a northern girl much the same as herself and not entirely at home in London or the office just yet. Julian, meanwhile, is loquacious and confiding, with an unforeseen vulnerability which he brings out like a special party trick. Oh, how she fell! It was the apotheosis of acceptance into this exciting society. He stroked her hair as she scrabbled in her purse to pay for their drinks; that was the first she knew that something was about to happen, possibly.

The last time he fucked her was two weeks ago now, back at his Highgate *pied à terre* whilst his wife took their young daughter to see one of those Harry Potter films. The whole visit lasted no more than thirty minutes and she was packed off in a taxi no more than five minutes after he'd come inside her. It was a long, uncomfortable and damp ride home to SE16.

She rings Building Services again. The same dumb woman answers, the same conversation takes place, as if the two of them have slipped through a wormhole to a parallel universe characterised by repetition and irritation. Marian has passed hunger and there is nobody left to go for a drink with. Her hunger and her anger have merged to become a dull, nagging ache. Two hundred people dead out there, two hundred. What is wrong with me, these days, that I don't care? Things like this – tragedies, I suppose is what we've come to call them – have so little impact.

Dempsey stands like a bad comedian's impression of a mad person, waiting for the lift, trembling slightly at the prospect of what he has to do. But the lift has seen him coming and dives on down past his floor to the basement and then back up again without stopping. The other lift is broken, a sign Sellotaped to the door apologises for any inconvenience caused and quotes an extension number for people to call if they want to find out more or forward a complaint form. Colleagues of one sort or another gather around him, some of whom he knows – but he stands well away, to one side, panting and staring at the wall. After a quarter of an hour or so a sort of holiday atmosphere prevails amongst the rest of those waiting; a frowsy temp and two young admin clerks engaging in wearying noliftbanter; two or three senior news executives allowing their enforced absence from meetings to loosen their tongues with each other. There is venal talk of office politics and wholly uninformed speculation about the air crash – these Far Eastern airlines, you can't trust them any more, not since their economies fucked up five or six years ago, there isn't the same level of maintenance, *you can't have everything.*

By the time the lift finally arrives, some people have drifted off having formed friendships which may very well endure for years. Dempsey stumbles inside and looks imploringly at his fellow travellers, hoping that they might read in his eyes that death could be but a few moments away for him, that here is a soul waiting to be saved. But the people in the lift look uneasy and move slightly away from him – maybe they know what I'm going to do, he thinks, and maybe they agree that it is entirely the right option. In reality, of course, they are edging away from a colleague who appears to be several sheets to the wind – although Dempsey himself feels oddly sober, an unusual state of mind these days.

He is alone when the lift ejects him at the top floor and he stands for a few moments, hyperventilating, trying to work out the way to the roof.

Marian rests her head on the keyboard. She's begun to get this reputation for being difficult and querulous and with each day that passes it is an impression which it gets harder for her to dispel. Querulous, difficult and – as a result of her relationship with Julian – gauche and naïve. She finds herself forever snapping at people these days, like earlier with poor Cassie, who is stupid, but means well, and she hates herself for doing it and isn't sure why it happens. Nearly three o'clock. This fuckpig roach of a workman is going to get a mouthful.

Where's the fucking roof? Where's the fucking ROOF? You'd think a roof would be easy to find, it should be right there, on top of the fucking building. Dempsey can't find it. He's wandered unhappily along countless corridors searching for that elusive stairwell, passing people at whom he gazes imploringly *stop me*.

Maybe I should jump from a window, he thinks, in death as in life slightly failing to fulfil his potential, lowering, metaphorically and literally, his sights. Plus, of course, it should be easier for somebody to stop him killing himself in a proper office environment.

He rejoins the main spinal corridor and, pausing briefly to gather his resolve, turns the handle on the door in front of him, the door marked 8106.

Marian has had enough. She has had *enough*, she is past caring; now she just wants to go home. The time at which she wants to go home gets earlier and earlier each day. She thinks when this cunt workman has come she'll wait until the job's done and then just leave, using a headache as an excuse. Or maybe she should just go home now? Why should she wait? Pinned to her desk by a faulty window; who, really, gives a shit, one way or another? Fuck Bavins. Fuck Julian. Fuck Chloe and, for that matter, fuck Cassie. Mentally she begins to prepare her exit, sickened by the tapping of the computers, the important work going on all around her, sickened by it all.

Then the door opens and an ill-kempt man in an open-necked shirt walks through, looking at the windows. Marian turns to look at him, her lip curled up in a sneer. Yes, yes, yes. *That's* the loser.

Dempsey stands just inside the door and peers around the room. He sees people with their heads down, working. He sees windows, lots of windows. He feels a slight racing inside himself, maybe his heart, he thinks, his heart preparing for the end.

It is a busy office, this one. Maybe too busy; who is going to take the time to notice? Who is going to reach out and stop him?

Oh! Look! There's my window. They've left a window open for me. Lucy, are you listening? You can't have everything. You can't have everything. The basement where the fire begins, the noose around the choking heart, the shadow drawn across the lung, the burnt rubber on the median strip, the plane that banks too soon, the rubber hose inside the car, the pills like Smarties swallowed whole, the black crab alive inside the gut, the sudden stroke, the sniper's bullet, the window for the drowning man.

He looks around once more and sees directly in front of him this girl returning his gaze. *Aaah, she knows.* She looks at him and he thinks surely this is the human being who might offer him a path back into existence. There is a bond between all of us, a fragile cord of humanity which we sometimes mistake for the supernatural, even for extra-sensory perception; but it is simply love, our souls reaching out for each other.

Like this girl now, someone he has never previously seen, but someone prepared to become his saviour at this last moment, her soul reaching out with love for his.

Stop me; stop me. He stares at her, his eyes wide with beseechment and gratitude.

Her own eyes narrow slightly and she stretches out her right arm and points towards the open window.

'You took your fucking time. Third one on the left, and make it snappy.'

He does as he's told.

Three Seconds with Sophie

Sophie's been slumming it down in SE14. The kitchen has a feral look, what with the bluebottles and the almost empty take-away cartons and the mountain of chipped and crusty crockery and the discarded lo-fat yoghurt pots with their aluminium lids gouged out and the confident mice and the inquisitive cats. Sophie doesn't go there any more – it was only ever a sort of depository, even before the gas was cut off.

She has no living room – that's where Béchamel sleeps – and the bathroom is almost out of bounds because of the state of the toilet bowl and the complete absence of hot water.

So she stays in her room, her twelve-by-twelve box on the second floor . . . up there it is usually hard to tell where the mattress stops and the linoleum begins, the whole room is a monochrome patchwork quilt of discarded clothes in Lycra, silk and cotton. Each night she burrows down beneath coats, blankets and sheets unwashed in months, the boombox left on to drown out the noise from the New Cross Road.

Famous or semi-famous people watch over her as she sleeps – Terence Stamp, Lenin, Elliot Smith, Hope Sandoval, Aleister Crowley, Rosa Luxemburg – and also tacked to the pale yellow walls are cute or risqué snaps of Sophie and Sophie's new friends and clever black and white photographs of trees, old people, derelict buildings, railway stations and Barcelona.

The lightbulb went about two weeks ago, so she has these huge white candles to read by and their sweet warm stink and the stale dope and the unwashed sheets and the sharper tangs of Malice and Loathing give the room an exciting, exotic flavour which makes her happy and convinced that she is, at last, in the right place.

Her skin has gained the coolest pallor; her eyes are grey subterranean hollows; her bob is growing out, will soon be gone. Friday nights, if there's nothing much doing around town, she'll drive back to Leamington Spa in her beloved black Beetle and each time her parents watch her swing too sharply into the drive they know that she will look exponentially worse than the time before. But they know, too, how much she resents their worrying. Her father, Ben, has given her two hundred K to buy a small flat – in Clapham, Clerkenwell, Fulham or those bits of Stockwell which are still, you know, OK – all Sophe would be required to pay is the rates, as Ben persists in calling the council tax. But the whole ghastly bourgeois process of buying property fills her with . . . with . . . *ennui,* it's simply not something she can deal with just now. Oh, I don't know – maybe next year, she tells her sad father each time they meet, still tense and jumpy from the amphetamine sulphate and the driving and the suddenly being-back-home.

Weekdays are spent at UCL where she's immersed in the first year of her Sociology degree. She's learnt so much in such a tiny space of time, things she'd never thought about before.

And course work aside, she's expanding her horizons

in all manner of ways, reaching out and taking hold of everything which was previously, for one reason or another, denied to her. There is pretty much nothing which she will not try: Red Bull, amphetamine sulphate, anal sex, livid curries, Lexotanil, blow jobs, *Red Pepper* magazine, Staropramen, abortions, Jamaican patties, cocaine, not washing, Charlton FC, night buses, dark alleyways, the occult.

And people, too; she's made lots of new friends and slept with lots of strange men. She's fucked four boys from her compulsory course unit in Comparative Social Structures and she's fucked two more from her optional year one module in Sociolinguistics. She's fucked a plumber, she's fucked the singer of a second-division indie band; she's fucked two drug dealers, a grocer and a junior professor of Ethics. She's fucked her two flatmates, Mark and Béchamel; she fucked a man who knocked at the door asking for directions to the tube (it's just over the little bridge, actually – you can't miss it); and best of all she fucked the poor tormented soul next door, a troubled and bedraggled man who believes that the Americans are secretly poisoning us all with potash and who, sometimes, late at night, she can hear howling across the rooftops.

She loves the area she lives in. The noise, the grime, the tangible threat in the air and the wild-eyed dogs and the dangerous children. She likes it all, she thinks the local whites are just fine, they struggle by doing what they have to with their difficult, impoverished lives, and the blacks, the blacks she thinks are terrific, so elemental – they embrace life, don't they? And, with a cool symmetry and open handed reciprocation, the area loves her in return, it really does. At the corner paper shop they have her *Guardian* and Marlboro

Lights ready each morning for her and one or another of the Pakistani brothers behind the counter will always tell her how beautiful or how tired she's looking.

And the landlord, Mr Milosevic, he loves her, though she is rarely on time with her £90 rent and keeps him waiting outside the house for hours in his two-tone 1989 Ford Cosworth.

And they love her on the tube and they love her on the top deck of the 53 during its interminable, shuddering crawl to the Elephant and Castle and they love her in the Grove and the Hermit's Cave and the Five Bells and the Pacific Bar and the Trafalgar.

And Paul loves her too, loves her to distraction and she loves him very, very dearly. But she won't actually *fuck* him because that might get in the way of a far more valuable relationship which, of course, transcends – and indeed, precludes – sex.

Needless to say, Paul argues from an antithetical perspective, feeling the way he does – but he certainly sees her point. He admits that if one were to sleep with absolutely everybody, then, perhaps, refusing to sleep with the person you loved really would show a depth of feeling. Maybe.

It's all very confusing. Sometimes, in his darker moments, which these days seem to multiply, he believes he must be the only man Sophie has exchanged more than a dozen words with and not fucked. But he also knows that she is so candid and guiltless and certain about sex that in a way it is both cheapening and futile to berate her about it. And it's, you know, her choice?

They are in her bedroom right now.

Paul is sitting tight, opposite her – it is the only thing to do, sit tight, when Sophie is speeding. After a dab or two of sulph, rubbed fervidly and sexily into her still healthy, pink gums, she becomes a sort of spectator sport, rather than something with which one might participate. There is simply no knowing with her, she is a fuzz, a blur of nervous energy, crackling with deconstructed energy, like static jumping on an old TV screen.

She kicks some dirty old clothes from a patch of green linoleum and clambers down to her knees, maniacally agitating the antique silver bangles and beaten metal charms which dangle around her tiny wrists. Then she jumps up as if in response to a sharply spoken order and rips out the disc from her small Technics system – she is *so* sick of Black Rebel Motorcycle Club, but then there's nothing much else she wants to hear so she puts the disc back in the tray and it's *Spread your love* hammering across the floor and she nods her head in time to the thick, dumb beat and over and over, these big cool sulky American boys implore her over some guttural riff all spruced up and pared down from 1974.

Then she jumps to her feet, and searching first through an engraved wooden box on her dowdy and rickety chest of drawers, finds and then lights a stick of incense which she sets to burn down on the windowsill. Smells of hot jasmine, unwashed clothes and bodies, amphetamine skin, grimy lino, stale dope, Malice and Loathing, candlewax and *spread your love like a fever, don't you ever come down.*

This is the first Paul has seen of her for two weeks, two weeks, she has been holed up at Dominic's virtually the whole time, Dominic's little *pied à terre* in Belsize Park. But she rowed with Dom all this morning and fled for the tube in tears. She tried calling him on her Nokia what, thirty or forty times . . . but the phone rang out unanswered – so at seven she dialled Paul's number and not so much invited him over as simply let him know that she would be in were he to maybe swing by.

Paul has been distraught, this has been a very difficult two weeks for him, they've spoken three times and on each occasion he's asked her out for a drink she's said oh yeah, OK, I mean maybe, perhaps, and left it at that. Even at the best of times it's hard to get to see her, for such a special friend. Her visits to Leamington begin on Friday evenings and if she's feeling like it she'll sometimes skip the Monday morning lecture on Evolutionary Psychology and drive back, fizzing for London, later that day or even early on Tuesday morning. Then again, some Thursday nights she'll play hooky from New Cross to meet up with old school friends and friends of the family at a flat in Eaton Square or down the Fulham Road or maybe the girls, Biba and mad Emily and poor Anna, down at Clapham Common, where she arrives breathless and street-smart, always sporting a new accessory from her life in that terrible, forgotten south-eastern quadrant – a small wrap of crack or a sultry bruise beneath one eye. Her voice, on these occasions, bristles with sarf lunnun slang and as one their hearts go out to her, this brave refugee from SW10. And no heart goes out further than Dominic's.

Paul took the call on the communal phone in his shared house, shivering with relief and excitement, and of course he'll be round. He had intended going back to Goldsmiths for the evening to work on a polystyrene and junk sculpture of the waterfront at Rotherhithe –

incorporating real river mud, black and fragrant, which he keeps in barrels outside the bathroom door – and then maybe a drink or two in the union bar, if he can scrounge the money. But these vague plans – formed in a lacuna, waiting for Sophie – dissolve into less than nothing when he hears her voice.

Before leaving he changes into his best underwear (pristine white boxer shorts), borrows a tenner from Simon, his housemate, and does a strange sort of rain dance by his bedroom window. He knows very well that if it rains, if it's really miserable outside, and if he can hang on until the last 36 has headed for its cavernous home at Peckham Bus Garage, then Sophie will take pity and not expect him to walk the two and a half miles back to Camberwell Green and he can hunker down beside her under those coats and blankets, his legs slotting in with hers as she drifts towards jerky, fitful sleep.

Yes, it's happened before . . .

And now, here she is. Chain-smoking Marlboro and asking Paul if he's been OK these last two weeks and, most importantly, is his work progressing? He tells her about his latest sculpture and how he was kicked out of the grounds of one of those big warehouse apartment developments by some private security guard, just for sketching, and he tells her about one of the gays, this sombre, ghost-like blond boy from Keighley who has been diagnosed HIV positive and has switched courses to Performance Art, the better to, you know, incorporate his situation into his art and then, last of all, he says he's missed her, he can't quite explain how much or how badly and she accepts this with a slow nodding of her head and a sad, meaningful smile.

And this proves to be the cue for her litany of anguish about Dominic, or 'Dom': his possessiveness and, more specifically, the killing passion, the compulsion which exists between the two of them despite – as she explains, and has explained a hundred times before – their very many differences, social, political and of course, economic. And much as Paul would like to block his ears during this, he listens and gently stops her taking another lick of speed and instead rolls a spliff from her stash in the wooden box on top of the chest of drawers. He watches as she flicks her ragged chestnut bob backwards and forwards, inhaling deeply on the blue smoke, her grey eyes softening with every draw.

At length she asks, plaintively: 'What can I do?' – a familiar question, this, for Paul, who tells her that, really, she can do nothing save accept that the iniquities and traumas are at the very essence of her glorious compulsion. This is Paul's simple diagnosis and, as always, she nods her head as if chastened and says yes, of course, you're right, Paul, I know, I know.

Sometimes she does things or says things which cause him to doubt she cares the slightest bit for him, despite her repeated assurances about their valuable relationship, which he nonetheless clings to, like a spider will cling to the side of a bath as the water rises beneath it.

The way she expects him to revel in the depth of passion existing between her and Dominic and be happy for her sake . . . doesn't this girl understand, he wonders?

And then, on occasions, she will do something which seems even more blatantly cruel, such as turn up for one of their drink sessions in the Grove unexpectedly accompanied by a tall, extensively pierced hippy with whom she will later leave, whilst Paul sits rigid and immobilised in his chair, his eyes smarting with humiliation. At times like that he finds himself almost hating her and he wonders what compels him to yearn for this affected young woman with her foolish, druggy vernacular and vapid histrionics . . . and, for that matter, her matchless self-obsession which he knowingly and willingly feeds whenever they are together . . . and her embarrassing patronage of this crummy slumland where she spends what, at most, four days each week? And then there's her smug, overweight, indolent parents whom he was once permitted to meet, in passing, and in front of whom she said fuck and cunt repeatedly and even dropped a dove and these two rich complacent idiots just smiled like lobotomised Buddhas and never said a word . . . they drive down in the Audi once every six weeks from, where is it? he looked it up on a map once, Ledbury or Leamington or Leominster, and whisk Sophe up to Joseph and Agnes B and Harvey Nick's and then maybe dinner at the River Café . . . and then they drive back with four carrier bags full of dirty washing because, sorry, but if we're honest, she isn't quite up to speed with the launderette just yet and . . . and . . . and . . . and . . . and so on, and so on. He gets quite worked up. He wonders why he persists, he cannot understand himself, he thinks all these harsh and nasty things about her and he wonders how he let himself fall.

And, in a more analytical way, he considers his compulsion when things are going well between them – or, at least, comparatively well – and he is often truly lost for an answer. She is no prettier, no more intelligent, certainly no more endearing than a hundred girls he has known. She is not the first to have refused to sleep with him, either. He wonders sometimes if his love has anything to do with her at all, if she is responsible in the slightest way for his feelings – if, in effect, it is any of her business. He considers that he has manufactured it all and that, this being the case, wouldn't it have been better if he'd done it with someone rather more accommodating, such as countless girls in his college or Debbie whom he knew at school in Sunderland or, let's face it, anyone – that fat woman in the local bakery where he buys his cheese and onion pasties every day, the woman with the drooling lips and the alopecia, even her, maybe? Would it make any difference?

But he knows that at present he is unable to stop himself, he cannot desist, and that he will continue to pursue Sophie, always hoping that in the end the scales will slide from her eyes and she will collapse towards him and yes, that will be a wonderful day.

By ten o'clock she is hungry and doesn't want to be left alone, which makes Paul's head swim with love, and cooking is out of the question, nobody cooks in that kitchen any more. So Paul rings Domino Pizza and orders a medium *Napolitana* which is delivered by a sweetly confused Russian boy about twenty minutes later. Paul takes out his ten pounds and pays him the £7.60 and leaves the rest as a tip at Sophie's insistence and, in the musty, flickering, candlelight, they eat, sitting cross-legged on the floor. Sophie loses her appetite after two or three tiny mouthfuls and then distractedly picks off the olives from her half of the pizza and grinds out another Marlboro Light into the base. He adores her insouciance about things like food and this casual sluttishness. Perhaps this is the attraction, he thinks.

And then, suddenly, she is swamped by tiredness and almost falls asleep still sitting there on the floor, two weeks of speeding and the Lexotanil and the stuff with Dominic catching her off-guard, exhausted, back in her little room. So Paul, with reckless bravery, says he is tired too and suggests they both go to bed. Sophie unquestioningly assents, she doesn't even mention walking home, although it is a fine, clear night, still quite early, he could even get the 36 if he left right now. But instead she quickly strips down to her white T-shirt and g-string panties in front of him and crawls beneath the coats and blankets where they lie at their thickest on the old mattress.

Paul feels giddy with longing. He extinguishes the huge white candles with trembling fingers, allowing the hot wax to drip down into the palm of his hand, where it cools rapidly, pleasingly smooth and pliable to the touch. He lets her settle first and squats down by the window where the incense has now burnt itself out and, through the bleary glass, looks down on to the New Cross Road.

The traffic tails back further than he can see and on the other side of the street men are piling out of the Five Bells with its late extension, staggering between the growling cars calling cunt to one another and barking back at the angry traffic. It is a delicious moment this, for Paul, this shuddering anticipation of being so close to her and he wonders how it can be possible for a person to feel like this and if the feeling will ever cease.

He locates Sophie beneath the blankets as much by

smell as any of his other overburdened senses. She is wearing Malice and its sharp sweet astringency rises above the staleness of the sheets and clothes. Her back is turned to him so, as unobtrusively as possible, he slides his body up beside her's, looping an arm gently around her waist. He feels scarcely able to breathe and clenches shut his eyes to savour this moment, this closeness.

Of course, there is his penis to worry about. He is careful to ensure that there is a corridor of air between his groin and the cleft of her buttocks and yet even so, he is sure she must feel the heat from his erection – it is such a relentless burning, as if his whole body had been melted into one point. He lies there quite appalled at what is happening to him, the physical effect, curled up next to this girl.

He begins to stroke her stomach gently with one hand, a light circular motion he half hopes she won't notice and then, after a few moments of this, he is sufficiently emboldened to brush her shoulder with his lips. This is absolutely as much as he dares and indeed, after a few minutes, she shrugs his mouth away with sleepy irritation and he stops dead, mortified.

But the burning will not subside and he cannot, cannot possibly sleep; instead he waits, not daring to move, as the traffic quietens outside and the room absorbs a softer quality from the darkness. The time by her radio alarm clock, the red numbers glowing from on top of a heap of sociology text books, reads 12.45 when he next begins to kiss her shoulder and with one tentative finger stroke a tiny area of skin beneath her fragile ribcage. But then a door slams somewhere downstairs and, with an inarticulate noise of complaint, she moves slightly away from him again.

Once more he lies stock still, wide awake and a little nauseous from the heavy warmth of their bed, the smell of the room and the intensity of feeling as he lies there beside her; that burning.

He wonders if he should simply grab hold of her, pull her towards him and kiss her – render his actions unambiguous and maybe, as a result, have her send him home – but at least this burning would ease. He lies there thinking he must soon burst whilst the walls of the room twist and flicker – he thinks he might soon burst and he must, he *must* touch her again.

So he reaches out with one hand and so, so lightly lifts her cotton T-shirt to stroke the small of her back and the light silky hair she has down there. And the pressure builds still more inside him.

She doesn't stir now, she is in too deep a sleep, he thinks, so he allows himself the luxury of this feeling and, emboldened again, moves his head up beside her own to taste the softness of her hair upon the pillow.

Then, with an exclamation he doesn't catch, she turns over to face him and he feels caught, eyes-opened and guilty. But this time, instead of a silent reproof, she lays one hand firmly on his arm whilst the other – and this he does not entirely believe, it is unprecedented, a quite outstanding development; his breathing quickens and he struggles for air and his heart races – slips through the opening of his best white boxer shorts and begins, with a practised lightness, to *stroke his penis*.

Then she takes hold of him with a degree more candour and determination, her hand moving up and down – something which renders Paul a borderline asthmatic. He looks her fully in the eyes but hers are closed so he screws his own eyes shut, buries his head in the pillow and gasps for air.

But this whole, quite incredible, episode lasts for just three seconds, if you adhere to an outmoded and deeply mechanistic belief in the linear concept of time. And as these three seconds conclude, Paul ejaculates voluminously and with very great force indeed. In fact he keeps on and on ejaculating, there's loads of the stuff, out it all comes, pint after pint, and he begins to wonder if it will ever cease. Sophie, the minx, trails the back of her hand across the top of his penis – what a wonderful trick, thinks Paul, vaguely, lost in a chemical oblivion – and delicately but decisively arches her body away from him to avoid the ostentatious spurting which continues for so long that Paul becomes embarrassed and wonders if there's maybe something seriously wrong with him.

When, eventually, it does stop, he opens his eyes to look at her and murmurs with what breath he has left in his quite supremely grateful body: 'I love you,' and moves towards her to kiss her on the lips.

But, her eyebrows slightly raised, she simply puts a finger to her mouth and says: 'Sssshhhussshh . . . now, go to sleep.'

And now he finds that he can, he can sleep, after all – although he is denied the pleasure of lying tucked up behind her, his legs interlocked with hers. They each cling to opposite sides of the mattress, well away from the vast lagoon of semen in the centre of the bed, a thick coldness which will still be damp when Paul awakes the next morning. His dreams are furred with a strange sort of exhaustion.

He opens his eyes to what must surely be a different world and gropes across the bed for her with a degree of familiarity he has never previously allowed himself to display. But she's already up, has been up for ages, there's an empty wrap of speed on her chest of drawers and now she's swigging from a can of diet cola. She's crouched down in the far corner of the room, punching out numbers on the Nokia and scrabbling in a pack of Lights at the same time. She holds the phone to her ear and lights a cigarette with jangling fingers and murmurs: 'Come on!' and clicks her teeth in frustration. Then she hurls the phone into her bag and jumps up, taking long deep drags from the cigarette, seemingly in the throes of making a decision. All the while Paul peers hopefully from beneath the coats and blankets. He wants to say something to bring back last night and its scarcely credible and very brief dénouement, but can think of nothing to say save for 'I love you,' which is what he says with slightly more expectation than usual. But she gives the impression of not having heard him, standing there in her short black cotton Copperwheat Blundell dress, her eyes fixed upon something outside of the bedroom, beyond the mattress and well beyond Paul.

And he knows exactly what she is thinking about – but even so he persists, suggesting breakfast at the Criterion, a small café midway between their homes, and knowing that, really, this possibility does not exist.

She looks at him abruptly, as if surprised, and shakes her head. 'No . . . I've got to go,' she says and adds, 'is it OK if you let yourself out?'

But she doesn't go, just yet, she stands there in front of him turning her Nokia on and off, disbelieving the 'no messages' signal. She shifts her gaze to his face and says with greater emphasis: 'I've got to go, Paul!'

And for Paul, the world slips back on to its more familiar axis. But he still cannot stop himself. 'Sure, of

course I can let myself out. D'you want to meet up at
the Grove later?'

He cannot drag himself from beneath the coats and
blankets for fear of losing all of the previous night in a
single moment. He thinks that if he stays there then the
fact of last night will stay with him. And maybe with
her too. He watches the blue smoke curl around her
head and merge with the grey daylight now filling the
room.

'I don't know,' she says, 'why don't you ring?'

'Where will you be?'

'. . . I don't know. I really don't know. I mean, you
can get me on my mobile. Look, I've really got to go.'

Ahh, the mobile phone. An instrument of exquisite
torture. When he calls her on the mobile it rings out a
few times – enough for her to check who is calling, he
thinks – and is then switched through to divert. Hello,
this is Sophie. I can't talk right now why not leave a
message bye.

She grabs hold of her black leather bag and,
blowing him a half-kiss, quickly walks out of the
room, leaving behind skeins of smoke which smell of
Loathing. Her skimpy pants from the previous night
lie on top of the Technics, next to a chrome tube of
lipstick. Paul hears her hurried footsteps on the stairs
and then the front door open and slam shut. He gazes
hopelessly around the room. Lenin and all the others
gaze back at him imperturbably. Outside there is the
incessant, bad-tempered traffic on the New Cross
Road.

Paul buries his head back under the covers and closes
his eyes. He is ashamed at the depth of desolation he
feels, frightened and ashamed that he could be so deeply
affected. His guts churn as if he had been poisoned.

It occurs to him, lying there, that the hurt and humiliation of the last two weeks, the endless waiting, had been obliterated in just three seconds. That's all it took. Remembering those remarkable three seconds makes him shiver slightly and he feels an involuntary twitch of excitement between his legs, which rather disgusts him. And he thinks about why she did it and belatedly realises that it was the simplest way for her to get a few hours of trouble-free sleep, away from his irritating caresses.

And then he thinks that even if he had known last night that Sophie's actions were purely instrumental, he wouldn't have cared sufficiently to stop her, he would have let her carry on and the end result would have been exactly the same – a lagoon of semen in the middle of the bed no less voluminous than had it been effected through love.

And this thought repels him and convinces him further that Sophie is entirely extraneous to this love affair and that her motives and feelings make not the slightest difference to the way in which he feels.

Maybe he fell asleep, for the next thing he remembers is a tentative knock at the bedroom door and Sophie's flatmate Béchamel peering around the jamb with his annoying little pixie-face and strange, sharp teeth. Sophie has slept with him too, Paul recalls. More than once.

Seeing Paul alone in bed, he asks: 'Seen Sophe?'

'Ummm . . . yes, she's gone out. Ages ago, I think.' Paul checks the time on Sophie's alarm clock. It says it is ten-thirty.

The pixie looks aghast. 'Oh shit . . . you don't happen to know where she's gone, do you?'

Béchamel is playing with his silly bloody ponytail in

an agitated manner whilst Paul considers his response. 'No, not really . . .'

'Not *really*?'

'Well, she might have gone to visit a friend in Belsize Park. She mentioned something . . . but it wasn't really clear, you know?'

Béchamel raps in frustration on the bedroom door. 'Shit,' he says again. 'The electricity people are here again. We need, um, money. Otherwise we're going to get cut off, apparently. I'm astonished they can still do stuff like that.'

'Oh, God, I'm sorry. You could always try her mobile . . .'

Béchamel gives a thin mirthless laugh. 'Yeah,' he says, 'the mobile. Hello, this is Sophie, et cetera.'

'Well,' says Paul, 'maybe you could ask the electricity people to wait for a bit, until she gets back from wherever she is.'

Béchamel looks glum, shaking his head. 'No, I don't think so; not this time. They look pretty determined to me, to be honest. I don't suppose you've got eighty quid, have you? You can get it back from Sophie – it's her share.'

Paul shakes his head. 'Sorry . . .'

'Well, I suppose that's that. This place is finally fucked,' Béchamel shrugs and leaves the room, pulling the door to behind him. Paul gradually hauls himself into a sitting position, dragging the coats and blankets around him for a vestige of warmth.

Something approaching resolve creeps up on him, in the bedroom there – an irritation maybe partly caused by the relentless monotony of the traffic outside, a perpetual, nagging growl he can never quite block out. When he thinks about last night he still feels himself stiffen, despite himself. He wonders why he is incapable of controlling himself and then wonders maybe it is the other way around: he has taught himself to tremble and shiver in Sophie's company, he has schooled his body to behave this way. It has been as ineluctable and as selfish as learning to breathe and as depressing a cycle as one could possibly endure.

He hears movement and voices downstairs, the electricity men poking around in the hall cupboard trying to search for the meter. Switching it off is such a simple operation, these days. Not like water, which takes loads of court hearings and other complex, costly stuff.

Paul climbs from the mattress and picks up his checked shirt from the floor. He sees, next to where it lay, half concealed beneath a pair of her black leggings, a thick felt tip pen. He thinks maybe I should leave her a note, something concise and emotive; he looks around the room for something to write on. But he can't think of what to say. It's not, in the end, any fault of hers, is it?

Then he sees her pants and gets a rush of excitement and, at the same time, a good idea. He holds the white cotton taut and writes four words:

'Thanks for the wank.'

In a moment of slightly unchivalrous contemplation he wonders if Sophie will, when she arrives home, realise that it is him, Paul, who has written the words. But then he drapes the pants over her CD player and begins to button his shirt. He hears, above the noise of the traffic, a furious yapping from an upstairs room next door, the sound of a dog in distress – except that there is something in the unevenness of this barking which is plainly human.

Downstairs he hears the meter men exclaim in jubilation. Sitting down to tie up his shoes, he catches sight of Sophie's alarm clock at precisely the moment at which the red numerals fade and disappear.

What the Thunder Said

1. Mr Squirrel

A lavender pink sunset over the little park on Peckham Rye Common, so warm and fragrant it might still be summer. Down by the artificial lake kids are throwing stones at Canada geese, aiming with a canny dexterity at the white crescents on the necks of these unwanted birds. The children laugh and shriek and congratulate each other when they score a direct hit – which is often, because the Canada geese are too fat and indolent to dodge the missiles and just float along on their tiny ocean of filth, impervious and aloof and suffer the pain. Away from the lake, mums and dads amble along tarmac walkways clutching footballs and jackets and tracksuit tops discarded by their children – for although the pensioners lined up alongside the bowling green might shiver, it is surprisingly warm for the time of year, for the time of day; a close, sticky warmth which rises in bubbles from the sub-aqueous black bed of the lake and hangs down heavily from the lime trees. It is October, but there is still the smell, everywhere you walk, of recently cut grass, of mingled sweat, of the shallow water of the lake and the clinging mud beyond, of juniper, of the sulphurous mulch the gardeners are now using to grow next year's tulips. You really could be fooled that summer hasn't left us, yet. There are even some swallows, here and there.

It's a kind of sunset, too, in the tiny clearing between the juniper bushes and the rhododendrons, where, beneath iridescent foliage, Denise concentrates for a final few seconds on the blow job she is giving to Eddie. Her back aches from the stooping and her black tights are holed at the knees, the skin beneath scuffed and muddy. But she is nothing if not conscientious; even here, she makes sure to slide her mouth right down and has one hand lightly clasped around his balls, all of which is a difficult operation with the rhododendron branches scraping across her shoulders and the sound, from the middle distance, of children shouting and laughing, like harbingers.

But in truth she is conscious mainly of Eddie's penis in her mouth – and in a strange, dislocated sense, of the green sunlight still shimmering through the trees around her – totally immersed in this act of benediction and supplication. Eddie is kneeling too, it is far too small a space for him to stand, although he would rather he were standing, much prefer it, especially now as he comes with the faintest juddering of his hips and exhaling deeply, he leans back on his haunches, it's like pissing uphill, he thinks. He throws back his head into the sharp green leaves and says the name 'Denise . . .' just loud enough for her to hear. He is not sure, later, why he said it at all. Who else would it have been? What was the point of that? Did he think it was someone else?

Looking up at the mention of her name, her mouth glistening a little, she shakes her hair free of twigs and swallows and grabbing him by the shoulders, brings his shaking body next to hers. Perversely, you might think, she likes that thick, salty, glutinous gloop on the back of her throat and more even than that the pressure of a male body close to her own. Out of convention and exhaustion they hug each other, a belated attempt to confer some emotional commitment upon this hastily convened event, and then Denise gasps with shock and pulls away, something moved in the soft green twilight just a few inches behind Eddie's ear. Registering her sudden disquiet, Eddie turns around in panic, quickly zipping his fly. Two brown eyes stare out at him from the lowest branch of a lime tree. Eddie is perplexed by how come the eyes are so curiously close together.

And then suddenly the eyes are gone, with a ghostly rustling and the slightest disturbance of air around their heads. Denise laughs in relief. 'Go away, Mr Squirrel.'

Eddie doesn't laugh, he is exhausted, he sinks back against a juniper bush, full of disgust and confusion. 'I thought for a minute it was . . .' but his voice trails off and he shakes his head. The squirrel is gone and in front of him Denise is kneeling there instead with one hand between her legs, her white cotton skirt bunched up around her thighs. Eddie feels repulsed. He smells juniper berries and freshly disturbed mud and her coffee breath and sweet citrine perfume and a thin film of nausea envelopes him. 'We'd better go. Julie . . .'

Again, he can't finish the sentence. He rises with difficulty to a stoop above her and brushes the dirt from his black chinos. He closes his eyes and tries, for a nanosecond, to pretend she isn't there.

From the south, somewhere beyond Beckenham, there comes a low, flat rumble of thunder.

Eddie shakes his head and gropes for the right words.

'This is a curse,' he says, watching her touch herself distractedly, and without conviction, as the green sunlight around them fades to burnt sienna.

She pulls her hand away and straightens her skirt, her eyes wide with irony. 'Yes, well, it's a shame you didn't take that view three minutes ago,' she says, 'and stop me.'

'Well, obviously I couldn't even if I'd wanted to. That's why it's a curse.'

'A curse from who, exactly?'

Eddie shakes his head. 'I don't know.' He smiles. 'I only know that it's a curse.'

'No, Eddie, it was just a blow job. You've had plenty of those before.'

Denise snorts with irritation and pats her backside free of twigs and caked mud, half leaning on the thin perfumed stems of the juniper bush. The last of the sunlight flickers across his face, like slow, distant lightning. She leans forward and kisses his neck; Eddie's muscles beneath stiffen with resistance.

'Now,' she says to him, in a malevolent stage whisper, 'let's see if your little wifey managed to locate the ice cream van.'

2. The Radged Fucko

They clamber through the bushes and step over the low log fence and walk together down past the bowling green to the park entrance, the lavender pink sky darkening above them.

He thinks about coming in her mouth and wonders why her mouth is the one he so implacably wishes to come in. It is, after all, only a mouth. But when she bent down to unzip his fly, back there in the strange green sunlight, he had to hold back even then, he hasn't known such a thing since he was seventeen years old. He cannot explain why this should be so, the compulsion of it all, the drive and the relentlessness of it.

He feels foolish and melodramatic having described their affair as a curse; ejaculation, like drunkenness, loosening his tongue. He almost always feels stupid beside her and, in some indefinable way, at a disadvantage. There is no reason why this should be so, he thinks.

An elderly couple, both wrapped up in thick coats against some imaginary chill – the man sporting a bizarre and shocking growth upon his nose which makes him look like a spiteful caricature, rather than a person – notice Eddie and Denise climbing out of the foliage. But they register nothing, not even opprobrium or disquiet and just continue their slow walk towards the lake.

Julie was left to buy three ice creams whilst Eddie and Denise, as Eddie put it, 'take in the new rose trellis' by the lake. Eddie regards his wife from a distance, sitting on a green bench just down from Mr Whippy, just sitting there waiting with that perpetually preoccupied look on her face as the cornets melt on to each of her wrists. The requests for ice cream were an absurd and, Eddie thinks, transparent diversion. Except that these days, two months into their affair, every ruse seems similarly transparent and ludicrous and yet is carried off without even the faintest whiff of suspicion from the injured parties.

Julie looks up and grins as they draw near, attempting to brush away a strand of her pale brown hair with her arm as a light wind ruffles the trees behind her. She holds out two of the ice creams, desperate to be rid of them, the thick bright yellow of the frozen chemical custard making Eddie's stomach heave and his senses merge into a thin film of nausea.

'Took your time,' she shouts, 'quick, take these, they're dripping everywhere . . .' and stands up to face them.

With exaggerated thanks they take the cones from her and walk together along the tarmac path, towards the exit of the park and Barry Road. Denise has got a spirit of devilment in her, she is hyper, she is full of something. She waits until Julie is looking in another direction and then fellates the ice cream for Eddie's benefit, smearing it all around her mouth and letting the thick molten gunk dribble down her chin.

There's another low rumble of thunder in the sky to the south, a faint murmur of complaint from beyond the edge of their eyesight. The wind brushes across the playing fields in front of them.

Eddie looks away from Denise sharply but cannot stop the imposition of excitement rising in his stomach. It rises up and makes his shoulders quiver and his lips become parched. He is holding Julie's hand but every time he looks aside Denise is there and she licks the top of her ice cream lasciviously or sucks huge mouthfuls with her eyes closed in mock rapture. Eddie thinks she is being cheap and dangerous and what's more mocking him in some way but he can't stop watching her eating the horrible ice cream.

Then the wind blows her skirt out from behind and the first drops of rain burst upon her blouse. Ahead of them three crows rise from the grass and flap noiselessly towards the lime trees.

Julie's not saying much. Eddie wonders what's wrong with her, perhaps she's found out somehow, he thinks. This is what he always thinks, no matter what the situation, no matter how small the likelihood of her finding out, no matter how extraordinary it would be if she were somehow suddenly to *know*.

And although this worry should make him circumspect and cautious, he instead drops back a pace, lightly touches the hem of Denise's jacket and whispers into her ear: 'I want you again.'

Denise glances over quickly to see if Julie has heard this and whispers back, with a degree more discretion, with discretion and irony: 'I thought it was a curse?'

'That doesn't make me want you less.'

Julie's now walking slightly ahead of them, having thrown the remains of her ice cream into a metal rubbish bin. She turns back and seems about to speak when she catches sight of the light brown stain on the front of Denise's skirt.

'What happened to you, Mum?' she asks, smiling.

Denise says nothing by way of reply because she doesn't understand what Julie is referring to. Eddie gets it, though. He has been watching his wife, watching and worrying, stuff clawing at his stomach, strange and disabling stuff like fear clawing at his stomach.

'Your mother fell,' Eddie says, with a smirk. 'She can't keep her feet any more, it would seem.'

Julie notices this weird edge in his voice, which she's begun to notice more and more often these days. She thinks it must be antagonism and tension. When they first married, Eddie was sulky and irritable whenever Julie insisted upon a visit to the in-laws. He objected to the amount of time Julie spent with her parents, it seemed unnatural and an imposition upon their relationship. All Julie would say is: 'We're a close family, OK?' And then, by way of a sort of recompense, she made this big effort with his family, too – or his poor beleaguered, perpetually irradiated, father, at least.

'You didn't hurt yourself, did you, then?' she asks Denise.

'No, never been better. Eddie was there to help. It's useful to have a man around, to help you up when you fall.'

Julie wonders if they've been bickering again, if there's some argument left behind in the park and which, for her benefit, they are unwilling to continue. She feels guilty at inflicting her mother upon Eddie all the time.

They walk on in silence. By the time they reach the eastern corner of Barry Road it's almost dusk and big grey clouds are banking along the edge of the sky, the wind skimming across the park behind carrying with it the occasional vast droplet of water which will, soon enough, lead to a downpour. Eddie is working later that night and is very pleased with the weather; it will be a good night to make some money. He imagines the guttural cough of the car radio giving him yet another job, something which involves him travelling miles – Bromley, Catford, Penge – to pick up a couple of girls eager to be out for the night and who will chatter and make him feel OK and then tip generously.

A little ahead of them, on Barry Road, there's an old man lurching and rolling across the pavement. He stops occasionally to support himself on garden walls and bollards. He is either very pissed, or dying, or both.

As the three draw level, approaching him tentatively,

he turns round and confronts them, grinning: 'Well . . . what do you think of the show so far?' he says, arms outstretched, as if presenting something magnificent to them.

He is unshaven and his teeth are totally fucked, either missing or blackened. His trousers are grime-encrusted, a mélange of dark stains and ingrained filth and his ragged tweed overcoat is held together with what looks like crocodile clips. His hair is matted taupe plastered over too large a head. A cut above one eye is still oozing blood.

He stands there, grinning in front of them, sort of menacing but too old and too whacked out to be much of a threat, really. Then the grin disappears and he looks from one to another of them as they try to pass by on the pavement. Eddie shepherds them all along and attempts, at first, to ignore the man.

'Hey!' the radged fucko shouts after them. 'I'll tell you what I think. I think it's all fucking rubbish. It all fucking stinks . . .'

This is a bit too aggressive for Eddie's sensibilities and notions of chivalry. He tells Denise and Julie to go on ahead whilst he turns back to remonstrate with the drunk.

'You want to watch your fucking mouth, mate, shouting at women like that,' he says to the fucko, sternly.

The fucko straightens himself up and gives a broad smile. 'Development,' he says, quietly, to Eddie.

'What did you say?' says Eddie.

'Development. Development,' says the fucko and spreads his arms wide open. And then, getting no response from Eddie, he shouts once more, for emphasis:

'Development!'

'Just watch your mouth, mate,' mutters Eddie, disarmed.

'It's all about development,' nods the fucko sagely, and then starts kicking a tree very hard. Eddie isn't sure what to do. He stands and watches him for a bit, laying into the tree and still saying 'development'.

'Development!' screams the fucko, as pieces of bark fly up and around him. 'Development!'

'You mad cunt,' says Eddie and with a shrug stops watching the fucko and instead rejoins his wife and mistress.

3. The Alligator

The thunder makes the windows shudder and the TV flickers in time with the lightning. They sit in Denise's front room drinking beer and watching a quiz show; Denise has her hair tied back with a blue ribbon, she is lying slouched on the floor, her back up against the sofa, drinking straight from the can. She should act her fucking age, he thinks, unkindly. Julie is in an armchair sipping her beer from a half-pint glass. Eddie, on the sofa, feels stretched out between them, hardly touching his can of Coca-Cola, leaning back as if forced against the sofa by an extra component of gravity, a chunk of gravity created for him alone. Denise is just inches from his left leg.

The quiz show contestant is a fat man who stands nervously in the spotlight, sweat running down his face like hot cooking oil. Eddie imagines himself up there, in front of all those people, and supposes he was asked: 'Why are you sleeping with your wife's mother?' and all he can come up with by way of a response is: 'It's a curse.' This, though, is not the correct answer and he loses all his money and is out of the game.

The fat man in the spotlight wipes his brow with a fleshy fist and smiles back at the compère. He is doing all right. Eddie tries to watch the show but he can't take his eyes off Denise; her skirt is tucked up again like it was in the juniper clearing in the park. Her legs are slender and waxed but there's a thickening around her waist which she is astute enough to conceal beneath big jumpers, loose blouses and men's shirts. But Eddie doubts the way she looks has anything to do with his feelings, his compulsion. Sitting there, he decides the thing has got to stop, he should never be left alone with her, he cannot trust himself.

What type of animal is a cayman?

Julie says: 'It's one of those monkeys, a little monkey, isn't it?'

Julie's pretty sure about this but the fat man's floundering in a pool of sweat, narrowing his tiny eyes at the lights.

'Fuck off,' says Eddie, 'it's a goat.'

'Could you spell the word, please?' says the fat man.

The compère says: 'c-a-y-m-a-n.'

'Goat,' says Eddie again and puts a finger up at either side of his head like horns in case Denise and Julie are unfamiliar with the concept of 'goat'.

'Nah, it's one of those little monkeys,' says Julie again.

'Fuck off!' says Eddie.

'That's a macaque,' says Denise.

'No, a macaque is a parrot,' says Eddie.

'That's a macaw,' says Julie.

'A macaque is a parrot as *well*. It's like a macaw but much smaller and can't talk,' says Eddie.

'It's probably an insect,' says Denise.

'What, a macaque?' says Julie.

'No, a macaque is a monkey. Cayman. It's a tropical insect. The answer's always an insect, on shows like this. Because there are so many of them.'

'Alligator,' says the fat man in the spotlight.

'Fuck off,' says Eddie, to the television screen.

'Yes, I can accept that, it's a small, alligator-like reptilian,' says the compère and the audience goes wild.

It is a peculiar world, thinks Eddie, when you can be given ten thousand pounds for knowing what a fucking cayman is. 'I thought it was a goat,' he says irritably, to nobody in particular.

Eddie slurps at his soft drink and checks his watch. He gestures outside with his can of cola and says to Julie: 'Should be on our way . . . might make some money while the storm's on . . .'

Julie looks across in surprise. It is three or four hours before he usually starts and, in any case, he shares the car with her dad who is still driving. 'People won't be wanting to go out on a night like this, Eddie,' she says.

Don't tell me my job, Eddie thinks, still angry about the goat débâcle. 'People always go out. And it was a bad week last week. I just want to be ready for when Jim's finished so I can head straight to the office,' he says. It's true that Eddie is always more anxious to start driving on a Sunday evening. The rent on the car and the payment to the office is £240 and until he clears that he is working for nothing, with penury hammering at the door. Usually the Peugeot gets an hour or two of rest between Jim clocking off and Eddie clocking on, but not on Sundays.

With the slightest hint of a smile Denise says to Eddie: 'Jim will be back soon; he likes to see his daughter, once in a while. And you can't go to work until the car's home.'

The fat man is now being asked for the capital of Guadeloupe. The correct answer will win him twenty thousand pounds. Julie, Denise and Eddie don't even hazard a guess at this one.

Eddie sinks back on the sofa, the gravity business starting its work again. He can't stop himself staring at Denise, slumped at his feet with her hair tied up like a schoolgirl, an elderly schoolgirl. Julie climbs from her armchair and says she needs a piss. 'Tell me what happens,' she says, nodding at the screen.

'What do you want to go for so badly?' Denise asks Eddie as soon as his wife is out of the room.

'I feel sick.'

Denise twists around and looks up at him, that same faintly ironic smile flickering across her face. 'I didn't start this, you know . . .'

'Nobody started it. It started itself. I still feel sick and I don't particularly want to share a drink with your fucking husband. My father-in-law.'

But despite this he climbs down from the sofa and squats beside her. He runs his hand up the inside of her leg, it makes the room sway about him. He forces his hand under the tight elastic of her knickers and as he does so she drops her can of beer and throws an arm behind her head. Upstairs the lavatory flushes; Eddie sinks a finger deep inside her and then, tearing at the nylon forces his whole hand into her and she is so wet he feels soaked through, not just his hand, but every part of him. He pulls her towards him and kisses her with such violence that she tries, at first, to move away – but then, opening her mouth wide she grabs hold of his neck and pulls him on top of herself. They both hear footsteps on the stairs but it is difficult to stop this kiss and Eddie wonders if there is any point in doing so, he feels himself swimming in a pool with no bottom and no sides. His mouth begins to hurt from the pressure of the kiss and his wrist is bent back at an angle of nearly ninety degrees and beneath him Denise is gasping, struggling for breath.

The footsteps reach the bottom of the stairs and just in time he rolls from on top of her and quickly walks into the kitchen as Julie comes through the living room door.

The kitchen is pitch black, he leans exhausted against a cupboard and closing his eyes, places his fingers in his mouth. He stays like this until a vivid fork of lightning illuminates the kitchen: the cooker, the fridge, the imitation-wood work units, the block of stainless steel kitchen knives all held, for a half-second, in a cold blue light. The thunder is instantaneous and he hears, from the living room, the TV fizz and the telephone ring out once in complaint.

Julie climbs back into her chair. 'What happened, then?' she asks.

'Oh, bugger, we missed it. I'm sorry. Looks like he got it right, though,' Denise replies, gesturing at the TV screen where the fat man is beaming and the figure '£20,000' flashes on and off behind his head.

'Where's Eddie?'

Denise gestures through into the kitchen. 'Think he's making a cup of tea. Or something.'

Julie shakes her head. 'What's wrong with him today? He's so jumpy all the time.'

Denise muses for a bit and then says: 'He feels sick, he says. But I think he's just annoyed about the cayman-goat business.'

4. The Girl from Lethe

The rain died by nine and since then he's had just three rides, to Forest Hill, then on to Stockwell, then picking up at Camberwell and back to base. Five pounds a throw, no tips, the last lot three black guys done up with that gold jewellery they wear and who the office made pay in advance and therefore, as a result, acted all insolent in the car. The car radio is blaring out this song about taking off all your clothes because it's so hot and Eddie is getting more and more irritated sitting there drumming his fingers on the steering wheel and he wonders if he should call it a day, things aren't going to get much better. The car's a dump, in any case. It reeks of tobacco from Jim's chainsmoking despite the red and black stickers Eddie put up on the dash and the back of the seats saying 'No Smoking'. Bits of Jim's lunch are stashed away in the trough next to the gear stick, curled-up sandwich crusts and smears of tomato ketchup, and on the floor of the front passenger seat dog-eared maps and an old copy of the *South London Press*. An empty Fanta can is rolling around down there too. Eddie doesn't see why he should clear it all out so he leaves it hoping that Jim will take the hint the next day – knowing, though, that Jim doesn't take hints, by and large. It is a strange and awkward thing having both the car *and* Denise on a time-share basis.

He thinks of Julie sitting at home in front of some long, brown, boring BBC costume drama, her feet up on the sofa, and suddenly the wet roads seem slightly more enticing. He thinks about Denise too and that familiar wave of revulsion and excitement sweeps over him and then, forgetting the sandwich crusts and the rest of the mess, he is overcome with a mawkish pity for Jim. He wonders what Jim would say if he found out and he can picture the scene, Jim probably just crying or something equally horrible, maybe passing out, and Denise, what would Denise do? Just stand there with that faintly ironic smile, he shouldn't wonder, unrepentant and somehow allowing the blame to reside with him, Eddie.

Yes, Jim would definitely cry, he thinks, and he wants to shut this picture out of his mind so he starts the car and does a U-turn and swings down Peckham Rye to McDonald's, where he buys a McChicken Sandwich and fries, which he eats leaning up against the car, throwing the paper box and wrapper at a litter bin which he misses by a yard, the carton ending up on the shining wet pavement. Denise is bad, isn't she? he thinks. He even suspected her of some sort of relationship with his own father, before the man got so irradiated and zonked out all the time he scarcely moved. Eddie's still not certain nothing was going on, if he's honest. Is that possible?

The radio calls him to a job in Camberwell, some girl wanting a ride to Balham. He finds her outside the pub swaying slightly, supporting herself on a lamppost, a pretty thing and, he reckons, not much younger than himself.

'Hello. Barry Cars. You the one for Balham?' he asks and the girl nods and climbs in the back where she sprawls out across the seat.

The radio's still on and churning out this old saccharine mush from the Cranberries but he could do with a conversation, so he says to the girl: 'You off out for the night, then?'

'No, going home,' she mumbles.

She has closed her eyes so Eddie doesn't bother her

any more until they get to the eastern edge of Balham, where he turns around in his seat and says to her, 'hey, whereabouts in Balham d'you want?'

She's asleep so he repeats the question and her eyes open and she looks back, a confused thing. 'I can't remember.'

'Oh. Thought you said you were going home?'

'Yes. I'm sorry. I get mixed up about roads and things.'

'Do you know your own name, then?' he says, good naturedly enough, but there's no reply from the girl, she's staring out of the window. He continues to drive, heading west, wondering if some sign or landmark will suddenly jog this girl's memory and after five minutes or so, as they're stuck in traffic lights by the tube station, she sits up and leans forward between the front seats and says: 'Yes!'

Eddie looks at her expectantly.

'It's Emily, definitely. You had me worried for a bit.'

He pulls over. 'Look, love, I can't just drive around all night like this. I need to know where in Balham you live . . . do you have anything on you with your address?' Eddie points at her little handbag.

She shakes her head. 'I don't think it is Balham, after all. I think it's, like, Camberwell.'

Eddie sighs and says are you kidding and the girl says she doesn't think she is kidding so the car swings round and they head back the way they've come. She's silently dozing, her head jammed up against the window, as the meter clicks on and on, past fifteen pounds, he hopes she has the money to pay. And what if it's not Camberwell, but really is Balham? He heard on another quiz programme about this man, Charon, who ferries the undead across a river. Maybe he could spend the rest of the night as a kind of Charon, Charon in a Peugeot, rather than a rowing boat, endlessly ferrying an undead girl between nowhere in particular and somewhere else.

He gets caught in traffic at Clapham Common and Denise, the thought of Denise, creeps up on him again. He can't fathom why she should have this effect but he's sure that in some way he knows, inside. He wonders if it's simply that every time he fucks her there's so much at stake, so much to lose, every fuck being charged with menace and fear and tension and this, he reckons, is probably how it should be. But maybe not, maybe it's something else altogether. Better not even to question the whole business. He pulls away from the lights by the edge of the common and he suddenly wants Denise again so much that his hands shiver upon the steering wheel. And then, bizarrely, this thing comes to him from God knows where, this utterly useless piece of knowledge he must have picked up somewhere along the line and filed away at the back of his brain and some complex and unfathomable process has resulted in its belated, pointless recall – simply this: the capital of Guadeloupe is Basse-Terre.

The Long, Long Road to Uttoxeter

Recurring prostate trouble plus a dream of being incessantly tormented by Kalahari Bushmen forces Graham to wake up and, without at first disturbing his snoring wife, climb slowly out of bed and pad with eyes sleep-dumbed and dysfunctional towards the bathroom. He hunches over the lavatory bowl, leans with his hand against the wall beyond and after the occlusion of aeons coaxes out a pitiful trickle of cloudy chemical yellow urine. And then, shaking his recalcitrant and exhausted penis dry, he lurches towards the sink to cup some water to his mouth. He curses his prostate and thinks to himself as the tap splashes up and into his face, yeah, this is it, things will never get better, it's a slow descent to the grave punctuated by incessant visits to the lavatory and other niggling bodily irritations, the arteries and tendons and joints all desiccated and hardening daily. Just the simple act of rising from bed, five minutes ago, took unearthly effort, like lifting up a car.

He is less gloomy of a morning, when his wife, Claudia, is up and about, but right now, trying to balance the tiresome servicing of his immediate bodily requirements plus allowing Claudia to sleep on undisturbed, he gets affronted by the sheer inconvenience of old age, and its insistence upon minor, nagging discomforts. Plus, he watched two television programmes this evening. One about the social structure of – and, inevitably, the iniquities suffered by – Kalahari Bushmen; the other a fictional drama during which the extremely attractive actress Anna Friel engaged in oral sex with a succession of disparate men. At the age of seventy-two, it would be nice to have some control over what one dreams, he thinks. Give me that, at least. But no, he got the bushmen. It is only when he stands fully erect, preparatory to returning to his bedroom, that he hears the quiet commotion first on the path outside his house and then at the front door. He is instinctively clammily afraid. He assumes of course that it's a burglar, burgling being a popular local enthusiasm treated with disdain or indifference by the police. But then, as proper consciousness is forced upon him by the circumstances, he realises that burglars rarely knock at the door and do not normally carry out their activities whilst weeping. Whoever is downstairs right now is doing both. A tremulous knock and a low, deep sobbing. Perplexed, he stands dead still where he is and listens. But then, when the knock comes again and he hears this voice call out, he dries his hands meticulously on the pink bathroom towel and, walking slowly along the landing, rouses his wife: 'Claudia . . . Claudia . . .' he says, 'wake up . . . there's someone trying to get in. I think they're in trouble . . .'

It's a long, long road to Uttoxeter. And Christian is not even half way there.

Earlier in the evening, he's pacing the platform at Cambridge railway station, waiting for the London train which is a little late, his hands and mouth and groin regions fragrant of very recent sex. The flickering monitor screen above him says the train will be five minutes late and therefore due in nine minutes, which is OK, so he smokes a last cigarette and walks along the edge of the platform up beyond the deserted waiting room and the shuttered snackbar and he wonders if maybe now would be a good moment to call Angela, his wife. So he reaches into his suit pocket and pulls out the Motorola but then there's an announcement from the tannoy about some service to Norwich and he shudders and thinks, no, that would have been a bad idea, calling his wife. He knows that it is guilt making him want to ring, guilt burning away at him like an ulcer in his conscience, so he puts the phone back in his pocket and turns around and walks towards a metal bench seat, designed to maximise his discomfort, where he sits himself down to drag through the final six or so minutes.

He is not meant to be here, on Cambridge station, you see. He is meant to be in Uttoxeter or, by now, on the way back from Uttoxeter. That's what he's told Angela. He has to go to Uttoxeter to deliver a lecture to the Turing Society, he said, Christian being an acknowledged expert on the life and works of Alan Turing. Always lie from a position of strength; nobody is going to challenge him about anything to do with Alan Turing, probably not even Turing's relatives if there are any left alive. Why Uttoxeter, Angela asked, as she was indeed expected to do and Christian looked up surprised and said: Why? Why? Are you joking? Well, because he spent an important three weeks in the town, of course, immediately before completing the first draft of *Principles of Computing*; for the followers of Turing, he says with a confection of patience and condescension, Uttoxeter is a big deal.

This is a nonsense: Turing never visited Uttoxeter,

so far as anyone knows. But coming from Christian, the writer of two books about the man, it is easily established as a verifiable fact.

'We're meeting in a place called the Three Oaks Hotel,' he says above the whine and complaint and chaos of the family breakfast, naming a hotel which actually exists in Uttoxeter, or at least nearly exists because it is really called the Two Oaks Hotel – a more subtle lie this.

'When are you back?' asks Angela, trying to force food into the throat of their dissolute daughter, Martha, who at the age of two is already anorexic or bulimic or something, refusing all food and getting thinner by the day, so thin and bedraggled she looks like one of those ponies rescued by the RSPCA from a gypsy encampment, all ribs and bad pelt and woebegone expression and which then, despite public sympathy, gets put down.

'This evening, but lateish, I suspect,' says Christian, with total honesty, swallowing a last mouthful of coffee and watching his daughter tip over a bowl of chocolate frosties with distaste.

'It sounds a bit dreary. Where's Uttoxeter?'

Christian had hoped she wouldn't ask this, but is prepared all the same. 'Miles away, up north. It's a real pain. I only said yes out of a fucking misplaced sense of duty. I mean, it is my subject.'

'Good luck. I really don't understand why they can't have these sorts of things in London. It's just inverse snobbery. You know I'm out 'til late too?'

Of course he does. It is a major factor in the construct of his planned deceit.

'Yeah, Moppet Bar. Have a nice time. Say hello to Miranda for me.'

Zinaida, the Ukrainian au pair, lurks nervously in the background, a small, pale shadow of a person, sharp, fragile cheekbones on a pair of waiflegs, watching the three of them closely, but comprehending nothing. She was born very near Chernobyl in 1986 and Angela thinks maybe some of the bad stuff got to her when she was in the womb. Apparently there is a species of vole living near the decommissioned reactor, on the Belarus side of the border, which have grown to twice their normal size and are super-intelligent, sort of Extreme Voles. Maybe the radiation has precisely the reverse effect on humans, Angela says, because Zinaida is tiny and stupid.

So, anyway, Christian chose Turing for his deceit because he's an expert on Turing and he chose Uttoxeter for more complex and fiendish reasons. Firstly, he's almost convinced Angela has never heard of it. He's almost never heard of it himself. He's said it's 'up north' but she has no idea that, more properly, it is in the north midlands, a little to the south east of Stoke-on-Trent, according to his AA map. Christian's guess is that she will forget the name of the place, but even if she doesn't, he's got a safety net. Should she suddenly wish to call him – which is unlikely – she will have to remember the name of the town *and* the name of the hotel, which is asking a lot. Further, Directory Inquiries will not have a Three Oaks Hotel in Uttoxeter. And it is likely that even if she attempts to spell out Uttoxeter, she will miss the second 't', the pronunciation of the place being misleading in this regard. So she will have trouble trying to find Uttoxeter and great trouble trying to find his designated hotel. Even if she persists, for God only knows what reason, and tracks down the Two Oaks

Hotel and finds that there isn't a Mr Veevers there at all, he can say well, no, I was at the Three Oaks Hotel, as I said and that, really, should be that. And if, upon his return, Angela should say look, I tried to ring you but there's no such hotel as the one you mentioned he can say oh, what, you mean the Two Oaks Hotel, etc.

Are you still with me?

And really, there's no reason why she should try to track him down at all because he's not even away for the night, just most of the evening.

Angela has been 'up north', as she calls it, only once. She went with some girls for a weekend in Blackpool and hated the place. They stayed in a B&B and went clubbing. All she talked about, when she returned, was the cold and the rough, dreadful people with their appalling, good-natured bonhomie. They went by train and it's quite likely she passed through several Staffordshire towns on the way – Leek and Stafford, for example. Maybe even Tamworth. But not Uttoxeter. There is a branch line to Uttoxeter, the Stoke to Derby branch line, in fact. But she would not have travelled on that. Christian checked.

Nor does Angela like horse racing very much, which is the only other reason anybody from London would have heard of the place. There's a race course there.

You need to know somebody very well in order to lie to them convincingly, he thinks. Really, you need to love them. And he certainly loves Angela very much indeed. He would do anything, almost anything, to shield her from pain.

On platform three the Norwich train draws up and the recorded announcement lists the various stations at which the service will deign to stop. It is a good job he wasn't on the phone to Angela right now. She might hear the announcement in the background and ask so, then, is this Uttoxeter place near Norwich and the whole edifice of his alibi would begin to deliquesce. He shivers a little, thinking about this and reaches into his pocket to turn the phone off altogether. Better to be safe than sorry.

It's only ten-thirty, so in any case Angela will still be out with her friends – Clara and Miranda, at the Moppet Bar – getting smashed on vodka and diet tonics.

And if she tries to track him down via the Turing Society she won't have much luck either, because there's no such thing. He made it up.

He wonders if he should light another cigarette as an anciently established superstitious means of encouraging the train to arrive, but then the tannoy crackles back into life, telling him his train is approaching the station and apologising for the delay which was due to a signalling failure.

At Diss.

So, why is he in Cambridge, after all? Well, for an illicit fuck, obviously. An illicit fuck with Joanne, whom he met two weeks previously at a book launch in Pimlico. Joanne is an English Literature post-graduate, a firm and youthful twenty-two years old with the bright, if slightly thyroidic, brown eyes of a squirrel. Her dissertation, which she explained at great length, is on science-based literature of the twentieth century – that great bore C.P. Snow, mainly, but a quick nod here and there to Djerassi, Levi, Gibson and Philip K. Dick. She talked very knowledgeably about Turing, not just his achievements but his tortured sexuality too. It is always a good sign if girls talk about someone's tortured sexuality, Christian feels. Anyway, he certainly couldn't have pulled the Uttoxeter stunt on Joanne with all her background knowledge about Turing.

The Scientific Imagining, she called her dissertation. So in a sense she is right up Christian's street and, sure enough, half an hour ago, he was right up hers.

By the way, he has told Joanne that he lives alone in a flat in Balham, whereas, in fact, he lives with his wife, daughter and strange au pair in Tooting. Tooting and Balham are very close to each other in south London, but they have different postcodes. Christian's *modus operandi* on such occasions is always to lie copiously and conscientiously to his wife, Angela, and quite indiscriminately to his more recently acquired partner (i.e. Joanne, on this occasion).

The train pulls into the station and Christian selects a carriage with not too many people in it. Being seen by someone known by the two of them – Angela and Christian, not Joanne and Christian – is an undoubted risk; but a very small one. In fact, on the train up to Cambridge he tried to work out what the odds would be. Lower than the average layman might think, maybe – perhaps one in a few thousand, once you've factored in the many variables. But high enough to swallow the risk.

It's one of those new hermetically sealed electric trains which is almost totally silent, just a faint hum from the overhead electric cables. Christian climbs aboard and sits in an aisle seat and puts his briefcase on the seat next to him, by the window. In the briefcase is the outline of his address to the Turing Society, a work of scientific imagining if ever there was one. Six pages – it took him the best part of an afternoon.

Was it all worth it, this labyrinthine deceit? Or is the

labyrinthine deceit the point? Christian can't make up his mind. Joanne is very pretty in a London Zoo small-mammal enclosure sort of way and, furthermore, every bit as sexually accommodating as he had expected her to be. On the way to the irritatingly trendy bar where she had suggested they meet that lunchtime, he wondered to himself what, exactly, might entail from this liaison. Sexual intercourse seemed highly likely, if not actually certain. He had reckoned the odds of penetrative sex as being about evens, with odds on in favour of some sort of low-level romantic or sexual activity, perhaps, at the least, an introductory wrist job. His calculations were deliberately on the conservative side, so as to mitigate against disappointment later on. But even in the bar, at one o clock in the afternoon, she had allowed her hand to be held across the polished wooden table and then held his back, so the odds started to shorten very rapidly indeed.

Not that he was absolutely convinced he wished to engage in penetrative sex; mentally he did, but physically part of him, a crucial part, often shirked its responsibilities on such illicit liaisons. He is not sure why this sometimes happens. It is not something he likes to think about for very long.

But Joanne was more interesting than he had at first assumed. The artwork in her little apartment was far from the usual stuff – not girlie Matisse or Picasso and lots of artsy photographs – but massive, properly framed prints (he assumed) by Bridget Riley and, oddly, that most male of painters, Lichtenstein. And when he browsed through her book collection whilst she attended to herself in the bathroom, perhaps washing herself or urinating or quite possibly applying one of those feminine hygiene deodorisers to her vagina, he was quite astonished to see the complete works of that yankee whacko Ayn Rand. There they all were – *The Fountainhead, Atlas Shrugged* and so on – all stacked up right in the middle of the shelf. Displayed proudly, you might argue. Christian has a thing about very right-wing women. He's not sure why. He is the only man he knows to have masturbated over photographs of Eva Perón, Allessandra Mussolini and Leni Riefenstahl. When he found out Brigitte Bardot these days voted for M. Le Pen's *Front National* he spent weeks trying to track down her old videos. There's something fascinating and unnatural about a woman who is intellectually or even instinctively right wing. Ayn Rand; lordy!

Christian wonders if it's late enough to ring Angela. He thinks maybe not, but he should turn his phone back on in case she rings him. A mobile phone turned off for too long is an unnecessary cause for suspicion. He takes the Motorola out of his pocket and places it next to his briefcase. The train glides like a guilty silver ghost through the Cambridgeshire night.

He grabbed hold of Joanne when she came out of the bathroom and pushed her back against a wall and kissed her, holding her lightly by the head, his hands mussing around in her fine, chestnut hair and then slipping down to the artful gap between her white T-shirt and the top of her grey cargo trousers. He stroked along the soft, pale band of flesh there and found that there was no lack of avidity in her response, nor did she break off and say no, no, please, I'm not ready or anything like that. In fact, she was more than ready. She said nothing at all but led him by the hand into her bedroom where she pressed up against him and began to undo the buttons of his shirt so as to gnaw and worry at one of his nipples with a rather acute, rapid action of her powerful incisors. So quickly did all this occur that he scarcely had time to register his new surroundings and was aware only of a muddled blur of white linen, the smell of clothes and sheets laundered with the aid of Lenor Spring Awakening Fabric Conditioner™ and another piece of op art or pop art obscuring fully one wall of the room. And the sweet, pale afternoon sunshine washing across her face.

On his first few occasions – dates, I suppose you'd call them – with Angela, he was surprised and perplexed by her reserve and containment. She doesn't really like me, he thought, each time he made his way home after an evening of thwarted burrowing and nibbling and poking around. But she did, it seemed. Because they've been together for six years now, during which period Christian has constructed elaborate deceits for seventeen extra-curricula fucks or moistly agreeable rummages. Averaged out, that means about three per year. But to view the statistics in so superficial a manner would be misleading. You see, there was only one in the first year, four in the second, six in the third (when they had Martha), five in the fourth and one in the fifth. This is his first such encounter this year. If plotted on a graph, it would prove to be an interesting and illuminating parabola. What are the variables, he wonders? What are the forces at work here? He does feel himself, on these excursions, to be unwillingly propelled by something – maybe genetics or even historical inevitability – and not the master of his own destiny.

Baldock. North Herts. Edge of the Chilterns. Hosiery, light engineering. Somewhat eclipsed by the new town of Stevenage in the last quarter of a century.

The train is making good time. He will certainly be early enough to catch the Northern Line tube train back to Tooting.

At one point, towards the conclusion of the act of intercourse earlier this evening, he became unaccountably distracted and ever so slightly panicky: he could not remember the surname of the girl he was fucking. He wondered if she remembered his and thought she probably did. Women may not know – in strict geographical terms – where they are, exactly, but they tend to remember who they're having intercourse with.

Even before ejaculation, the first strategies for exit had begun to form in his mind, and he pondered the conundrum as to whether he should ever see her again. Angela had already begun to fizz upward in his consciousness and then swim before him, her eyes clouded with reproach.

In only thirty per cent of these unsanctioned couplings has he seen the girl more than once.

Joanne hung with her head flung back over the side of the bed, her hair splayed out across the floor, which required Christian to cling on to her waist so they both didn't fall off, and then after a modicum of congenial thrusting, she came with the exhilarating whoops and pant-hoots of a troop of Rhesus monkeys, which was flattering, if alarming.

He reaches out for the mobile phone, thinking about it. By now, Angela will surely be staggering out of the Moppet Bar with Miranda and Clara, maybe being urged by Clara – who has recently divorced – to go clubbing or retire to Jimmy Heidegger's for a night cap. Christian picks up the phone.

And then, for some reason, he is suddenly catapulted

out of his seat and across the aisle. The thing happens so quickly he does not have time even to register surprise, fear or pain. Wham, wham, wham, goes his body; first against the side of the carriage, then the ceiling, then the floor. He is vaguely aware of screaming, in the middle distance and this terrible tearing sound, like a factory being torn in half by a giant alien, and a grinding and screeching, a feeling of weightlessness and then of gravity at its most intense, and then the lights go out and he is thrown once more up and sideways, his body wrenching this way and that in the turbulent air.

This is a train crash, he thinks to himself, with commendable acuity, as his head collides with the edge of a seat. And then his lights go out, too.

When he wakes up, he is cold. He can hear the distant sound of a man crying, an intermittent babble of voices and a light pattering above his head. It is rain, rain falling on the crashed train. He feels very weak and rather other-worldly, lying splayed out across two seats, hemmed down by something, facing towards the window, which is smashed, the metal edges buckled viciously inwards. He notices blood on the floor below him and soaking into the seats too. Is that my blood? he wonders. It must be my blood. There's nobody else here. Groggily he tries to collect himself. I should ring for an ambulance, he thinks, or the fire people. Or do they already know? He can see no blue flashing lights outside the carriage and can hear no sirens. And yet he has the feeling that he has been asleep for a long time.

I should ring Angela, he thinks to himself.

But first he must struggle up and find his phone somewhere amongst this wreckage.

'Help me, somebody, please help me,' he hears

someone moan quite close to him. Oh no, I must help that person, he thinks, reflexively, as soon as I find the phone.

And then he sees the Motorola. Miraculously, he is still holding it in his left hand. He remembers, now, preparing to call Angela when the crash occurred. But he feels dizzy and disoriented and his sense of perspective is askew. The phone, for example, looks as if it is yards away from him, and yet, there he is, still holding it in his left arm. He tries to close his hand around it and then stops trying because nothing happens: his hand will not obey the command. I must have snapped a tendon or maybe broken my arm, he thinks, or – he gets frightened – maybe it's a neurological thing. And yet he does not feel in great pain. He tries to reach towards the phone with his other hand and this confuses him because, try as he might, he cannot get anywhere near it.

And then the bewilderment lifts a little and he realises the true nature of his predicament. There is nothing wrong with his sense of perspective. His left arm – and the phone – are indeed a good distance away. Several yards the other side of the smashed window.

And, quite clearly, no longer connected to the rest of his body.

At this point, he passes out once more.

He is not sure if he is dead, alive and unconscious, or fully conscious. He feels himself to be lying in the same place, splayed across the two seats of the train, pressed down by something heavy on his shoulders and his back. He can see his arm out of the shattered and corrupted window and senses a sort of vague nostalgia for it. That's my arm, he thinks. I've had it for years, that arm. And look at it now, lying there in the dirt, alone and untended. Goodbye, arm, he murmurs, goodbye! And the arm lifts itself a little from the ground and offers him the faintest of waves. Goodbye, Christian, it says.

A sharp spasm of pain jolts him into a semblance of wretched lucidity. He is moving, floating through the cold night air with its veil of pale drizzle, floating on his back, up, up, up, he goes, except it is not floating really because his passage is uneven and every jolt sends an electric shock of outrage through his left shoulder, the shoulder without the arm on it. He groans and gibbers.

A huge man's face slips into view, grey and mottled in the deep shadows cast by the klieg lights. You're all right now, the face tells him, everything's going to be all right, you're being taken care of, everything's all right. Blue flashes strobe across his own face and he smells petrol, hears engine noises and then, above all of this, voices discussing something, the something being him, he realises after a few moments. Lost blood. Trauma. No major problem other than amputated left arm. Is he in pain, a voice asks? I should fucking well think so, someone replies from behind, with a dry laugh. Dunno maybe cracked ribs, few cuts and bruises nothing internal so far evident. Got off lightly, then. Morphine . . . no, twenty mils . . . no more. Can you hear me, sir? Can you hear me, sir? Hello, sir, can you hear me? They're talking to him, now, asking him something.

'Yes,' says Christian. 'I can hear you. Does anybody have the right time?'

Somebody laughs again.

'Yes, mate. It's eleven-thirty. You got plans for the rest of the evening, then?'

That same massive face appears above him. 'What's your name, sir?' it asks, and Christian mumblingly replies before a band of greyness washes across his line of vision until his whole sight is obliterated and he drifts back into a sort of comfortable but dissonant limbo-land.

His shoulder does not hurt any more, just now. There's no pain anywhere. But he is gripped by this terrible anxiety and restlessness. He lies flat on his back in the intensive-care ward of Cambridge Royal Infirmary, little lights blinking around him, contraptions attached to him and in the background the murmurings of his fellow patients and the occasional clatter and sound of footsteps. What time is it now, he wonders to himself.

He must ring Angela. She will be home and may have started to worry, surely. But, along with his arm he has lost his phone. How is he going to explain all this in the morning?

He attempts to consider the problem logically, banishing the panic. He is in a hospital in Cambridge when really he should be on his way home from Uttoxeter.

It is not inconceivable, he thinks, that Angela might be convinced by an argument that says Cambridge actually *is* on the way home from Uttoxeter. Her knowledge of geography is truly appalling: she had imagined that Blackpool, for example, was a hundred or so miles from London, and possibly in Wales. The length of the journey for that weekend jaunt astonished her. In Richard Adams's novel about bunny rabbits, *Watership Down*, the rabbits are deemed to be incapable of counting above four. Everything over that amount is called 'H'rair', whether it be five or five thousand. All 'h'rair'. Angela's phrase 'up north' works in much the same way, thinks Christian, swamped with affection. 'Up north' is everywhere beyond a thirty mile radius of Waterloo Bridge, whether it be to the north, south, east or west. Newcastle, Leeds and Bedford are 'up north'. So, too, are Aberystwyth, the Isle of Thanet and St Ives. She knows, however, that Salcombe is in Devon and, furthermore, 'in the West Country', because her mother has a flat there, where they stayed one damp Whitsun very early on in their relationship, a sort of experimental attempt at living together which went so well that the very night they returned to London a mini-van was booked for Angela's stuff.

Christian tries to prop himself up on his left elbow and then remembers that he doesn't have one any more. So he props himself up on his right elbow instead. We learn to adapt and survive very quickly, don't we?

Outside the glass observation window of his room a nurse hurries by with a tray of implements. In the corridor he can hear new arrivals being shunted around and consoled: it must still be quite early, he thinks. Poor unfortunates are still being delivered from the train crash. He does not at any point consider himself a poor unfortunate. He has a problem to wrestle with.

So: tell Angela that he changed trains at Cambridge? Christian considers the potential dangers of this escape route. If he tells her that he is a victim of that big rail crash near Baldock then she will take a greater than usual interest in all the relentless news reports of it. There's a very real possibility that they will show maps of the route the fated train took. But the graphics would probably be cut off at Cambridge, wouldn't they? They wouldn't put a map on the television which showed Cambridge in relation to Uttoxeter? Unless they were deliberately trying to spite him.

But, he muses, one of her friends, or maybe her bloody father, if they asked about how come he was on this train near Cambridge . . . the cat would be out of the bag, then. Her father would know the precise location of Uttoxeter. He would swoop on it. You do not travel through Cambridge to get home from Uttoxeter, he would say. There's something fishy going on.

A new idea presents itself, somehow. Not an explanation for the arm mishap, as such, but a means of at least buying himself some time. Time, you see, feels very short. So what about this: Christian discharges himself from the hospital and makes his way home, probably via a taxi. By the time he gets back Angela will be asleep; all he needs to do is murmur a quiet hello darling and climb into bed and pull the covers tightly around him. The following morning she will be up quite early for her day shift as a supply teacher at St Bernadette's School. Tomorrow night she's due at her parents . . . well, they both are, but he could cry off, ring from work saying he had stuff to do at home, or was tired. Again: he would be snugly in bed again by the time she returned. If he could swing this, she would see him, head on, for at most ten or fifteen minutes over the course of the next thirty-six hours. If, during that brief crunch time, which will be undoubtedly nerve wracking and awful, he were to drape his jacket over his shoulders, rather than wear it properly, if he ensures that he is largely turned away from her, or at least conceals his left side, if he does all that . . . *then it is entirely possible that she will not notice the fact that one of his arms is missing.*

This will give him time to fabricate a plausible excuse: a hit and run accident on the way home from work, a terrible explosion in one of the labs – or maybe he lost the arm when it got trapped in the lift doors at the university. It doesn't matter now. There are thousands of ways one could lose an arm, after all. The great thing about this plan is that it buys him time.

Christ, he thinks, it's workable. What are the drawbacks? Christian's mind switches into its familiar and comfortable mode of binary analysis. He would have to get out of here – and back home – quickly, for the thing to be successful. Secondly, there's a problem with Zinaida. Even after Angela has left for work, she would still be around for the whole day, observing him. Although stupid, she might notice something was amiss. But even if she noticed she couldn't tell Angela, because she doesn't speak English. She's an au pair and she doesn't even know the English for 'child'. She certainly won't know the English for 'arm' and 'amputation'. Could she conceivably mime it to Angela when she came home, mime the fact that Christian's arm was missing? It's not likely. Why would she?

Martha, however, is a different story. She may well notice the missing arm – but she won't care. She'll think it's another one of those bizarre adult foibles, losing an arm. And Angela will simply assume she's talking rubbish, as usual, if she does say anything.

He would have to be very careful and perform with great chutzpah and fortitude – but he's managed that before. Why not now?

His mind spins through the variables.

He'd have to meet people at work head on. And they'd notice his arm problem. He'd have to tell *them*. What if one of them were to ring Angela *before* his arm were officially, so to speak, missing? The colleague, whoever it was, would be bound to say at some point, I'm so sorry about your husband's arm. Why, what's wrong with it? Well, it's gone, isn't it? And then he'd have the tricky problem of explaining to Angela why he forgot to tell her he'd lost an arm. And he'd have to fabricate *two* excuses; one for Angela and one for his work colleagues and ensure that the two were not brought into collision with each other, like matter and anti-matter. And they do sometimes ring her, his colleagues; she knows one or two of them socially: Stuart in the media centre and his girlfriend Sally *who is the departmental secretary!* In other words, the first person to see him every morning.

And he'd have to go to work in order to be out of the house. And Angela always rings him at work so he can't *say* he's going to work and then hide all day in the Horniman Museum, or something.

Could he claim he lost his arm on the way to work? It's difficult and it would buy him hardly any time at all to get his mind straight and sort out an excuse.

Christian shakes his head, causing minor tremors of pain to slither down the side of his body. It's not feasible. It's just not feasible.

The safest route, he thinks, is to somehow get himself to Uttoxeter, or at least the Uttoxeter area. Stoke, maybe. Or Derby. Check into the local hospital and say look, I've had a spot of bother with my arm. Can you help me? Then he'd need to fabricate only one explanation for the missing arm and he would be spared that traumatic thirty-six hours of deception. But he'd have to get to Uttoxeter pretty quickly for the thing to work. Now, what if he . . .

'Mr Babbage . . . Mr Babbage . . . are you awake?'

Christian is dragged from his reverie by a harassed looking doctor with swept-back black hair staring down at him. Christian is confused. Who the hell is Babbage? Is that what he told them his name was? It's quite possible. Charles Babbage, of course, the other important figure in the history of computing.

'Yes, I'm awake.'

'How are you feeling?'

'I'm fine.' Christian tries to shrug nonchalantly but it doesn't work.

'Ow,' he says. His days of shrugging nonchalantly are over.

'You'll be feeling very weak: you lost a lot of blood, which we have largely replaced. And I daresay you will suffer various symptoms of shock at both the crash and the trauma as it directly affects your body. But there are two bits of very good news.'

Christian smiles up at the man. He could do with some very good news. 'Yes?'

'I know it may not seem like it, but you seem to have escaped pretty lightly. No serious internal injuries or bleeding. And you have been only mildly concussed.'

'Good,' says Christian.

'Secondly, your arm was sheared off very cleanly indeed. We think there is a ninety-to-ninety-five per cent chance that we can reattach your arm successfully. It may take a long time for it to work properly . . .'

'You've found my arm?'

'Yes. It was lying by the side of the track. At least, we assume it's yours,' the doctor laughs.

'Was the phone still with it?'

The man looks at him rather curiously. 'I have no idea. I will check for you, later.'

'And you think that you can reattach my arm?'

'Yes, absolutely.'

'When?'

'Well, within the next couple of days . . .'

'Oh, no, I'm sorry . . . that's out of the question.'

'What?'

'If I have to wait that long, I'd rather do without the arm. I have to be home, you see, this evening. Or this morning, whichever it is.'

'Mr Babbage,' says the doctor, 'we cannot possibly reattach your arm tonight, not least because you are still in a state of severe shock. You might not survive such a lengthy operation and I certainly wouldn't be prepared to risk it. And you most certainly can't go home. The stitches in your arm are temporary; you shouldn't be moving about at all. And of course you are concussed.'

'Yes, I'm aware of that. And I respect your point of view. But if the operation cannot be performed this evening then, regretfully, I'm afraid I will have to forgo my arm entirely.'

The doctor appears perplexed but then smiles at him once more. 'Look, Mr Babbage. It's best if you get some sleep. If the pain begins again, just call the nurse on the buzzer here. We'll talk about this further in the morning. Now, if you'll excuse me, I have some pretty terrible injuries to deal with. A terrible, terrible, night.'

And the doctor walks away.

Christian waits until he is out of sight. And then he rips the plastic drip tube from his solitary arm and climbs out of bed. His clothes are in a plastic bag on the chair beside the bed. He dresses, leaning against the bedside table to balance himself, struggling with his trousers, almost toppling over as he tries to slot in the left leg. His shirt is covered in blood, so he drapes his jacket over his shoulders and buttons it in the middle over the loose, pale green, hospital night shirt. He catches sight of a reflection of himself in the window. He looks a bit of a mess, if we're honest. A dark cut over one eye. And a suit jacket with the arm ripped off above the elbow. Still, needs must. Peering around the door jamb, he tiptoes down the corridor, muttering to himself, Uttoxeter, Uttoxeter.

The disquieting thing is, nobody bothers him. He walks through the reception area for the intensive-care ward and the nurses, marching swiftly hither and thither, and the doctors wiping away the sweat from their brows, affixed to clipboards, pay him not the slightest attention. He walks quickly towards the lifts and waits with exasperation for the lift to arrive.

Outside, the world is ablaze with light and noise and an epidemic of activity. On black tarmac shiny and greasy with rain and artificial light, ambulances swing into the forecourt and discharge their cargoes and spin away back into the night. Up the steps to the main entrance is a frantic procession of humanity; doctors called back off their rest periods, the first relatives stumbling blindly towards God knows what; journalists and media monkeys spaced out across the horizon announcing death tolls and injury lists and whose fault was it and can the hospital cope . . . Christian crouches down low behind a privet hedge, the rain splattering across his back and trickling down his back towards the terrible absence below his shoulder. He runs in a strange, crab like motion, keeping low all the time, ducking ever lower, tracing the hedge as it prescribes the perimeter of the forecourt, aching from the effort of stooping so low but adrenaline coursing through his body and obliterating the vaguest edges of a formless ache in his body, which will later become excruciating pain when the drugs have worn off. Those press monkeys, more even than the doctors, must not be allowed to see him.

Get a taxi, get a taxi. A nice warm taxi, where he can doze and marshal his thoughts, a taxi with one of those vanilla-scented de-odorisers hanging from a little cardboard pine tree above the dashboard and with a driver who is friendly but not too solicitous. He needs money, but he can find a cashpoint on the way. Oh, and he needs a phone. To ring Angela.

But where, exactly, is he? He curses himself for not having become better acquainted with the geography of Cambridge city centre, for not having properly prepared, in advance of his liaison, for some alarming eventuality, like being hospitalised and losing a limb. Such carelessness, he thinks, is not like him.

He is in a wide arterial road flanked on either side by broad grey-brick Victorian villas. He can see the city centre lights way ahead of him, to the right. Which way is north? The stream of cars and ambulances arriving at the hospital, three hundred yards away, approach from the right. The crash occurred south of Cambridge so he must, surely, turn left. That must be north. The drizzle washes his face and brings about a state of comparative mental alertness, but also the glimmerings and twitchings of pain in his left shoulder. He puts his hand up to where his other arm should be and folds the ripped ends of his sleeve over his bandaged stump. And then he walks, turning every few seconds to scour the road behind him for an approaching taxi.

And then he sees the telephone booth, on the other side of the road.

Jamming the receiver under his chin and feeling peculiarly off balance doing so, he bungs twenty pence in the slot and punches out the number of Angela's mobile phone. He will tell her that he is still in Uttoxeter, there having been a problem with the trains. He cannot tell her about his arm because she will worry and start doing things like making phone calls here there and everywhere and his deception will become immediately evident.

The phone is answered with a blur of static.

'Hello, darling,' he says, 'I've had a problem . . .'

'Higrippley ygggr . . . velociraptor gambit tetrahedron,' says Angela, between bursts of coruscating white noise.

Christian shouts down into the malodorous mouthpiece. 'I've had some trouble . . . I don't know if you can hear me . . . I'm still in Uttoxeter . . .'

'Krishnan Guru Murthy . . . bilious conceptual verkehesampfel,' Angela replies, before the phone cuts out altogether. He hangs up, sweating a little, exhausted by the exertion.

But he rang her, at least. Hearing her voice – even that electronically mutilated approximation of it – swamps his senses with love and yearning, for a second or two. But: did she hear him? He is wondering about this when he notices a sticker on the wall beside the telephone, advertising a firm of minicabs. They are called City Cars and offer a twenty-four-hour service. He is advised that he may hire one of their special stretch limousines equipped with a mini bar and television if he so wishes and also white limousines for weddings. He rings the number.

'City Cars,' says the man.

'I need a car.'

'There's an hour's wait, mate. It's chaos, you know, what with the rail crash . . .'

'But I need to go to Staffordshire . . .'

'Staffordshire?'

'Yes.'

'Where in Staffordshire?'

Christian pauses. Where will the nearest hospital be? Derby? Uttoxeter? Stoke? Another lamentable failure to prepare. Why hadn't he thought about all of this properly! 'Stoke,' he replies.

The man tells him to wait a minute and Christian hears a clunk as the phone is put down. And then: 'Yeah, well Stoke's a hundred and thirty pounds, mate.'

'That's OK,' says Christian.

'Car will be with you in ten minutes max. Where are you?'

'Um . . . near Cambridge hospital. In the main road. Near where all the television people are.'

'Theobalds Road. OK. Wait there by the phone and we'll be with you.'

Bang bang bang went the music in the car. Bang bang bang went Christian's head and neck and shoulders.

'Yo more bangin choons for you coming right up this is BBC Norfolk takin' you thru the wee small hours with heavy heavy multi techno garage, house and conservatory for the good people of East Anglia, south Leicestershire, the western edge of Northamptonshire – as far as Oundle and the Rockingham Forest – what used to be Huntingdonshire and Lincolnshire all the way to the Wash. Hey listen up, going out to Milly,

Theresa, Galileo and the Radical Lowestoft Possee, stay cool, we've got yo' bitches some fishy fishy beats from Formal Gravadlax Intifada: "My Name IS Ern," yo, wicked . . . um . . . shit, man, I missed north Essex . . .'

What on earth was the man talking about, Christian wondered, as the car bounced and shimmied in time to the horrible song? Maybe it was something to do with his concussion, not being able to decipher what would normally be coherent sentences. Maybe that was the trouble with the phone call to Angela: she was making sense, but some switch had flicked in his brain and the stuff got downloaded wrong. Christian sweated and shifted uneasily in his seat as Formal Gravadlax Intifada pounded out of the in-car quadrophonic speaker system behind, below and beside him. There was no vanilla-scented de-odoriser on the dashboard, just a cocktail stick upon which was appended the flag of Pakistan.

'Could you turn the music down a little,' Christian asked the driver, a young Asian lad who, so far, had not spoken to him at all save to ask for the money up front. Christian had said he needed a cashpoint so the driver took him straight to a branch of the Woolwich and watched as he struggled with his wallet.

'Uh, yeah, sorry, mate. Trying to keep awake,' said the young man.

'Just that I'm feeling a little under the weather.'

'Sure, yeah, I can see. Lost your arm.'

The driver flicked the radio off altogether, opened a window and put his foot to the floor. The wet road hissed like a thousand little snakes, the driver started humming to himself the four-note refrain from 'My Name is Ern' and Christian drifted into a queasy slumberland, beset by gibbering creatures, angry little red and black demon things stabbing at him with their nasty pitchforks, and shimmering white lights.

It was at a roundabout – where the A511 meets the A42, near the old coal mining town of Ashby-de-la-Zouch, in north Leicestershire – that he awoke with a sudden and terrible misgiving. He had been dreaming, a dissonant and hazy thing constructed by some hidden part of his brain, dreaming about Angela. She was preparing breakfast for Martha and something trivial, he can't recall what, made her laugh, she had this huge, compelling laugh and her eyes would come alive and then narrow and sometimes water with hilarity. Christian especially loved Angela when she laughed and he moved across to hold her in his dream but he couldn't because he had only one arm so he stroked her shoulder instead and flapped at her with his spare sleeve. Then she sat down and began to read the newspaper.

Fuck! The newspaper!

Christian was sweating heavily now in the thick warmth of the car. His armpits, he noticed, gave off a strange and unpleasant chlorinous tang.

'We've got to go back.'

The driver looked across at him. 'What?'

'I'm sorry, but we've got to go back to Cambridge. Quickly. Can you do a U-turn here? Go round the roundabout and head back they way we've come?'

'Why have we got to go back? We're more than halfway there.'

'I'm sorry, I'm sorry. We've got to go back. I've forgotten something.'

'What have you forgotten?'

'My arm.'

The driver slowed the car and pulled into a lay-by.

He turned around in his seat and faced Christian. 'Listen,' he said. 'Look, I don't understand any of this arm shit. But it'll be one hundred and thirty quid just to go back to Cambridge from here.' His face was devoid of sympathy or understanding.

'That's OK, no worries. I want you to wait for five minutes outside the hospital and then we'll carry on back to Stoke.'

What had occurred to Christian was this. The media interest in the rail crash – and its survivors – would be immense. At some point, perhaps a couple of days into the coverage, somebody would do a story about the strange case of the unclaimed arm in Cambridge Royal Infirmary. There would be many photographs of the arm. With captions saying stuff like 'Is This Your Arm?' It was entirely conceivable that Angela would *recognise his arm from the newspaper photographs.* And then the game would be up. Further, the arm was last seen holding his mobile telephone. Even if she didn't recognise his arm from the photograph, or think it a little suspect that her boyfriend had lost an arm and here was this arm being advertised in all of the newspapers, then she'd certainly recognise the mobile telephone number which they would undoubtedly print alongside the arm as an aid to identification. They had a name too, of course – Charles Babbage – but that wouldn't distract her for very long. She would put two and two together. She would know that it was his arm.

The little digital clock on the dashboard read 02.46 when the car turned around and headed back along the A511, towards the M1. Little knives of pain began to shoot through Christian's shoulder and the bandage around the stump of his arm glowed pink. He tried to sleep, but those jabbering red and black devils filled up his head whenever he closed his eyes. Now they were poking him with their horrid tridents and sniggering about his arm. Where's your arm, Christian? they asked, cackling and poking. He closed his eyes shut against them and focused upon Angela; Angela poking him in the ribs to get him up of a morning, Angela smiling up at him as he arrived home from work and that habitual 'Hibabegoodday?' which he wished, which he yearned, to hear again.

The scene back at the hospital was much quieter now. Most of the TV trucks had gone and there was no longer an anguished procession of ambulances into the forecourt. The passion had been drained from the event. This rail disaster was now entering its second, more dangerous phase. Rational contemplation of events and the time for the authorities to start thinking about stuff like who to blame and so on.

Christian paid the driver one hundred and thirty pounds and told him to wait. He presented himself at the reception desk of the hospital, feeling calmer than, really, he should. A young girl in a pale blue uniform and the name Yvonne Shepherd pinned to her breast looked up at him, clocking the absent arm and the sweat and the blood beginning to show through the stump below his shoulder.

'Hello. Can I help you?'

'Yes. I'm in a terrible hurry. I would like you to return my arm which, apparently, you still have.'

'Your arm?'

'Yes. I was involved in the rail crash, during which my arm was severed from the rest of my body. I want you to give me my arm back, please. I realise that this sounds an odd request.'

The nurse was silent.

'I need it very quickly. I have a taxi waiting outside.'

'Your name is . . .'

And then her question was answered.

'. . . Mr Babbage!'

The doctor who had previously spoken to Christian, the one with the swept-back hair who had so crushed his hopes by telling him that they could reattach his arm within the next few days, suddenly appeared at his side.

'What the hell do you think you are doing?'

The doctor stared, transfixed and appalled.

Speaking was beginning to take real effort for Christian now; energy was flooding out of him. 'Hello again, doctor. I simply wish to collect my arm and proceed on my way.'

'Are you joking? That's absolutely out of the question. Look: you're bleeding! If you do not return to your bed you will die. We have had the police out looking for you! Are you mad?'

Christian paused. 'I am not mad. I appreciate your concern. And all that you have done for me. But I have to leave. I have no choice in this matter. And I wish to take my arm with me. It is, after all, my arm.'

The doctor shook his head. 'It is no longer your arm. It is now our arm. It became our arm when it was separated from the rest of your body and delivered to this hospital in a Safeway carrier bag. You have no legal rights whatsoever over your arm.'

Christian closed his eyes. Why was everything conspiring against him? 'Please,' he said. 'Please give me my arm.'

'What are you going to do with it?'

'I'm going to take it to Uttoxeter.'

'Why?'

'I know a man. In Uttoxeter. A famous arm surgeon.'

Nurse Shepherd giggled.

'What are you talking about?' the doctor gasped.

'He's, uh, very good with limbs. Putting them back on. He's an old school friend.'

'What's his name?'

Christian thought for a moment.

'Gates. Bill Gates. *Doctor* Bill Gates.'

'I don't believe you. I just don't believe you. Look: we can reattach your arm. Do you understand? But if you leave now it is entirely likely that you will die. You will begin to lose more and more blood: those are temporary stitches in your shoulder. You are in shock; you are very badly injured. And listen: whatever it is that is so motivating you to behave like a madman, the consequences cannot possibly be worse than death, can they? We will not give you your arm, Mr Babbage.'

'We-ll,' Christian replied levelly. 'Can I at least have the mobile phone?'

The nurse giggled again.

The doctor stared at him for some moments and then waved his hand at the nurse. 'Oh, give him his fucking arm. Babbage: you are going to die.'

Christian scoured the forecourt for his taxi driver. But the taxi driver had gone with his £130, it seemed. Christian carried (in his right hand, obviously) his left arm. It was in a plastic carrier bag surrounded by ice cubes. The phone was there too, but dysfunctional, because the hospital people had put it in with his arm so it was soaked with water and blood and just made this annoyed beeping sound when he tried to use it.

Pain pulsed through him at every step. What shall I do now? he wondered. Do not think for a moment that he had not considered the possibility of confessing all to Angela. But it was a prospect far, far, worse than anything else he could imagine.

Quite apart from anything else, Angela had a thing, a bad thing, about amputees. She really didn't like them. There were lots of things which, irrationally, maybe, she didn't much care for. Offal, for example. Jazz music. Christmas re-runs of *Morecambe and Wise* or *The Two Ronnies*, especially Corbett. They made her feel she was old. She didn't like sushi, geese or anal sex, either. But amputees really worried Angela. He remembered her once rushing to the television to change channels simply because some poor legless chap was being interviewed about landmines. Amputations horrified her.

But, of course, she would not end her relationship with Christian simply because he'd been unfortunate enough to lose his arm. *She would need an excuse to do so.* And his infidelity provided the perfect excuse.

So Uttoxeter, then. He walked back down Theobalds Road, past the telephone booth, under a damp moonless sky, heading north-west. The plastic carrier bag had begun to leak. A pink watery liquid left a trail along the pavement. But there was a darker red, too, dripping behind him and the bandage and the bunched up sleeve of his jacket was sodden. The earth beneath his feet had lost its usual comforting solidity and the streetlights flickered and shimmied in the air before him.

Pain now occupied most of his brain. He could think of almost nothing but the pain; it occupied him, it took him over. Almost. He was just able to muse, with

87

irony, on his predicament and on the terrible psycho-logical traumas which had beset Alan Turing. I may be in trouble, Christian pondered to himself, but at least I'm not a latent poof.

And if nothing else, this proves the degree to which I love Angela, doesn't it? The lengths to which I would go, to protect her. You think I'm doing all of this for my own sake? he enquired of an imaginary audience. It's all for Angela. That laugh she has. When her eyes narrow and crease up. And her expression, too, when she cried; a long slow and noiseless tightening of the face, the lips stretched wide in misery, the tears coming at first silently. Yes, he would give his left arm not to see that happen. He'd give his left arm, and more. She should not be encumbered with the misery of his transgressions. Anything would be better than that.

And then, a few hundred yards further on this shimmering blackness swamped him and the pain seemed to recede or at least become of little consequence. As a child he'd had a dream, a bad dream, in which he got shot in the stomach and instead of pain there was just this feeling of being drained from the inside and an unbearable heaviness. Something like this hit him now and he sunk down to his knees on the swaying pavement, thinking now just let me sleep, let me sleep. I can work out the rest in the morning. I need energy to think. If I sleep here . . . he raised his head a little.

The road was black; everybody else was sleeping. Oh, to sleep! Maybe if I can find a room to lie down in, just for a few hours . . .

. . . and there, look, in a house close by, a solitary light was shining in an upstairs window. Somebody was up. Christian crawled towards the light. Blood trailed black and thick behind him. Help me, he heard a voice inside him cry, help me.

I hadn't thought that it would be like this, he whispered to himself, as the door in front of him was finally opened.

The hospital authorities said they'd come back for the arm, but they never did. The ambulancemen told Graham to put it in the freezer. It's still there.

That Big Ol' Moon is Shinin' Down

On the BBC local early evening news, Kenny Douglas pleads with the cameras for the return of his wife, Nicola. Blubbing on the sofa next to him is their only child, Danny, a three-year-old with Disney cartoon eyes and a mop of black hair. Because of the big policeman, the lighting technician, the pretty young reporter and the fat, red-eyed hack from the news agency, Danny now perceives a danger in his circumstances which the mere absence of his mother for nearly a week had not quite instilled.

'Where's mummy?' he asks, poignantly and on cue.

Where indeed. The detective inspector, standing just out of shot at Kenny's side, has been exuding sympathy and gentle concern all day, but a handful of his colleagues are already out combing the railway embankments, the urban copses, the alleys and wastelands of Camberwell, Denmark Hill and Dulwich.

'Nicky, Nicky, come home now; wherever you are, come home for me and Danny,' Kenny croaks to the camera for a third time. He just can't quite get it right, the cadence and the timbre. They're patient with him, though, the television people; they know he's going through an awful time. Just imagine how it must feel, they say to each other, as Kenny runs a hand through his hair which is now greasy with sweat beneath the thick television lights.

Nicola 'left home' without so much as a note, it's all a bit of a mystery and look, here we are with the police involved. Kenny's father Maurice sits in the kitchen, well away from the journalists, and later tells the policeman he thinks it's all a complete waste of time, this palaver – she's run off with a fella and she's not coming back.

Is that what he really thinks? Just how likely is that?

Because, for the rest of us, watching at home, one simple question occurs: How long will it be before Kenny is charged? And then, maybe a subsidiary: what is the good of this ninety second television drama, apart from to give the local population the chance to see the perpetrator before the blanket goes over his head?

Does it help the police? Their minds are pretty much made up. Officially, the case is still open, of course – but in the view of the DI and his subordinates poking about in bushes and wastebins, the door is ineluctably closing. So why this televised charade? What are the signs they are watching for? A lack of sincerity in the crying? An injudicious slip from Kenny off camera, perhaps during a conversation with his father? A sudden, blurted confession provoked by television's confessional idiom and the anticipation of an audience eating its tea at home?

And quite what we, the viewers, or voyeurs, get from the whole thing is unclear. It is less 'news' than a sly, black joke, or a statement of the patently obvious. And the real pathos inherent in it – Danny's evident bewilderment and tears, a bowl of wilted tulips on the table behind the two of them, a brightly coloured ball on the floor, pictures of the three of them, Kenny,

Nicola and Danny, on the self-assembly sideboard unit, stage left – is simply the emotional detritus of a familiar scene.

★

Poor Nicola. Gone for five days, not staying with any known friends, no contact, indeed, with anybody known to her. Or even not previously known to her. The little film ends with a close-up shot of a photograph of Nicola, head thrown back and laughing, brown hair hanging down behind, a picture taken on their last family holiday, on Santorini. You can just about make out the black, volcanic sand in the background.

How happy were they both then? Had they an inkling of what was to come? From the thin straps on Nicola's shoulders you might guess that she was wearing a bikini. Had she been swimming? Had they been swimming together, splashing around and playing the fool? Was the laugh, caught on camera, a genuine thing, or was it a forced laugh for the sake of the family snapshot album? And what about Kenny – presumably he was the photographer on this particular occasion – hunched behind the camera, watching her, watching her . . . and wondering what, exactly? Did he force a reciprocal laugh each day as they walked towards the beach or back up to the restaurants and bars for an evening of retsina and light-hearted holiday chit-chat? Or was the happiness of this holiday a genuine thing, despite the darkness behind the picture? In a way, you sort of hope it wasn't. And you wonder about Kenny, mulling over the imperative of his situation, endlessly fretting what to do, how to make everything work out all right.

Kenny admitted to the police, almost immediately, a long-standing affair with another woman – exotically enough, a night club singer called Tequila Mockingbird.

It has not yet been explained where the two of them met, Kenny and Tequila, but meet they most certainly did – and continued to meet, off and on, for the best part of two years.

Tequila does cover versions of country and western songs in some of the local pubs and private clubs, so maybe that's where they hooked up, on one of Kenny's drinking nights. She usually ends her spot with that old favourite, 'Blanket on the Ground.' Up, up, up those long stairs to the big chorus, Tequila grabs hold of the song and wrings its pretty neck. I'll get the blanket from the bedroom and we'll go walking once again, to that spot down by the river, where our true love first began. Just because we are married don't mean we can't sleep around . . . hold on, that's *slip* – Tequila and Kenny – not sleep. How many other British people, unfamiliar with the multitude of sexual euphemisms utilised in the American vernacular and further hood-winked by Billie Jo Spears's wide, southern twang, misread the injunction entirely? In truth it's a song about the necessity for sexual desire or what we might loosely call romance to outlast the onset of marital boredom or enmity. But also the warning that in order for it to do so you need to play a role to keep that thing – whatever it is – alive; a role every bit as taxing as the one Kenny is playing now, with the sweat running down the back of his neck and one arm thrown around his increasingly confused and frightened child.

So maybe Kenny heard Tequila sing this song and one way or another the words got to him, hit some kind of chord – albeit, you might argue, a strange chord. Various friends have all testified that Kenny was utterly devoted to Nicola and Danny – although not sufficiently devoted, it would seem, to remain faithful to her. Sufficiently devoted instead, it's possible to guess, to hold the concept of devotion in higher esteem than he does the person to whom he is supposedly devoted – and, consequently, to find the prospect of mentally hurting Nicola the worst crime imaginable and the trauma of leaving her (and Danny, of course) unthinkable. What's the difference between devotion and fidelity, anyway? And of what, precisely, was Kenny more scared: Nicola's reaction to his affair or the necessity of bringing one or the other of his relationships to a painful close? And to what extent did Kenny, in his quandary, take into account, or attempt to second guess, the views of Nicola and Danny? We can assume that those two had no say in the events that eventually transpired and that, further, both would have objected to the dénouement had they been afforded the right of veto. We know that Kenny is a rather sensitive man, although not very bright. What a fatal combination. We can grope towards his final rationale because it has become such a familiar one, played out with crushing regularity on our television screens and in our newspapers.

'I could never hurt Nicola,' he tells the detective inspector, apropos of nothing, apparently, after he has filmed this little drama for the evening news programme. And in one sense at least, he is telling the truth. Now all we need to know is how he killed her and where he's hidden the body.

Sometimes Eating Marmite

Mick's last girlfriend, Helen, had this strange medical condition which endowed her skin with a distinctive and powerful taste, somewhere between Worcestershire sauce and Marmite.

Mick didn't know what the cause was, whether it was just a cutaneous thing or maybe endocrine-based or simply dietary – and it wasn't an issue he felt they could discuss easily, so he never brought it up. But licking her was a neverending pleasure, from the nape of her neck with its tiny vibrating scillia right down to the soles of her little feet. The flavour was at its most concentrated in those pouches, grills and vents which served as an entry point to Helen's body and at its weakest on her fingers and knees.

Mick adored the taste, it was the thing he missed most about her when the two of them split up, the most likeable and desirable thing about her. Helen was, as the Americans put it, crazier than a shit-house rat, an extravagantly disturbed young woman and largely because of this their relationship was often troubled and difficult. She should be sectioned for her own good, friends told Mick after some traumatic episode in a restaurant or bar, they'll give her drugs and ECT and maybe invasive surgery and it might sort out her skin ailment too. But Mick thought this was overstepping the limits of his responsibility and sovereignty. They lasted about six months, living together, and then one day she was gone, no explanation, all of her stuff removed from the wardrobe and just this cryptic and slightly ominous note left on the kitchen table: 'Mick: don't try to clean the Gaggia.' More madness, he thought. But nonetheless he left the Gaggia alone.

What actually happened to Helen was this. One evening, when Mick was away somewhere on a computer software sales training course, Helen discovered that an emissary of Satan had taken up residence in their open-plan kitchen. She arrived home from work, sagging with tiredness, and there he was, this demon, a furious whirling cloud of evil some four feet high, suspended above the Mexican stone floor tiles. All the evidence pointed to Satan – the stench of excrement, the numbing coldness which reached deep inside her and an immediate sensation of impending chaos and dissolution, of hopelessness and decay. When she advanced, gingerly, towards this spinning mass of darkness its speed increased perceptibly and a tiny green demon with red depthless eyes detached itself and shot behind the split-level Zanussi cooker, causing sparks to dance like fireflies above the white ceramic hotplates.

And then, from behind the appliance, it spoke to her.

'My name is Legion, for we are many,' is what it said, equably enough.

So, hearing this, she advanced no further and, holding a hand over her nose, rang Mitchell, her downstairs neighbour, and waited nervously for him in the corner of the living room, sipping from a glass of Sancerre left out from the night before.

By the time Mitchell arrived, the cloud of evil had disappeared; but the stench and the coldness remained and one of the tiles above which the devil had spun was scorched black and still hot to the touch. Mitchell thought the smell was from the river, running thick and black like oil outside, and the coldness because the central heating wasn't on, but he kept these views to himself, having run into Helen a couple of times before and knowing, therefore, that his uncomplicated observations wouldn't go down too well. Plus, he couldn't explain the tile – what could scorch Mexican red granite except maybe a creature from hell? Mitchell agreed with her about this but couldn't think of much else to do, so he stood in the living room as she drank her wine and wondered idly what the devil was doing in south Docklands and just how monumentally bored he must be.

At length, Helen put down her glass of wine and, touching Mitchell lightly on the shoulder, confided in a whisper: 'He's still here . . .'

Mitchell nodded and scratched his head. 'Ummmm . . . where, exactly?'

'I think he's inside the juicer.'

Mitchell peered cautiously at the copper and chrome machine gleaming on the white steel worktop. He told her he could see nothing. Helen shrugged and walked away.

'Oh, perhaps he's gone, then. I don't know. What difference does it make? He'll be back, sooner or later.'

Mitchell nodded again. 'Well, OK. But just you let me know if he, ah, manifests himself once more and I'll be up here in a minute with the paraphernalia to deal with it. Mr Muscle, and so on.'

'Thanks, Mitch,' said Helen, walking with him to the door. 'You've been a great help.'

The next morning Helen lay awake in bed waiting

for the devil to return. She heard noises in the kitchen but was not unduly concerned: not all unexplained noises are necessarily the devil. Sometimes, she thought, the world tilts a little on its axis and things slide about and occasionally collide. The telephone rang out from the living room and she knew that wasn't the devil either, but most likely Mick, ringing up from his sales training course to see how she was. Or maybe people from work wondering where she'd got to.

Then the apartment was silent.

She dozed off, into this tilting world, and awoke again at noon, roused by the telephone, which she declined to answer. She dressed without washing and sat for a while on the arm of her white sofa, watching the kitchen for signs that the devil might still be about.

She sat like this for an hour or more, staring mainly at the Gaggia and the blender and the juicer and the expensive, under-utilised Hotpoint dishwasher. At length a brown-furred creature with cloven hooves manifested itself in the middle of the floor and began rummaging furiously through the refrigerator, apparently searching for something to eat.

It seemed quite at home and entirely oblivious to her presence, inspecting Marks and Spencer's tubs of taramasalata and hummus and probing with thin, furry fingers inside the remains of the chicken from which Helen intended to make soup. Helen was once again assailed by the stench and coldness of unequivocal evil, and the dinky electric lights in her kitchen – the neon ceiling strip and the halogen lamp built into her cooker hob and the tiny spotlamps above the blender and the juicer and the Gaggia – flickered and crackled and spat out gobbets of indigestible light.

The demon grumbled as it rummaged through the fridge, growing more dissatisfied and exasperated and aggrieved with every item of food it inspected. A bowl of aeoli was hurled in fury against the white-tiled wall of a worktop unit; rocket, curly endive and purple sprouting broccoli flung backwards into the living room. Eventually the creature howled in desperation and dematerialised inside the Gaggia, leaving behind in the still air a skein of noxious, yellowish smoke.

Helen felt she had seen enough. She returned to the bedroom and opened the wardrobe doors and her chest of drawers and threw the entire contents into three cheap suitcases. She zipped the bags shut and, using the back of an unopened bill from a mobile telephone company, scribbled a short note to Mick which she left on the kitchen table.

She took one last look around her apartment and then walked out, slamming the door shut behind her. Nothing which happened in this flat conformed to rules she could comprehend.

Mick, of course, knew nothing of this; he just got the note: 'Mick: don't try to clean the Gaggia.'

Anyway, Mick is now married to Mandy, who, dispiritingly, tastes of nothing, her skin has no flavour at all and Mick craves the spicy astringency he lost when Helen moved out. So, some nights he settles down in front of the television and with the orange bombs from the latest war detonating softly around him he eats Welsh Rarebit with Worcestershire sauce or slice after slice of Marmite-coated bread, washed down with a cup of tea, and the tang stays on his lips and tongue as he unobtrusively licks Mandy.

But it is not so good, this way of doing things, the rush he gets less immediate and compelling in its impact and sometimes, as he is licking her neck, he has to stop and roll his tongue around his mouth to remind himself of the flavour he craves.

Of course, Mandy doesn't know about the business with Helen, any of it, and Mick can't bring himself to explain. In his more reflective moments he wonders why it is that some people taste of stuff and other people taste of nothing at all and the reflection depresses him a good deal. He gets depressed a lot, these days, and isn't sure why. Maybe it's boredom. He feels boredom pinning them down in their tiny Docklands flat, like a giant fist in his stomach. And he feels this boredom and thinks sometimes eating Marmite isn't enough.

And there are problems with Mandy too. She also appears to be crazier than a shit-house rat. She does these strange things. Mick wonders if he is to blame some-times, if maybe he turns these women mad. Statistically it's a long shot to have two successive women who are totally doolally, unless there is something within him which yearns for mad women or something within him which turns normal women mad.

Whatever: Mandy's started doing stuff to which there is no logical answer, nor any feasible means of escape. One night, for example, Mick comes home from work to find her crouched in a ball at the top of the metal staircase which leads to their bedroom. She's crouched there, her head between her knees, rocking backwards and forwards as if she were about to tip over and roll all the way down to the bottom. Mick took his raincoat off and stood there watching but didn't really know what to do. He stood in the hallway looking up at Mandy but she just stayed there, rocking backwards and forwards, backwards and forwards. He wondered briefly if maybe he should climb up and talk to her, ask her why she's doing this, what's the point of this whole business, but then decides it is better not to get involved. She'll either stop of her own accord or she'll stay there, rocking backwards and forwards. One or the other. So Mick makes his way into the lounge and with this slightly prickly feeling, as if he were now being watched, grabs himself a beer from the Neff refrigerator and stands uneasily in the kitchen, drinking and mulling things over.

Sure enough, a couple of hours later Mandy just comes down stairs and says nothing about it, just picks up a book and starts reading. By this time Mick's got the TV on so there's no obvious reason to quiz her about the hunched up rocking business, not now that she's apparently OK and happy just to sit there reading.

Truth is, the reading worries Mick more than the crouching, frankly. She's begun reading all the time, all hours of the day and night, which would be OK except it's always stuff from the nutters' section of their local bookshop. It would be OK if it was Jane Austen or Helen Fielding or the usual stuff women like to read. Gabriel García Márquez. Scott Fitzgerald. You know. But it's never things like that, it's always *Was God a Dolphin?* Or *Mysteries of Runic England* or *The Cancer Conspiracy: Why They Want Us to Die* or *Kabbalism for Beginners*. And such like.

Again, Mick doesn't understand and reckons the best policy is not to get involved, but sometimes, sitting there on the sofa watching her read with her head bent down over the print, oblivious to the outer world, he feels she is a participant from a different universe and different structure of time and that maybe it would take only the lightest tap on her shoulder to send her spinning away deep into space and out of reach for ever, maybe down a black hole, which is something else she reads about from time to time. *Black Holes Explained. Explore the Space–Time Continuum from Your Own Bedroom. Wormholes: A Beginners Guide.*

When she is reading and there's nothing much on television and he's not out with his cabal of friends, Adie, Sophie, Colette, Troy, Twix when she's over from Guadeloupe and so on, he wonders about their life together and whom he should blame for the boredom and the fact that it's all going terribly wrong and how can he explain the dislocation which seems to exist in their home and why is she just, sometimes, absolutely barking and so on. And he decides that he can't blame anybody, not even himself.

And he's perplexed too because sometimes he thinks he must be still in love with his last girlfriend, Helen, and at other times he thinks nah, it was just the Marmite really. Love or Marmite? Hell, it's a difficult question.

What he really wants is to be unfaithful a bit, but he can't, the prospect utterly terrifies him and he refuses to properly contemplate such a thing, especially after the last time and the horrible things that happened. He hates the thought of being unfaithful to Mandy and he can see the hurt and the incomprehension in her wide, flat face whenever he thinks about it. And he's also sort of ideologically opposed to infidelity for complex reasons associated originally with Karl Marx, he dimly remembers. But there's a problem here too because he's also ideologically opposed to bourgeois domesticity and monogamy, so the vestigial tail of his revolutionary politics is of little help to him in his predicament.

One day they're sitting there in the lounge, Mick just

lolling, occasionally reading the South London Press, Mandy with her head in another one of her books, when Mick remembers that her birthday is only a few days off and asks her what she would like in the way of a present.

She looks up from the book and smiles at him and says: 'A particle accelerator.'

Mick takes this deep breath and frowns and thinks about it for a minute and says: 'A particle accelerator? Are you sure? Aren't they sort of quite big things?'

And Mandy puts the book down, becoming animated for the first time that evening and says: 'No, they don't need to be, not any more. You can get one to fit in your suitcase these days. They've made them much more . . . compact.'

Mick says: 'Oh,' and they're both quiet for a bit. Then he asks her: 'Where do I get one from, then?'

'Well,' says Mandy, 'I should reckon you could find a pretty good one down the Tottenham Court Road, in one of those electrical shops.'

So much against his better judgement, the following Saturday Mick wanders up and down the Tottenham Court Road asking perplexed computer salesmen if they do particle accelerators, or know anywhere he can find one, sort of not too expensive, the kind that fits in a briefcase, etc. They're all very sorry but they can't help him, they haven't a clue what he's after. So in the end he buys her a Goodmans Fourway compact disc player, cassette tape deck and radio and a boxed set of Linda Ronstadt CDs, although, if he's honest, he's not sure that she'll like Linda Ronstadt, she's never shown much of an interest in country music before. But hell, he tried. At least he did that. And the Ronstadt set was on offer.

One salesman, this young Arab bloke with a thick

fake gold chain around his neck, says to Mick what do you want a particle accelerator for and Mick explains briefly and the salesman says simply: 'Leave her.'

Leave her. Why? What would be the point of that? It seems, despite the situation, the most unlikely and least desirable of all options. Where would they both go next? He imagines the trauma and the upheaval and the unnecessary pain inflicted upon the two of them and the misery and the removal expenses. But thinking about what the salesmen said, on the bus home, the notion of infidelity raises its head once more as a potential alternative to this strange stasis and almost simultaneously this voice comes in his head saying infidelity bad bad bad bad bad bad bad bad bad bad bad bad bad bad bad.

Since meeting Mandy two years ago he's been with another woman only once and the horror of it all has stayed with him ever since. Anna was part of that coterie of friends – Adie, Colette, etc. – with whom he escaped down the pub every now and then and one night he agreed to an innocent drink with her alone when Mandy was back home with her parents in Sunderland. The innocent drink at the Five Bells turned into a slightly – but only slightly – less innocent joint back at Anna's flat in New Cross and, thinking about it, Mick can't remember when the border was crossed between the licit and the illicit.

The drink Mandy would have been OK with and perhaps the joint too, although suspicion would have clouded her face at the lateness of the hour and the, you know, location. Certainly when, out of fraternity and absentmindedness, Mick started stroking Anna's left foot, running his finger along from ankle to toe and then delving in between the toes and lightly kneading the soles of her foot, certainly then Mandy would have called out you know, hello, time out, that's it, just stop. And then thirty seconds later they're fucking like polecats on the Goan dhurry in Anna's frowsy front room, illuminated by the soft glow from her Chinese lantern and sometimes the weird, ethereal, blue flashes from electric trains making their way south to Sutton and north to London Bridge, just outside the front window.

Mick shudders just thinking about it, infidelity is a course of action barred to him, so maybe its just a case of suffer the fist of boredom in his stomach and maybe she'll stop crouching on the stairs and reading those books after a bit. But then, the Marmite Problem still nags away at him, too, and he ponders the question: do I crave the taste of Marmite because I associate it with Helen or do I crave Helen simply because I love the taste of Marmite? It's a hard one, that.

Back on the dhurry with Anna, Mick is inside her and can't believe how good it feels, he had forgotten that slightly fizzy warmth and the excitement rolling around his body, a sort of perfect sensation which makes him think hell, why didn't I do this before, this is quite good, really. She has her legs crossed behind his back and is forcing him into her and he pulls the strap of her dress from over her shoulder and tears at her bra underneath and then sinks his head down and bites away gently at the soft pale flesh along the top of her arm and her light brown hair is strewn across her face and her eyes are closed and her mouth is open and it's this deep pink, the deepest pink you've ever seen, and she has one hand holding his hair at the back of his head quite roughly, scrunching up a handful and tugging at him every now and then, which is nice, and the other down between his legs cupping his balls and he wishes, really, that this could go on and on for ever.

Which is sort of what happens.

It goes on and on and Mick is at first supremely grateful that he is able to continue fucking her without even the need to think about holding back but then it goes on and on and on some more and worry begins to embed itself in a corner of his temple, a small sharp piece of worry like the point of a tiny star. And so he carries on, the thrusts becoming imbued with less and less conviction and he tries desperately hard to concentrate on what he is doing, to think about the physical act in the hope that it will jog his memory in some way and he stops gnawing at her arm and he realises she's not holding his hair any more, or his balls and he keeps trying to concentrate and he knows that she hasn't come and he certainly hasn't and he has the distinct impression that he's not going to and he can't fathom why this should be and he worries some more and he looks at that deep pink mouth of hers except now it isn't deep and pink any more because it's closed, tightly shut, the lips stretched taut in an expression of determination or endurance or acute discomfort, Mick isn't sure, and he's beginning to lose all sensation in his penis, it's as if he were buried deep inside a vacuum, not a vacuum cleaner, which would be preferable, and even pleasurable, maybe, just a vacuum, an absence of everything and he lifts his head up, still deep inside her, and he gasps for air and growing very bored indeed he looks out of the window . . .

He lets out this long high shriek and his body becomes rigid and immobile.

Through the ethereal blue flashes from the electric trains he can see faces pressed up close against the glass, familiar faces looking down at him with expressions of consternation, opprobrium and disappointment.

He pivots round inside Anna and strains towards the window. The faces see him looking and peer back.

'Go away!' he shouts and Anna tries to twist from underneath him to see who he is talking to, panic etched across her forehead. 'Please go away!' he says again as another electric train, a long one, maybe returning to the depot at Hither Green, who knows, rumbles by outside and the identity of these censorious voyeurs is suddenly made clear.

Mick recognises, with some surprise, the face of the Foreign Secretary, Mr Jack Straw. And that's not all.

Next to Jack is the Archbishop of Canterbury, Dr Rowan Williams, with his extravagant ecclesiastical beard. And straining for a better view behind this pair is the presenter of *Crimewatch UK*, the BBC's popular early evening police-based interactive magazine, Nick Ross.

He shrieks again, seeing Nick, and tries to pull himself out of Anna; but nothing happens, he's held fast. He pushes down on the dhurry with the palms of his hands and attempts to wrench himself backwards but there's no give, no give at all, maybe her muscles have contracted in some weird way and tug and strain as he might he can't get out of her.

He looks back up at the window, supporting himself on the palms of his hands. There's an entire queue of people there, all pressing and jostling to look in on this squalid and absurd scenario taking place in Anna's front room. He sees the junior Home Office minister Beverley Hughes and Andrew Neill and the Radio Two presenter Jeremy Vine and the stern-looking newsreader Fiona Bruce and that gay comedian

Graham Norton and that man who walked to the North Pole whose name escapes Mick just now though he recognises the face and there's the manager of Arsenal, Arsène Wenger, shoulder to shoulder with the tennis sisters Venus and Serena Williams, just in front of the head of the Roman Catholic Church Cardinal Cormac Murphy O'Connor who has, perched on his shoulders, Little Laura Brown, the six-year-old girl who had all those operations in America and who is now being sent to Disneyland at the expense of some tabloid newspaper because the operations were no use, as it happened, in the end.

Mick is beginning to feel nauseous and has started scratching at the floor in a bestial manner, trying to drag himself out of Anna but he still can't do it and now she's really, really, panicky and is asking him in ever-rising cadences what the fuck is going on and shouting at him get out get out get out get out but Mick is deaf to her protestations, the only thing to register on his consciousness is the queue by the window which, he realises, stretches all the way down the New Cross Road and round the corner into Queens Road and probably beyond, if he could see that far. There are members of his family mixed in with the array of celebrities and establishment icons, he can see his father attempting to explain something to John Prescott, the Deputy Prime Minister, and his mother standing sad eyed and doleful beside him. And look, there's his dentist, Dr Khali, and his locum Mr Brennan and next to them comes Mr Cox who took him for Maths in fourth year and whom he once heard mutter, under his breath, but distinctly enough to hear, 'fucking stupid boy' one time when he'd messed around in class and . . . anyway, there they all are, lit by these blue flashes and staring in at him and he can't get out of this girl, which has never happened before, not ever, and now she's crying, these long anguished sobs with her head pressed down against her Indian rug.

And after a while Mick stops struggling thinking maybe its like one of those plants in the jungle where the more you struggle the tighter you get trapped, so he tries to relax a little. And then he sees that the queue outside does indeed have an end, miles back down Queen's Road, and he wishes he hadn't looked. Slightly apart from the stragglers – a few Lib Dem MPs he can't put a name to, the disc jockey Nicky Campbell and Paul McCartney's wife, Heather Mills – and standing off to one side, her wide face wet with tears, is his wife, Mandy.

After a while – it seems like hours but it's probably only seconds – there's an audible gurgling sound from Anna's vagina, like water disappearing down a plug-hole and with a sudden pop! Mick is free. He is inexpressibly happy at this development. He rolls from on top of her and lies on his back on the floor, exhausted. The people at the window have gone now, he is relieved to discover, but Anna is still crying softly beside him.

'You OK?' he asks.

'Yes, I'm OK,' she says.

Mick starts exhaling huge gusts of air. 'What happened, back there, honey?' he ventures, a little nervously.

'I'm not sure. Must have been a contraction of the muscles or something. Why were you howling like that? It was fucking terrifying, Mick.'

'Oh, you know, just that feeling of being trapped, or something, I suppose. I just lost it for a moment,' he says.

Anna lost most of her clothes during the struggle. She yelps as she climbs to her feet. 'Owwwwww. My feet hurt.'

Mick looks at her feet. Bizarrely, the toes and half of the feet are shiny dark brown. He notices her standing on her heels.

'Jesus,' says Mick. 'I'd get that looked at, if I were you.'

'Yeah,' says Anna. And then she adds: 'It was a bad idea, really, wasn't it?'

So this whole episode deters him from being unfaithful again. Even though he fully realises that Anna's flat is on the second floor and that therefore Jack Straw and all the others probably weren't looking in through the window, in reality.

Sometimes he thinks he should ring Helen and perhaps exorcise this feeling he has, get himself clear about everything. But he hasn't spoken to her now for more than two years and hasn't a clue where she is. If he was pushed, he'd guess maybe Rampton. Which is another thing: if he got in touch with her now there'd probably be acrimony and unpleasantness, not least at the manner of her departure, plus she owes her payment for the mortgage, etc. Thing is, he can't imagine such emotional upheaval were Mandy to move out; one minute she'd be there, the next minute she'd be gone and nothing of her would stick to the walls of the flat, the way it did with Helen, he thinks.

It's eleven o'clock and Mandy is reading one of her books, curled up on the sofa, her head cocked to one side, engrossed as usual. The book is something technical about uranium. Mick sits on the floor watching the latest fighting from the war. There's a film of an Israeli soldier being used for a live blood transfusion by the Syrians and then some good shots of the bombing of Aleppo, followed by a very brief interview with the American Secretary of State. The war's been going on for ages and even Mick, an avid viewer at the outset of hostilities, has grown bored by now. He asks Mandy if she's enjoying her book and Mandy says yes, it's very informative. 'I know almost all I need to know now,' she adds.

The telephone rings out: Mandy leans across and picks up the receiver and says: 'No' and then puts the receiver back down. She tells Mick: 'Wrong number.' Mick gets to his feet and pads through to the kitchen and places two slices of thick-cut white bread in the toaster and then fills the kettle for tea. He feels the fist in his stomach but pushes it away and stands watching the red filaments turn the bread golden brown. He takes the jar of Marmite out of the cupboard and licks around the rim of the jar. The toast pops up from the toaster. The kettle starts to boil. And the Gaggia sits there, doing nothing, doing nothing at all.

Headhunter Gothic

It is three o'clock in the morning. An inglorious summer, chilly and brief, has shaded into autumn. But that notwithstanding, James has the quaint, almost archaic, suspicion that he is blessed.

This rather pleasing notion flickered across his mind a few moments ago – ironically, at precisely the time at which an event transpired some eighty feet above his head and which will, pretty soon, lead him to a very different point of view. Just watch this space, as they say.

James means blessed with regard to women. He does not mean blessed *in toto*, with regard to absolutely everything. Just women.

But even on its own, that's not such a bad thing to be blessed with, now, is it? he asks himself, inhaling his cigarette smoke and leaning back happily against the wall.

He is bathed – rather unflatteringly – in the jaundiced aurora of a sour sodium night light, down at the bottom of a stained and chilly concrete stairwell. Above him he hears the occasional indistinct murmur of voices, or footsteps, and every so often the urgent report of a car door and a subsequent, brief, frenzied hubbub. He does not mind these intrusions over much. It simply makes his chosen hidy-hole all the more private and agreeable.

He is astonished that he was able to persuade the girl to accompany him. It is this astonishment which prompted the immediate suspicion that he was blessed. All he said to her was: 'Um, why don't we go down there?' and she replied, after scarcely a moment's pause: 'Yeah, OK.' And then followed him down, flight after flight, without further demurral.

That's a remarkable thing, he reckons. It was not something he had expected. Then he asked the girl out for a drink 'sometime next week'. At the Grove, he suggested, or maybe the Hermit's Cave, both pubs which are local to the two of them. He did that as soon as they reached the bottom of the stairwell. And, to his jubilation and even greater astonishment, she has replied, with a sort of weary inevitability: 'Yeah, OK.'

So, there they stand, smoking their cigarettes. His a Camel, hers a Marlboro Light, the sweet, musty smoke mingling in the cold yellow air, James all unkempt and bleary-eyed as if he had just got out of bed very, very hurriedly indeed – which, in fact, is exactly the case, as it happens.

Some cigarette ash has spilled down the front of the girl's uniform. Reaching over, James brushes it off with an ingratiating tenderness. 'You have very beautiful hair,' he says.

But this is a lie, or at the least an exaggeration. She has adequately lustrous, thick black hair cut a little too short – probably for professional reasons – for her thin pale face. It's OK, really, as hair goes. It's clean and there's no overt evidence of alopecia. But beautiful would be stretching the point.

The girl sniffs and smiles, slightly embarrassed. 'Thank you,' she mutters, eventually, straightening her dress. 'Look, I'd better be getting back. Sister will be wondering where the hell I am.'

She stubs her cigarette out on the concrete wall, causing sparks like tiny suns to spin down all too briefly, burning out before they hit the floor. She adds, a little archly: 'You'd better get back too, for that matter. Heaven knows what stage things are at . . .'

James nods rapidly in agreement and, covertly checking the name tag on the front of her uniform, says: 'So, Colette . . . do you have a mobile, so that we can finalise that drink?'

'Sure,' she replies and rattles off a bunch of numbers which James embeds in his Nokia. 'But don't call me before lunchtime, please; I'm on lates next week. Come on, move. Let's go.'

They climb the stairs, Colette in front, pacing them out two at a time, James wheezing a little behind her. Halfway up she says to him: 'You'd be surprised to discover how many men in your position try to cop off with the nurses. I think it's what the psychologists call a defence mechanism.'

James ponders this for a moment. 'Are they often successful with you, then?' he asks.

He watches her shrug as she climbs. 'Fairly often. It makes no difference to me.'

This brutish revelation forces James to belatedly reappraise the belief that he is blessed. Maybe it's not just me; maybe most men are blessed, he wonders now. Or maybe it's not a case of being blessed. Maybe all you have to do is ask.

Colette lets them in through the side door of the hospital, quickly slicing her ID card through the metal slot. The lobby, where they murmur goodbye, is almost pitch black. As James's eyes struggle to make sense of the darkness, strange phantoms and ogres lurch out from the walls, amorphous and lumpen silhouettes which seem to beckon him hither. One such is standing sentinel by the far wall, its arms outstretched, a giant monster head watching him with malice as he steps gingerly across the linoleum. But as the molecules of darkness and light slowly dissolve inside his brain James sees that it is not a monster after all, but a great big cuddly teddy bear. He realises that he must be in the waiting room for the post-natal clinic.

And then, just as he's recovered his equilibrium, he's startled again by a voice close behind him.

'Take the door on the right and climb up two floors. G'bye.'

He looks back through the grey gloom, but Colette is already gone. Where did she disappear to? And why the fuck was she whispering?

As he pounds up the stairs, guilt bites into his stomach with every step. Even from the landing on the first floor he can hear the shrieking, a terrible, terrible rending which makes him feel even more guilty and a little frightened. He reaches the second floor with laboured breath and skids through the deserted reception bay to the ward, tears past the front desk and then – momentarily dislocated in his panic – is unable to remember in which room he is supposed to be attendant. Everything is quiet: the shrieking has stopped and James looks wildly from side to side, cursing in exasperation. Where should I go?

A multitude of doors lead off at an angle on each side of a long corridor; so which one is her fucking room? He can't remember. He stands there, frozen with indecision, panting.

A black woman in a pale blue uniform comes to the rescue, poking her head from a doorway just ten feet away. 'In here, Mr Thwaite. You jus' missed the big party.'

'Oh shit, God, I'm sorry . . . I just nipped out for a cigarette,' he gasps, shaking his head, 'I just nipped out for a cigarette and . . .'

But then he stops burbling because he is inside the room and it is as if he has stepped into the middle of the final scene of a particularly unpleasant Sam Peckinpah movie. Or, better expressed, a still shot of the final scene of the movie because the participants, viewed from James's vantage point in the doorway, seem frozen in time and space, almost as if they will never move again. What has been happening here? he wonders. Has there been a gun battle, or was there a lunatic loose with a machete?

'Christ . . .' is, in the end, all he manages, by way of a greeting. And then, again, in case it was missed the first time: 'Christ . . .'

There are three men in this tableau, presumably doctors – all of them, anyway, dressed in white tunics. Or, at least, tunics that were once upon a time white. It doesn't look as if they will ever be white again. Now they are tunics that appear to have been designed by Jackson Pollock during his red-only phase. These men all turn to look at him as he stands there, stricken, in the doorway, like the first horrified witness at a car crash. There's an elderly Pakistani doctor whom he hasn't seen before splattered from head to toe in blood still holding these enormous . . . Christ, what *are* they . . . Giant pliers? . . . Some kind of medieval instrument of torture and religious instruction? Another man unfamiliar to him – short black hair, with the thin-lidded eyes of southern Asia – is bent over, brandishing an oversized kitchen plunger which even now is still dripping gore on the white linoleum.

And there's Doctor Anderson, whom he knows from his last visit here, resting up against the window, in a state of considerable exhaustion. There's blood and some kind of gristle adhering to his chin. He waves a tired wave as James gapes at him from the doorway. Hi again, Jim, he says.

And then there's the midwives, both of whom have also been comprehensively doused with blood from whatever carnage has recently taken place. The woman who showed James into the room is now busying herself winding down some cumbersome metal attachment at the base of the bed. The other woman is washing her hands in a corner sink, the water running pink and lumpy down the plug hole. God, the room is stiflingly hot, he thinks.

And then he sees Angela. He had almost forgotten her. Little Angela, lying back in bed, her legs still hoisted high up in the grotesque stirrups, the green medical sheet across her lower half flapping in the breeze from a recently opened window. He takes a big breath and averts his eyes from the complicated, livid mess beneath the green sheet and walks over to her side.

She looks awful. She looks like she's been ship-wrecked, or is dying of cholera in a Bengal slum, or something, he thinks. Her hair – usually chestnut – has somehow lightened to a sort of distressed taupe and lies plastered to her head in thick, greasy clumps. Her face is grey and slack from the pethedine and the exertion.

But she still has the energy left to smile at him. 'Hi, sweetie,' she croaks. 'Late again, huh?'

He takes her hand – strangely cold and yet clammy from sweat still drying – in his. 'Sorry, sorry, sorry . . . I just nipped out for a cigarette . . . I . . .'

'That's OK, don't worry. Probably better you weren't here, to be honest. Bit of a struggle, really.' She looks around the room. 'They were all quite heroic. Hey . . .'

She lifts something up towards him, a bundle of white he hadn't noticed her holding, or had somehow expunged from his mind. She starts to unwrap the layers of cotton surrounding the thing.

No, no, he wants to say, don't bother, not on my behalf, please, plenty of time for that later. But he can't get the words out. Instead it's Angela who speaks.

'Charlie,' she addresses the lump in her arms, '. . . say hello to Daddy.'

James stares with horror at the creature before him. What in God's name is it? It is a fucking nightmare being, with its cone-shaped skull, elongated and twisted at the top; green and yellow face dripping with alien mucus and huge, clever, black eyes.

'Ugh,' James can't help but say.

The eyes swivel in his direction and hold him in a malevolent stare.

James tries very, very hard – give him his due – to summon up affection for this thing. But, hell, you know, it's difficult. 'Hi, Charlie,' he mutters at last, reaching out towards the hideous beast with a tentative hand.

Charlie suddenly breaks the stare and starts, instead, to cry very loudly, the noise of several cats being tortured by a gang of adolescent children.

'Isn't he beautiful?' says Angela, returning the bundle to her side.

★

To James's vague irritation, there is no time in the following week to meet Colette for a drink at the Hermit's Cave or the Grove or anywhere else, for that matter. His entire life now consists of running menial errands – making cups of tea, washing up after meals, pelting to the shops for emergency supplies of nappies, laundering befouled baby clothes. That and attempting to keep the house like most normal people have houses – a task which is proving quite impossible. Muslin shawls coated in pus-coloured goo litter the hallway and the kitchen and the living room; hideously grinning toys in eye-blinding colours are scattered across every floor. And here and there you might, if you're lucky, find a pungent nappy or a bag of odiferous wipes cunningly concealed beneath a cushion.

And the smell of excrement and rancid breast milk pervades every corner of their home, despite James skittering around all day with a can of Glade.

Of course, he tries to keep away from the nasty little creature itself, as much as is possible. He even tries – and manages, for the most part – to avoid being in the same room as it.

He is excused, for obvious reasons, the chore of breast feeding – something for which he is supremely grateful. And he has devised a cunning rationale to avoid the even worse job of changing its nappies. The baby is, at this age, 'mum-centred', he says to Angela, reading from a parenting manual. He holds the fatuous tome aloft and quotes: '. . . it is important, then, that the father does not come to be associated exclusively with the unpleasant things in the child's life, such as changing nappies and the mother exclusively with those things which are pleasurable, such as being fed . . .'

It could all lead to serious problems later on, he assures his wife.

And, bless her, Angela doesn't object to this argument, particularly. In fact, she seems to revel in the whole filthy business, despite its repetitive, stultifying boredom and the inevitable stench. She is perpetually tired – that's true. And she misses her friends (who now avoid her as if she had smallpox or diphtheria). But, inexplicably, she adores Charlie and does not cavil even at dragging herself from too brief a sleep at three o clock in the morning for the selfish little bastard's early-morning feed. James always screws shut his eyes as he hears her rise from beside him to assuage the keening wail of complaint from the cot at the foot of their bed. He feels a bit guilty on these occasions, to be honest.

But then, his guilt is mitigated by the fact that the little beast doesn't seem to like him very much. In fact, more than that, it seems to bear him ill-will. How James has come to dread those moments when Angela, sagging with exhaustion, says: 'Can you hold him for a bit?' and the rank bundle is passed between them. Then, James gingerly takes hold and starts the text-book approved rocking motion – but the creature inside isn't fooled for a single second. It opens its big black eyes and fixes James with that stare again, the stare it gave him in the hospital ward. It doesn't even cry, it just stares, with wickedness on its mind. The stare seriously unnerves James. How come it knows how to stare? It's not meant to be able to focus properly at this age. That's why it's got that stupid fucking mobile of different-coloured canaries hanging over its head all day – so that the eyes learn how to focus. But it has no problem focusing on James. It focuses on James with a cold, dry look of loathing. And then, usually, it vomits on his shirt.

When the creature was about six weeks old, a strange thing occurred. Angela had passed the bundle over to James and retired upstairs to the bedroom for a nap. Charlie had kept her awake for longer than usual the previous night. She looked like a sepia photograph of a racoon.

As soon as she'd left the room, James put the bundle straight down in its Moses basket and sat on the sofa, reading a magazine about nice clothes, attractive women and sport.

The thing started crying.

'Stop crying,' said James.

It continued to cry.

'I said stop fucking crying,' said James.

The crying became a little more insistent.

So James went over to investigate and, when he did so, the crying stopped and the baleful staring began.

'Stop staring,' said James.

But the creature continued to stare.

So James poked it in the throat with a Perspex ruler.

'I said stop that fucking staring.'

And he poked it again.

But the thing just looked at him with the same menacing expression, and then – this is the strange bit – opened its tiny mew of a mouth and said, quite clearly: 'Desailly.'

James dropped the ruler in shock.

'What did you say, you little fuck?'

The thing stared at him some more and repeated: 'Desailly. Desailly. *Desailly.*'

James shook his head sadly. 'You are a nasty, weird

little fucker,' he said and sat back down to his magazine.

Two days later James is ensconced on the sofa with a mystery ailment. For thirty-six hours he lies motionless in the same set of clothes, swamped by lassitude, or nausea, or both, an arm flung out behind his head, sweat dribbling down the front of his shirt. He scarcely has the strength even to wonder about his illness, whether it's food poisoning, or a flu bug, or merely the slenderest tentacles of something more ominous still, something which will never go away and will, in the end, after horrific medical treatment, most likely do for him. He feels, oh, drained and powerless.

During this time poor Angela is forced to run the house, look after Charlie *and* cater for James's occasional plaintive demands. 'Could you possibly bring me some cordial from the kitchen,' he asks, from time to time. This odd affliction has affected his vocabulary. He keeps using words like 'cordial' and 'ague', as if he were the wan-faced, invalided heroine of a great Victorian novel. That's how he spends his confinement: talking in an archaic manner and watching the golf on Sky.

Charlie, meanwhile, continues to shit, piss and eat entirely oblivious to his father's suffering. But from his vantage point on the sofa, James views the little creature, growing in health and with looks that improve by the day, with a combination of fear, suspicion and dread.

Even when he gets better there is none of the exultant relief which more usually accompanies the withdrawal of an illness. Instead he frets about returning to work and, when at work, frets all day about returning home to a manifestation which he truly believes is out to get him.

As you have probably guessed by now, James no longer thinks he is blessed in any way at all. He is beginning to believe, instead, that he is cursed. He has a solipsistic and peculiarly black and white perception of fate, you might think. Blessed or cursed, one or the other, the pendulum swinging on an almost daily basis. We can't be sure why he's like this about life; he was not, after all, brought up an animist or a Roman Catholic. But equally, we cannot be certain that everything he claims to have witnessed is simply the result of a childish and paranoid imagination. 'Desailly' is certainly an odd thing for a six-week-old baby to intone. And then there's the horrible, unnerving staring. And there are still more things which convince him that something awful might be brewing up, in the none too distant future.

For example, at night the house seems to be collapsing around them. James lies awake sweat-filmed, eyes wide open as the walls and floor and the roof come under attack from million upon million of rapacious insects: silverfish, woodlice, devil's coach horses, fire beetles, earwigs, wood weevils, cockroaches, cater-pillars, crickets, dust mites and things much smaller still, with unmemorable and inarticulable Latin names. This constant munching is a row James can never block out, these days, and sometimes he rises from his bed beside Angela to investigate and – stealthy in the darkness – quite often catches them at it: chewing away at the linoleum in the kitchen, gnawing through the wood in the skirting board, tapping at the windows with their frothy soft wings. They run like hell when he appears, scurrying under cabinets and chairs or simply melting away into the night. On several occasions recently he has hidden behind the sofa to await their arrival, springing out at the last second, just as they start their dastardly work. Ha! he shouts. GOT you! And then begins an orgy of stamping and snarling.

How can Angela not hear them? he wonders. The only thing to wake her is Charlie; otherwise, she sleeps and sleeps, her face a luminous milky-white as it hugs the pillow, like those strange fish you find at the very bottom of the ocean – built for the darkness and happy within it.

She doesn't hear the insects and she doesn't hear the constant, droning roar of air molecules as they smash about above her head, either. She just hears Charlie. And yet for James, in the dead of night, this constant activity constitutes a clanging fugue he can never subdue, even if he wanted to.

And then there's the bird in the garden, the big black bird which he had never noticed, until a few days before. It sits on the tiny square of lawn, peering through the kitchen window with its black eyes.

'It's a crow, Jim,' says Angela.

'It's too big for a crow. It's a rav . . .'

'It's a crow, Jim. Just leave it.'

A week or so after the 'Desailly' business, there's another, similar, crisis. Early one evening, Angela hears crying from the Moses basket in the back room and, physically incapable of movement, lying prostrate on the sofa – which is now employed almost exclusively as a surrogate hospital bed – begs James to attend.

'What do you think he wants?' James asks nervously.

'Oh, he probably needs changing again,' says Angela, hovering before the welcoming embrace of a semi-coma.

James tiptoes into the next room. The creature is crying quietly and insistently but as soon as it sees James, it stops the crying and starts on with its staring business. This time its eyes are a little narrowed: in so far as it's possible to ascribe conscious thought patterns to a creature so young, it appears to be concentrating upon something vitally important to it.

James picks up the Perspex ruler and tentatively prods at the nappy: it is, indeed, noisome and replete. He grunts with distaste. He lifts the beast out of its basket and turns it around. He undoes the plastic tabs on the side of the nappy. He takes the nappy off very carefully and places it on the floor. He lifts the creature's bare arse towards him and prepares to wipe it down when . . .

'Jesus fucking Christ!!!!!'

The arse detonates with a guttural cough and a vast stream of excrement − the colour and toxicity of uranium oxide − splatters against the far wall, the door, the carpet and, most copiously, James's face. He drops the thing on its back in the wicker cot.

'Fucking hell!!'

'What's the matter, sweetie?'

'It's whole fucking arse has blown up, that's what. Jesus. Jesus.'

Retching, James removes pints of simmering yellow shit from his face with a whole wad of wet wipes. The stuff clings and burns like napalm. It smells like the decomposing corpse of a tramp. James gags and heaves with every dab of the cloth.

When the worst of it is off, he advances upon the foul creature with his trusty Perspex ruler held out before him. 'You grotesque, disgusting little cunt,' he tells it, prodding the ruler in its fat neck.

The creature looks back with those big black eyes, quite unbothered.

'Babayaro,' it gurgles. '*Celestine* Babayaro.'

Nobody believes him, of course.

James is on a brief, late evening furlough at the Hermit's Cave with his friends Adie and Clara and Clara's smug, awful boyfriend, Troy. He had been prepared for their laughter and their disbelief but even so, now that he has to suffer it, he is both irritated and affronted.

'I'm telling you,' says James, banging his hand on the table and swallowing another vast gulp of lager, 'the horrible fucking thing has started reciting the names of the Chelsea team. There's no fucking mistake about it. It's seven weeks old. It's not meant to speak at all. And it can recite the fucking Chelsea team. It's fucking possessed, I'm telling you.'

'Possessed by Ken Bates?' says Adie.

They won't stop laughing at him, any of them. Clara pats his arm. 'His name's Charlie, Jim. And he's your son. You've just got to get to know him a little bit . . .'

'If you showed him a smidgeon of affection . . .' says Adie.

'I can't! He won't let me. Adie, you can't imagine it. He fucking hates me. He wants me out of the house. And he knows I support Leeds and that there's this historic enmity between us and Chelsea dating back to the 1970 FA Cup Final when we totally slaughtered them but they sneaked a winner from that donkey David Webb.'

'In the replay, wasn't it? Osgood scored as well. Through ball from Charlie Cooke. Straight down the centre. Bang.'

'Shut up, Adie. Jim, you're being ludicrous. Are you suggesting Charlie's been flicking through thirty years worth of football annuals?'

'No, you're not listening to me. I'm suggesting the fucking thing's possessed.'

'Now, Jim,' Troy butts in with a condescending reasonableness which makes James want to spew, 'look at it logically. He's not really reciting the Chelsea team. All he's said so far, according to you, is Desailly and Babayaro. Now, linguistically the first sounds a baby can make – the easiest sounds for his still forming palate – are 'd' and 'b'. Desailly is probably an approximation of daddy – you should be proud!'

James does not much like Troy. The fact that James has fucked Clara a couple of times back in their college days goes some way to explaining the not entirely latent tension which exists between the two men.

'OK, Mr Jean Fucking Piaget,' James sneers, 'how do you explain Babayaro?'

Troy laughs, looking at Clara for help, spreading his hands out wide: 'Oh, come on, think about it! What did he say? Babababababababa . . . I mean, whoever heard of a baby saying something like that! Get a grip, Jim – he was just babbling and your brain filled in the rest.'

'It said *Celestine* Babayaro, Troy. Even fucking Lineker has trouble saying that. I've sired a monster.'

'Jim, honey, he didn't say . . . what was it, Troy? . . . Cel-whatever-Babayaro. You're obviously under stress. And stress, well . . . it's like Troy says, your brain is overworked and psyched out and it's doing things it shouldn't be doing.'

Hearing Clara side with Troy like this is too much for James to bear. He slams his pint down, foam spilling over the table, his lips flecked with the spittle of impotent fury. 'Clara, don't talk to me like I'm an imbecile or a fucking madman! I know what I heard. I just know, OK?'

Other people in the pub look over at them during this outburst. It's all getting a bit too much. As if by synchronicity, the four of them go silent and concentrate for a while on their drinks. James wonders if he should tell them about the insects too but thinks, no, maybe not just now.

Over at the bar Geoff the Fat Landlord barks out last orders and, grateful for the interruption to this intensely embarrassing scene, Troy stands up, smooths his hair back and asks cheerfully if anyone wants a drink. He is mightily sick of the subject of James's bloody baby.

But before anybody can reply, James breaks in. He's not shouting any more, but there's something just as scary about the enforced evenness of his tone. 'We're not having another drink. We're going to sort this out,' he says.

'What do you mean, sort it out?'

'Come back with me and hear for yourself. Angela will be asleep. The beast will be snoozing after its eleven o'clock slurp from my wife's tit. Come on back with me, all of you. I want you to believe me. You have to believe me. It's important. It's driving me up the fucking wall.'

They mull this idea over for a few seconds.

And then Adie says: 'He's at Southend now, isn't he?'

'Who's at Southend? What the fuck are you talking about?'

'David Webb. Went there as manager last season, I think, after a spell at Yeovil.'

Fifteen minutes later the four of them are crouched in the pungent, soft gloom of the master bedroom, James in front brandishing his ruler, Clara with her eyes wide with concern and worry about her friend, Adie attempting to stifle his sniggers and Troy hanging back, dubious about the whole enterprise.

'What's the ruler for, Jim?' Clara whispers, although she has a pretty good idea.

'It's to poke the little fucker. Now shussh or you'll wake Ange.'

The darkness of the bedroom closes in around them, thick and warm, illuminated by Angela's gentle snoring and her sweet milky animal smell. The baby is on its back, eyes closed and silent.

James pokes it in the throat with his ruler.

'Jim!' says Clara.

'Shhh,' says James, and thrusts the ruler at the child once more.

Charlie opens his eyes; the pupils flicker indiscriminately around the room in confusion.

So James pokes him again, hard, in the belly.

And then this happens. The child's lips curl up and he *chuckles*. A light, happy, gurgling spurt of laughter, accompanied by an adorably excited waving around of the arms.

'Aaaaaawwww sweetheart,' gushes Clara, scarcely able to control the volume of her voice. 'He's laughing, Jim, look!' She leans over the cot and offers Charlie her finger, which it grasps firmly in its tiny paw. 'Oh, bless him . . .'

James is disconsolate: 'It's never done that before. It fucking knows you're here,' he growls. He raises his ruler aloft once more but Clara grabs hold of his arm.

In a furious whisper she says: 'Jim, if you poke that baby again I'm going to punch you. There is nothing remotely wrong with him. He's a lovely child – far better than you deserve.'

Adie adds: 'Looks pretty normal to me, mate.'

And Troy, with an expression of weary resignation says: 'Can we go now, please?'

And getting no reply from James – who appears, for a moment, catatonic with suppressed rage – Adie, Troy and Clara climb to their feet and tiptoe towards the door.

'Bye bye, little honeylamb,' says Clara, stroking the child on the arm.

James shakes his head and sighs and whispers: 'Go on down; I'll be out in a minute.'

Clara hovers in the bedroom doorway. 'Don't poke him, Jim. I'm warning you. In fact, give me the ruler.'

James sulkily passes the ruler to Clara and crouches back down by the crib. He hears his friends giggling on the stairs.

He is left with the thoroughly unpleasant alternatives that either the creature is much, much cleverer than even he gave it credit for, or he's imagined the whole thing. He sits on his haunches, not quite knowing which is the worse of the two. He stares down into the cot. The creature looks back at him impassively. He's not chuckling now; he's not doing anything. He's just a baby lying in a cot. James leans forward and gently rearranges the blankets below Charlie's head, placing his son's bedtime companion – a small white lamb called Baa Baa whose fur is stained and matted from repeated chewing – back on the pillow. He tucks the blankets in around the bottom of the cot, covering one of Charlie's little feet, which is poking free.

He is about to get up and leave when, suddenly, Charlie stares straight at him, reaches out and grabs his hand and in a low, guttural, whisper, intones: 'Jimmy . . . Floyd . . . Hasselbaink . . .'

'Why, you little bastard . . .'

'Yes. Jimmy Floyd Hasselbaink. Go on, run downstairs and tell them, you wanker. They won't believe you. And I'm not saying it again.'

Down in the hallway James virtually manhandles his friends through the front door and out into the night.

'Look, thanks for coming,' he says, his face a mask of strained equanimity. 'I've been . . . I mean both of us have been, Angela and me, we've been under an awful lot of stress recently. I'm sorry about this evening . . .'

They stand together and watch him, unconvinced.

'I just wanted to say thanks for popping round. It was, you know, important to me . . .'

'Is Charlie OK?' Clara breaks in, a little shortly.

'What? Charlie? Yes, Charlie's fine, he's fine. He's, ha ha, sleeping off his midnight wake up call . . . Look . . .' he adds, opening the front door with one hand and pushing first Adie and then Clara through it with the other, 'why don't we have a drink next week some time. At the Grove? Does me good to get out of the house. Angie too, I reckon. Brain gets a bit frazzled stuck inside . . .'

They all seem reluctant to leave, though. Go home, thinks James, biting his lip, just be on your way.

'You absolutely sure you're OK?' Adie asks.

'Oh, yes, yes, totally fine. Bit tired, really, that's all. Think I'll turn in, get some rest,' James replies, rubbing his temples whilst decisively escorting Troy through the doorway. 'See you all soon! Have a safe journey home! Bye bye!' he says finally, closing the door and immediately drawing the heavy security bolts across.

Troy, Adie and Clara stand together on the pavement outside James's house, a bemused huddle which isn't quite sure what to do with itself. The street is deserted, almost silent save for the distant murmur of traffic from the Camberwell Road.

'He's not well, is he?' says Adie, to a general nodding of heads.

'It's a difficult thing, having a baby, especially if you're as highly strung as James. We ought to keep an eye on him. Fancy poking his own son with a ruler! It must have hurt the poor mite,' says Clara.

'He wants to watch out the fucking Social doesn't get him, doing stuff like that. It could leave bruises,' Adie says, rubbing his hands together. It is such a cold night, maybe heading for the first real frost of the season. It's late November now and dark most of the time.

'He hasn't gone to bed, you know.'

Adie and Clara turn around. Troy's moved away from the other two, hands on his hips, peering in through the front window.

'What's he up to now?'

'Take a look.'

The living room light is off, but the door to the hall is slightly ajar and there's just enough of a glow for them to see their friend quite clearly. He is hunkered down behind the sofa on his hands and knees, clutching a jackhammer, waiting.

St Mark's Day

Trisha and the kids are off at Flyworld ©, '400 Square Feet of Shit', as the brochures proclaim. It's something of a tradition for those of our lineage round about St Mark's Day, April 25, when there's a palpable warming of the breeze outside and the not too distant smell of summer hanging above the lawn and the blackthorn hedgerows and the lime trees. Maybe I'll join them later – though, then again, maybe not because recently it feels like I've become immune to all the quote excitement unquote of being around so many similarly fervid buzzing bodies, the frantic diving and scrabbling and vomiting, the clamour and the rapacious fucking and the occasional violent side-shows as everyone gets a little too stoked up and overheated and tempers boil over. I think, reader, you know what I mean. You've been there. The sinister ichneumons are always around, too, looking for hosts for their hideous children, which is one reason why you never find our more genteel, civilised brethren – the moths and the butterflies – taking time out at Flyworld ©. Plus those guys are not mad on shit, anyway.

Anyway, this is why I'm here now, thinking things over, just circling the light in the living room. And there is work to be done, a few little odds and ends to be tidied up with everybody safely out of the house.

Without me to keep watch, I reckon Trisha will lose

a good five or so of our twenty-seven benighted offspring and the truth is we rowed this morning, me saying look, why make the effort, it's Flyworld-no-© in here, there's shit everywhere you look, they've just had a fucking baby and the human standards of cleanliness and hygiene have been forgotten, maybe albeit temporarily. And Trish waggles her pretty scape sadly and says it's not the shit, that's not the point, it's a day out, it's a family thing, when did you get to be so fucking joyless, Clive – look at the kids, all of them, buzzing around by the window, they're desperate to go.

And indeed little Jermaine and Bryony and poor, dumb, Edmund, the runtiest of runts, are flying head first at the glass trying to pulverise their way through, bang bang bang bang they go, and they're young and stupid and know nothing and I rate their chances of surviving Flyworld © about one in twenty absolute tops, and Edmund one in a hundred, but Trisha is resolute and there's this horrible, debilitating, acrimonious exchange between the two of us and then a dangerous silence before they all file out shrieking with glee through the ventilation grill behind the gas boiler and the house is quiet.

What gets the kids going, apart from the promise of all that glorious shit, is the chance to see the St Mark's flies make their first appearance. According to our popular mythology the laws of physics preclude a creature as ungainly and heavy and inept as the St Mark's from achieving any sort of flight. That cumbersome black undercarriage and two pairs of elongated, limp tarsi and a pair of flaccid palps should by rights drag them back down to earth and thus evolutionary annihilation. And in fact they don't fly too well and rarely climb higher than a bed of nettles and you watch them and think right, any moment now, nemesis in the form of an avian predator, a robin or a thrush, or maybe just gravity will strike and that's it for the St Mark's flies, for another year. But somehow, the St Mark's flies get by.

The kids are avid to watch all this and have been pretending to be St Mark's all around the house, plummeting from the arm of the sofa to the carpet and giggling and now they want to see the real thing, knowing that this will most likely be their only chance to do so.

And I think they hope to maybe strike up some sort of conversation too or ask for autographs and that's OK because the St Mark's are easy-going, self-effacing and approachable, which is more than can be said for most of the multitudes of kith, kin and mortal enemy spinning out their cheap holidays at the frantic, tawdry hedonism of Flyworld ©, with the barkers and the coloured balloons.

Here's a thing, though. Trisha and me, we met at Flyworld ©, during the last desperate whirl of bacchanalia just before the big autumn sleep. There she was, just inside the gates, this vision, dancing in the air surrounded by a virtual swarm of swooning, just-hatched stone flies with their soft and frankly hopeless gossamer wings and Trisha spinning above and around them in this peculiarly elegant ellipse or maybe a trapezoid which later became so familiar and then, in the end, unaccountably irritating to me. Lust-drunk, we flew straight back to my house and the kids were set down to mature in a large piece of unsmoked bacon which had fallen down to ripen behind the refrigerator. Hell, those were heady days, believe me!

And maybe remembering our first meeting was

behind some of the fury this morning. She thinks I've become too comfortable, too attuned to and obsessed with the rhythm of this house, its frequent, dangerous interlopers and the worry and irritation of a burgeoning arachnid population – much worse since the new baby arrived – and of course the life-cycle of our own, dear, kind hosts. The mewling baby has meant a glut of food and new breeding opportunities (which, for some reason, I feel disinclined to take advantage of. Tiredness, maybe). But you can't argue that it's not made for a comparatively easy life, the new arrival. However, problem is, the change in our circumstances has not gone unnoticed outside and underneath either. The various baby smells stretch down the block and around the corner and everyday brings a plethora of grimly opportunistic visitors, usually nothing more threatening than educationally subnormal bluebottles who, bereft of wit, fly straight into the myriad of spider webs which now festoon each corner of the kitchen and living room and connecting hallway, or maybe occasionally a sluggish, early wasp from the big nest in the attic, fooled into an early summer by the fact that the heating is on full blast all the fucking time. No, stupid, it's not July. Wasps are so gullible. When it comes down to it, they're just glamorous, dumb ants.

But it's the stuff at floor level which has got more worrying. Silverfish slither around the gloopy mess beside the sink; black beetles and cockroaches hide beneath the cooker. There are black ants scurrying around the slatternly melamine work surfaces, in search of powdered baby milk and spilt sugar. And even those fucking weird things from the damp grey earth beneath a stone, devil's coach horses, have colonised the cool and musty pantry. I try to explain to these enormous, stinking creatures, in words of one syllable, that there's nothing for them here, just shit, so leave guys, do yourselves a favour, make for the garden. But the coach horses can sniff a slug from forty paces and I can't disguise from them the glistening bejewelled trails leading haphazardly from the front door to the cellar and the kitchen and the coach horses just wave their fat tails at me and say in that coarse, primitive lingua franca of the garden, minda your owna fucking business, mosca, shadduppa you fucking face.

And apart from the new spiders which make even the most elementary navigation of our home a tricksy business – especially the frankly fucking terrifying *tegenaria gigantea* now installed in a crumbling plaster crevice to the left of the kitchen window, growling and slavering and uttering dire threats and imprecations whilst nimbly skittering across its deadly, cloying web or sometimes just sitting there, waiting, waiting, it's face contorted in a rictus of evil – things are changing with the humans, too, and I mean more than just the rather mundane advent of a human infant.

Thing is, there is a suspicion of entropy in the air. More than a suspicion, in fact.

Hell, I mean, we're all grateful for the mess, for the patent lack of energy to go that inch or two further and sweep up the breadcrumbs. Heaven, after all, is a slovenly house. But there are issues with the humans, bad issues.

Thing is, I think the man is going mad.

I watched him the other night scurrying on all fours across the living room floor after a pair of perfectly amenable cockroaches. He'd been waiting for them to appear and when they did he was on to them – with a fucking hammer. I mean, why break a butterfly on a wheel? I shouted out a warning but too late, too late. Just another brown gungy mess on the carpet. And he didn't stop there, either. He was off after the silverfish next, although with less luck.

And this is the problem: the increased insect activity has tipped him into a psychosis which will only find its release in the extermination of all of us. Obviously, it's a paranoiac fury whose subject has been transferred from the baby – which, according to human social convention, he is precluded from attacking with a hammer – to other small and inarticulate creatures whose murder will attract no opprobrium. That's my theory, anyway. Whatever the case; once, we were left alone. Now fear stalks the home. And this means that either I limit the incursions of my brethren to a sustainable level or we all suffer the consequences.

I swing down to the window. Outside, in the tiny garden, a walled rectangle flanked by impoverished shrubs and tired perennials, helibores and geraniums, an ichneumon is poised above some helpless fucking caterpillar – a cabbage white, I think – its enormous ovipositor trembling in the breeze. It catches my eye as it plunges the thing in, a look on its face of disinterest or maybe even contempt. We are thought of as decadent by most denizens of the outside world, which I think is a bit fucking rich. Especially from those creatures who rear their prey in the still living bodies of other animals, if you'll forgive me for sounding sententious for a moment.

I wave to the ichneumon and mutter a silent prayer for the caterpillar and its dead parents. Imagine, to be orphaned at three weeks and then devoured alive. Who'd be a caterpillar?

Anyway; the first task today is to deal with the

thuggish cleg which I saw banging its way around the bedroom first thing this morning, as brazen and conspicuous and threatening as an insect could possibly be. Nasty, provincial, unsophisticated, biting beasts they are, with no conception of tact or subtlety. Quite what it's doing here is anybody's guess; we're miles from the nearest livestock, their usual hang-out. They love thunderstorms, the clegs (a strange affectation, in my opinion – but each to his own), and there's been not even a suspicion of rain for days. It's a noisy and dangerous presence. Maybe I can persuade him to beat it. And then again, maybe not.

I fly through the living room, down the hall and up the stairs and check out the spare bedroom, through the open window of which Mr Cleg must have blundered, unbidden and unwanted. He's not there now. This is potentially good news – he may have left the way he came in. But I suspect otherwise. Call it ESP if you like, but I can feel his presence in my house and I've a good idea where he's got to.

The master bedroom is dark and has this sweet, heavy, milky smell. The woman is asleep in the bed and her ludicrously demanding and indulged child similarly reposed in a cot alongside. She sleeps when- ever the child sleeps, which isn't often. Usually it cries, especially when the father is around. Trisha gets irritated by it, the constant mewling and even more by the mother's limp and cadaverous appearance. She should look after herself better, Trisha always says, watching the woman stagger from room to room under some new baby-related burden. Somehow Trisha gets to be reproachful to me about the man's alternately slothful and eccentric behaviour, as if that's what I'm like, too. It may sound absurd to you, but she accuses me of forgetting what it is to be an insect and of the freedom such a state necessarily confers.

And for lo, sure enough, there he is, the cleg, making a circuitous approach to the cot, circling and then flying away, checking out the best seating for lunch. I fly across and join him in a holding pattern but he breaks away and lands on the top edge of the yellow blanket pulled just below the baby's face. He doesn't even bother to register my presence. I rub my wings in an approximation of nonchalance and then glide down beside him.

'Hi, friend,' I say, with cheerfulness. 'Name's Clive. Don't get many of you guys in these parts. You lost?'

The cleg looks at me curiously. 'Am I lost?' he asks, the deep rasping, country bumpkin voice laced with sarcasm. 'Am I lost? Now, let me see . . .' He affects a ruminative expression. 'Here I am, hungry for lunch and scarcely two centimetres from the soft skin of an immobilised, prostrate and perfectly delectable infant. In the great scheme of things, that doesn't strike me as being especially lost . . . *Clive.*'

This is not a promising start. I persist with my friendly and unassuming demeanour but come straight to the point. 'Suppose there's no chance of persuading you not to bite that child, is there?'

The cleg fly snorts. 'I think less chance than there is of me persuading you not to wallow in shit, house fly.'

'It's just a friendly request, is all. I have to live here,' I tell the creature.

The cleg grins at me and moves a few centimetres on to the child's face. 'Where's the baby,' he squeaks in a mocking, cartoon voice, covering his huge compound eyes with his flimsy antennae. Then suddenly he pulls them away. 'There he is!'

A bite from a mosquito is a subtle and delicate operation. Often humans don't realise they've been bitten until the anti-coagulant has long since done its work and the mosquito is gone. Not so with a cleg. I'm telling you, it's possible to *hear* a cleg fly's bite from thirty yards away, those great big jaws chomp down and the pain is instantaneous and intense.

The baby lets out an appalled wail. The mother wakes immediately with an expression of inarticulate panic, tears back the bedclothes and stumble-rushes to the cot.

'Christ!' she gasps, brushing hair away from her eyes and watching a rivulet of scarlet blood trickle down on to the blanket. She picks up the baby and cuddles it, wiping the blood away with her nightdress and looks around the room for the culprit. The cleg is circling the light triumphantly, replete for the moment, baby blood fresh on its hard bristles. The woman sees it but, sleep-dazed and encumbered with her son, is not quite sure what to do. Jesus, she looks wrecked, the poor cow, all grey lines and red eyes and sunken pallor, her hair matted and the colour of taupe. She looks like she's going to die, or has already died, maybe, like a may-fly clinging on through the humid depths of August. She grabs a magazine from beside the bed and swats awkwardly and ineffectually at the cleg. The cleg hardly needs to swerve and simply hangs above her in the air, cackling to himself.

'Quick way out of here?' shouts the cleg.

'Try the spare bedroom, first right out of the door. Top window is always left open, the way you came in,' I mutter, grudgingly, hidden from view on the outside of the bedroom curtain.

'Much indebted, much indebted. Thank you, *Clive.*'

And he's gone. The air currents ruffle the hairs on my back.

The woman is still hugging the baby and making cooing noises at it and kissing its forehead but it nonetheless continues to wail like a fucking creature possessed; the blood on its face is even now still flowing. The cleg bit deeply.

And the upshot of this will be, the man will go on another killing spree with his hammer. And maybe he'll throw in an aerosol insecticide and sweet-dripping, mesmerising flypaper this time. I worry about this every day and wonder what the hell I can do. But I get no moral support. Trisha is pretty laissez-faire about the state of the house. Bring one cockroach, bring on ten, is her mantra, whatever shall be shall be and so on. If the man persists with his campaign of annihilation then we just move somewhere else, come on, Clive, she says, exasperated, you're worse than he is, pointing to the madman hunched up on the sofa, his brain under alien control. We're not meant to be like that. We're flies, she says. We don't worry about stuff. We stay, or we leave.

And of course she's right. Traditionally, we do not inflict ourselves upon others of our brethren. But the notion of moving on is too exhausting for me to contemplate; another house to suss out for spiders and this time with twenty-seven kids in tow, I just think nah, it's too much too late in life. Sometimes I see death fizzing and shimmering before me in the middle distance, like columns of dancing air warped by summer heat, except it's no mirage, death really is just out there, in the middle distance.

Not that we have short lives, as you conceive of it. You may pity us what seems a paltry allotance, but it's not a short life really. It's all we know, or expect. And now I reckon that I have about one quarter of my allotted span left. Maybe a fifth. Who knows? The days are uncountable.

I thought about killing him, the man. But you guys are getting resistant to our toxins: maybe we insects should put our heads together and come up with something new. A few days ago – after another orgy of violence directed this time at an harmless if aesthetically questionable pair of slugs who'd made it to the entrance of the kitchen and only then realised that they weren't traversing the garden wall, after all – I slipped outside through the hall window and buzzed low down the street looking for shit. Thank God pooper scoopers never took off in this neighbourhood. I found what I was looking for in about five seconds, a long, gleaming, pale brown dog turd the end of which deliquesced into a pool of diarrhoea, evidence of a typically remiss dog diet. I swooped down and nibbled and then took off vertically straight back into the house through the same window and glided low and noise-lessly to the hastily manufactured ham sandwich on a plate by my host's left elbow. I padded around on the bread, puked a few times, padded some more, rubbed my front legs together and then swung up and away with a quick '*Bon appétit*' and watched from the wall all feverish with the excitement of a job well done as he consumed his despoiled lunch. It was a risky business, I could have been flattened against the table in a nano-second, and all he got as a result was a three-day bout of mild food poisoning, probably streptococci, which allowed him to wallow like a big jessie on the sofa and whine at his wife.

I'd hoped for toxoplasmosis at least. Blindness,

dementia, etc. Maybe even kidney failure. But no; instead just that vague physical unease and lassitude and a markedly increased commitment to wage war against the rest of us.

Back in the master bedroom, when the whirl of activity has died down, I find a companion sitting doggo on the curtain. It's a member of that most unfairly maligned and equable of species, the mosquito. You have some big animus against these fuckers, don't you? But you're barking up the wrong tree. Hell, they've adapted to malaria, why can't you? This one's a male, so of not even minor irritation to humankind, but I assume his wife is zumming around in a room nearby with her delicate and hungry proboscis. I bumped into this character yesterday and we exchanged the usual pleasantries; he told me he'd be gone pretty soon, back to hang out at the dank and stinking brick culvert a few hundred yards away from this house, from whence he was born. I signal a cheerful hello to him. He shakes his head in sympathy.

'Cumbersome bastards, those clegs, but there's no reasoning with them,' he says.

'Tell me about it,' I sigh. 'What I want to know is why the fucking oik was here at all. You could smell the farmyard on him. Must have flown miles.'

'Him and plenty of others,' the mosquito replies. 'There was a bush cricket in the living room yesterday: totally bizarre. I asked it what it thought it was up to but all I got was, you know, na na na na na na na.'

The mosquito rubbed its big back legs together in a passable imitation.

'Plus,' he goes on, 'what's with the cockchafers and the centipedes? Totally out of order. House is falling to bits. I'd get out, if I were you. There's something weird afoot. And there was a fucking raven in the garden yesterday.'

'Thought about leaving, believe me,' I tell him.

'Our fourth child, Alex, got eaten by that huge fucker in the kitchen, the tegenaria. I shouted out but he couldn't hear because the radio was on, just flew straight into the web . . .'

'I'm sorry . . .'

'Yeah, well, kids, you know? Anyway, we'll all be out of here as soon as Emma's had her evening repast . . . watch it, she's pulling the curtains . . .'

We both take off and almost collide in the widening gap as the curtains are pulled back. We settle as unobtrusively as possible in the middle of the bedroom wall. Looks like mum's decided to take the baby downstairs, maybe to treat the cleg bite, although she needn't bother: the cut will heal up and be gone by this evening, without a risk of infection. Me and the mosquito tarry a while in silence, each of us with our own thoughts. I wonder a bit about the centipedes, evidence that the house is returning to a sort of primordial state, the thin patina of human involvement diminishing by the hour. Next, the woodlice will come, but whether anybody will be around to greet them is a different matter. Trisha is, as ever, absolutely right. Dissolution is not something we're equipped to battle against: it happens and we succumb. You, meanwhile, battle – and succumb all the same, that extravagant expenditure of energy like the thinnest of vapour trails across an evening sky, clear and sharp before blurring almost imperceptibly into nothing at all.

After a while, the mosquito mutters a brief goodbye and spins away to join his mate. From downstairs I can hear the building blocks of the evening argument being put slowly in place, human voices rising in cadences of complaint and antagonism. And beyond all that, the brush of insect wings against glass, of insect feet upon linoleum and carpet, of insect jaws upon wood and stone and the gentle ticking of the clock on the wall.

Fucking Radu

1.

. . . so we're supposed to be having this special evening for Anna in a wine bar on Battersea Rise and we're all sitting there being strenuously upbeat and cheerful about her legs when Biba walks in with this tramp or psycho and we all stop and look and wait for the explanation.

It's so typical of Biba, you know? We're all here for Anna because she's leaving us to go to America to see if they can do anything with her legs and she might well be dead within the year and for the first hour instead we're all saying hey where's Biba, where's Biba and you *know* she's going to make one of her entrances, because that's what she does, she hates anyone else getting all the attention, even when they're dying, like Anna probably is.

She always does it.

Like turning up for my twenty-first in a burqa claiming she'd 'embraced' Islam and then not drinking or talking to men all night and being really picky about the food. I mean, hello?

Anyway, she stands in front of us looking super-cilious and self-important and this deranged, filthy homeless person starts gazing at the bread rolls with lust and the Sancerre too and you can see this stain on the front of his trousers where he's, like, wet himself and really, if she'd stopped to think about Anna, not to mention Saul and Dipak who run the place and are currently looking over very apprehensively from the far corner, then she'd just have, you know, given the tramp some money and left it at that.

Toby, who was sort of Anna's boyfriend before her legs hardened and she stopped having sex, stands up and hugs Biba and says hi Biba hi and we thought we'd lost you and where have you been and then, sort of matter-of-factly, who's your friend? And with this helpful cue and the attention of the entire assembled thong, Biba turns to the dosser and puts her arm around his shoulder and there's this solemn expression on her face, like a reporter on a Channel Four programme about poverty in the north-east of England or something and she says slowly: 'This is Radu, guys. I met him down on the Brompton Road where he was begging for money. Like, you know, off people in the street. He had this hanging around his neck . . .'

And then Biba takes this filthy piece of folded-up cardboard out of her Furla handbag and opens it out and holds it up for everybody to see.

It goes:

My Name is Radu.
I Am Romanian Refugee.
I Need Money.
Please Help.

Well, we all read this thing in silence and look at the tramp suspiciously and the tramp looks down at the floor and occasionally gives these furtive, passionate glances towards the food and then Biba says: 'He's from, you know, Bucharest, which is like the capital city in Romania. I knew you wouldn't mind if he joined us for the evening – he's on the run from the secret police and they are so complete bastards, anyway.'

And then having said all this and sort of entirely wrecked the flow and the atmosphere of our evening, all of us not really knowing what to do or where to look, Biba goes and puts on this big sympathetic expression and says: 'Now, Anna. How are your legs?'

And then Anna starts telling everybody what's going on with her legs and at this point I sort of tune out completely because it is so gross and hideous and terrifying and I look at her for a moment and just *pray* she doesn't take off her fucking blanket because that's something that always freaks me out completely, you know? And I'm aware that this sounds callous and uncaring and so on but I'm like, Anna, I can deal with the fact you're really ill but just don't show me, OK? I don't actually need to *see*. And while I'm effecting my mental blackout and not really taking much notice of what's going on around me, which is a familiar mistake, a chair is procured by Saul and suddenly Radu the fucking Romanian-Tramp-on-the-Run is seated down nice and comfortably making these odd catarrhal snuffling noises right next to *me*.

And as he settles himself down I get assailed by this astonishingly vivid stench of over-ripe Parmesan, stale breadcrusts and piss. Oh, *so* delightful.

But still I say to him, really slowly, like you speak to foreigners, children, the elderly and the physically handicapped, Hi. Nice. To. Meet. You. I'm. Emily. Would. You. Like. Some. Wine? But he just grimaces with incomprehension and grabs one of the bread rolls and gnaws at it like an educationally subnormal wolverine so I'm, you know, OK, fair enough, just eat then, knock yourself out, Radu, what the fuck do I care?

And from my right Dominic pours me another glass of white wine and smirks and murmurs to me ah, good, found yourself a new friend, ha ha, and I just glare at him and then he says so, Emily, have you seen Nic recently?

And this questions is even more irritating than his reference to the tramp.

I last saw Nic about seven months ago when he was supposed to be managing this witless indie band called Formal Gravadlax Intifada and we were at one of their predictably depressing gigs in Camden and he'd been trying to get money out of the landlord or owner of the bar as per the contract and the band's idiotic singer, this floppy haired pain called Ripple or Flake or something, was having this absurd flounce in the background because the PA hadn't worked properly thus depriving the nine members of the audience from hearing his whining voice for most of the night and, anyway, everything was a little fraught and Nic just turned to me with this really resigned expression and said I've just had, you know, enough.

And I give him this big consolatory hug and say well, fine, don't worry, just ditch them they're totally shit anyway especially the singer someone should take him outside and kick him around a bit, maybe tear off his fringe and spit on his shoes and Nic says er no, I meant I've had enough of *this*, of you and me. It's going nowhere. Our relationship.

It occurred to me then: where exactly had he been expecting it to go? Sheffield? Lanzarote? Mogadishu?

And I'm, like, just stunned by this statement and stop hugging him and just stand there for a moment wondering what to do and then I do what I usually do at times of acute crisis, which is go over to the bar and order a vodka and slimline tonic and drink it down in this big gulp standing in between the guileless, black-clad indie boys with their endless autistic maundering about who is best Dogshit or Rapemonkey or Anal Prolapse Alert and have you heard the new Cuntmonger single and so on and so on, all stuff which I've never really understood and when eventually I look up the landlord is gone and Ripple or Flake is gone and Nic is gone too and the sleeve of my jacket is soaked through from having leant in a puddle of Carlsberg and it stinks and I can't afford to have it dry-cleaned more than once a year.

And that's the last I've seen of Nic, if you want to know. And Dominic's question is irritating because it suggests everybody thinks I'm sitting here yearning or something and that maybe it's partly true, maybe I still carry something of Nic around with me, something of Nic is still smeared across my forehead like that thing Christ had on his hands, stigmata, I think, except in my case with much less religious significance.

When Anna's problem began, when it was just her feet, Nic used to keep referring to her as Gregor and suggested that we should throw rotten fruit at her and keep her locked up in a room – which was just like Nic, this dead original surreal humour, incredibly funny but sort of totally insensitive also. Plus, he tells lies.

Anyway, on my left Radu is on to the olives and dips and still not that keen on smalltalk so I'm forced to be polite to Dom despite his totally depressing question

and Dominic in any case has been sulking for most of
the evening, sulking big time. He's just split up with
Sophie and I reckon, knowing Dominic, he might well
be thinking of making a play for Biba tonight, he's
always liked her and it would be the sort of final
possible permutation because Dominic's slept with all
the women except Biba and Biba's slept with all the
men except Dominic, we need new blood around
here, really, but it looks like Biba turned up too late
plus she has the tramp with her so Dominic's sort of lost
the energy and has just resigned himself to sulking
instead. To get my own back I ask him if Sophie's
seeing anyone else which brings forth this big ironic
laugh and the rhetorical question uh, what do you
think, Emily?

And then he pours more wine, we're moving on to
red by the look of things, and he asks another question
about Nic which I just totally deflect saying, you know,
just whatever and then there's this sort of unspoken
agreement that we should call a truce, no more Nic or
Sophie stuff, so instead he starts telling me about this big
vineyard his father's bought in, uh, the Ardèche, which
is in France, and then begins this comprehensive
rundown on, like, grapes and the different wines of
southern France which makes me glaze a little but I
hang on listening because the alternative is bad, the
alternative being to engage Radu the Tramp, which is
just not on.

I quite like Dominic, mind, even though he's a
complete fascist and hates this vast list of social groups
including women, pensioners, foreigners, gays, lower-
class people etc. etc. he can still be, I think, quite
charming, if you phase out and ignore the shit every
now and then, some of the whining public schoolboy

self-pity and the misplaced sense of superiority and worst of all the awful blazers. So I try really hard to concentrate and show an interest in the micro-economics of viticulture and tilt my head to one side to look entranced but . . . but I can't do it, I just can't do it. Something is eating away at the back of my mind, maybe the stuff about Nic or maybe it's poor Anna's legs or even Radu the Tramp and I can't focus upon his dissertation. And then my favourite daydream sweeps down on me, this thing where I feel myself attached to the earth by a sort of electrical cord around my waist and I press this button and the cord lets me float further and further away, spinning out through space, past all the space junk and the planets and the asteroids and the big stars and the supernovas, out further and further towards a place where nobody exists and nobody knows me and where it's silent and black and really fucking cold.

And there's this other button which, if I press it, the cord would snap off and just leave me drifting away for ever with no chance of returning, the earth by now not even a speck or a glimmer all those light years distant.

Of course I've never pressed that other button, in my daydream. But it's nice to know it's there.

And I suppose it must be my totally vacant expression which gives me away because Dom stops in the middle of this fascinating exposition of the fermentation processes and says he, Emily, Emily, hello, what's the matter?

And this big feeling of foreboding comes crashing down on me and I look him in the eyes and grab hold of both of his wrists and say, *sotto voce*: 'Please, Dominic. Whatever happens, don't let me fuck the tramp tonight.'

And Dom sort of half laughs, not quite sure if this is a pass or not, you can see the cogs turning inside his brain and he mulls it over and decides it probably isn't, because it isn't, and just says come on, Em, get a grip, old girl.

But I can't get a grip.

Simba, who couldn't make it this evening because of her job – she makes hummus for this big deli down the Fulham Road and has just won a huge order for some artist's party so she's like up to her armpits in the taupe gunge right now – once said that the great thing about us all, meaning the gang, was that the friendships ran so deep . . . yeah, we've all slept with each other over the years and sometimes it's got a bit awkward like when Sophie was sleeping with all of the men except Raj *and* two of the girls, but in the end none of that really mattered because our friendships endure. That was the word she used, endure. Even then I thought Simba, shut up, just shut up, that's the E talking, go dance a while. And now as I look around the table at us all I really wonder if the thing keeping us afloat is maybe as fragile and tenuous as the surface tension of blood, a skin so thin it would break at the slightest troublesome current. Or maybe it's worse than even that and we hang around together because we're too tired to do anything else – anything, you know, better. And by luck I reckon Simba stumbled upon exactly the right word when she was wittering on, the word being, you know, endure. Yeah, that's right, Sim, it's a small pool of people fucking each other and when we're not doing that we endure each other.

And I'm thinking all this and feeling pretty depressed anyhow and I look all the way down the table again and oh fuck, Anna's got her blanket off.

I see two glistening black limbs, shiny and hard.

And I can't really tell you about the rest of the evening.

Make something up. Treat yourself. And me, for that matter. I think my life would run on rather clearer lines if somebody else filled in the blank spaces, the clanging hours of stupor and semi-coma.

All I remember is things started to slip round about nine-thirty, after the coke and the langoustines. And the next thing . . .

And the next thing . . .

Well, yeah, sure, you can guess the next thing. Fifteen hours later I'm woken by this horribly familiar collection of smells — stale breadcrusts, over-ripe Parmesan, piss — and I look across the bed and I'm like fuck fuck fuck fuck fucking fuck how did *this* come about? I close my eyes and offer up this desperate prayer. And then maybe it's answered because I suddenly notice I'm in Biba's spare bedroom — waxed walls, Conran lamps made of bandages, framed photo-graph of a dead turbot — so I guess I must have crashed out here and maybe, just maybe, it's OK because in that case it's just possible I didn't fuck the tramp, it could just be a case of not enough beds to go around, you know?

So instinctively I put my hand down to the inside of my thighs and the prayer, it seems, wasn't answered, the prayer was actually totally ignored, because there's four million proto-Romanians dried to a crisp down there and so I'm fuck, fuck, fuck etc. again.

And suddenly I hear Biba from downstairs open the front door with her precious, mewing laugh and then Dominic's voice comes spiralling upwards and even though I'm still half asleep I just *so* don't want to be here, you know? And I strain to hear the conversation and Dominic's asking if I'm up yet so I climb out of bed and dive for Biba's third-choice wardrobe and nestle down and pull the door shut tight behind me, curled up on the wooden floor amongst the shoes and the discarded underclothes and the dresses she hasn't worn in years. I hear one of them knock at the door and then come into the room and then Biba says oh, that's odd, she was here a few minutes ago when I brought her some tea, she was fast asleep, and I can hear Dominic quietly sniggering and then Biba again, in her most affected fucking stage whisper, go: 'Do you know, I think she might just be in the wardrobe . . .'

And I'm like thinking to myself fuck off, just *fuck off* and leave me alone and then the wardrobe door is pulled open and it's Dominic's stupid grinning face looking down at me. And I'm really mad now so I grab a shoe, jump up and smash at his chest with one of Biba's nasty, strapless, f-m stiletto heels and shout you bastard, you bastard, I begged you not to let this happen and Biba – she's howling with laughter – tries to wrestle the shoe away from me and the cheap heel snaps off and Dominic collapses in hysterics on the bed and this makes Radu wake up and clearly he thinks the secret police have come for him because he's out of bed in a second screaming stuff in Romanian.

So that was my start to the day. How was yours?

And I crawl home disgraced, unwashed, and half-way, on the tube, try so hard to rationalise it and be, you know, philosophical. It's just something that happened, OK? Why should I flagellate myself? We've all done it, well most of us, and if Biba tries to bring it up in company I've got a couple of stories of my own which she's pleaded with me not to divulge. That night at Astra's enlargement party, for example, when she was spectacularly monged out and vaguely remembered going back to some guy's house and even more vaguely remembered some desultory act of sexual intercourse taking place and then woke up to find this strange head on the pillow next to her and she's like uh-oh, time to leave. So she sneaks out of bed really quietly, pulls on her clothes and makes for the door but she can't, for some reason, find the door handle and she's really puzzled and a bit worried about this and then she looks down and sees it's like two feet off the floor. And she wonders for a moment about this and looks around the room and notices that *all the fixtures and fittings are no more than two feet from the floor* like the light switches and handles to the cupboards and stuff and there are these weirdly low tables and she just fucking freaks at this and is out of the house in a nanosecond, tearing for the tube, aghast, crying.

So, OK, Biba, honey; here's the deal. You want me to tell them about the dwarf? One word, just one fucking word . . .

The man I'm sitting next to on the train has shifted his entire body away from me; as far away as he can get, holding his copy of the *Independent* at an angle so it forms a barrier between the two of us. I don't blame him. I must smell awful. I just fucked a tramp, for God's sake.

How can I *do* stuff like that? What happens to me, when I'm not watching?

The saving grace is that I was clearly in no fit state to have given the man a blow job.

But it's not much of a saving grace, really.

I mean, it wouldn't sound very redemptive in a confessional, would it? I fucked a tramp but I didn't suck his cock because I was too whacked out to make my mouth work properly.

Deep inside the tunnel the lights flicker out and then on again and then out as the train comes to a gradual stop. We seem to be stuck there for like aeons and my fellow passengers start grunting and fidgeting and clicking their teeth and tutting with impatience but for me, it's fine, just fine. It's the best thing that has happened so far . . . please, we could stay there all day; just keep the lights out and let the day pass by hundreds of feet above us, all the noise and the traffic and the crush of people, especially the ones I know personally, all going about their business, oblivious.

A faint musty breeze blows through the darkened carriage, the ghost of some other train far off down the line and then we hear the distant clattering of wheels receding and then there's this perfect silence, beautiful silence.

And then the lights flicker back on like a second hideous daybreak.

Back home I run along the landing and lock the bathroom door behind me and strip everything off and lean over and turn the hot tap in the tub on full because what I need, I think, is something fucking scalding, something which will actually remove a layer of skin as well as the grime and filth and Parmesan stuff and trampcum. I bung in some bubblebath and as the tub fills up and the steam rises I lean against the washbasin and gaze in the mirror and then gaze away again really quickly, repulsed, because actually the mirror idea was a very, very thoughtless act and then I

sit down on the toilet and rest my head in my hands.
Next to me there's two Cap'n's Table Fish Fingers
glued to the wall, the work of Jamal, who's doing art
at St Martin's. They've been up there for ages and the
orange batter coating is beginning to flake off leaving
a greyish-white indeterminate flesh behind. It's only
when I avert my gaze from this particular obscenity –
the sole ornamentation in our bathroom, by the way,
and one to which I objected saying, you know, how
about a painting of a boat or some seashells or
something – that I notice the big thumb print on the
inside of my thigh. It's not a bruise; I am not about to
claim that force was involved in last night's grotesque
copulation. No, it's a dirt thumb print, a smudge of
Brompton Road grime.

Then I hear this peculiar noise coming from the
bath, really strange, there's a collection of high pitched
whines and an occasional soft popping like someone
opening a bottle of champagne, but not very good
champagne. What the fuck is this all about, I think, and
rise from the lavatory seat and push away the molten
clouds of steam and then I see the source of the noise
and it's oh, Jesus Christ, no, that's it, that's all I need,
because down there floating on top of the boiling
water, their little shells poking through the fragrant
bubbles, are Muppy's terrapins.

Well, Muppy's ex-terrapins.

And distraught I stand there and think what should I
do and then I turn off the hot tap and turn on the cold
and when the water's cooled down I scoop the dead
reptiles out of the bath with one of Muppy's face
towels and sort of swaddle them and leave them outside
his bedroom door, all wrapped up. I wonder if maybe
I should leave a note too but I can't think of what to

write except I'm really, really sorry but honestly Muppy what were your fucking terrapins doing in the bath and I'm too tired to write even that, I just want a nice bath and to sleep. Anyway, maybe he could make soup with the bodies.

So I run the water again, having first rinsed the bath free of terrapin stuff. And I soak and soak in it and the bizarre thing is the water went dark grey after five minutes or so, utterly disgusting and I towel myself down really vigorously and crawl back to my bedroom and huddle down under the covers and cry for a few moments and then sleep hits me, and I sleep for ages, even though, if we're being pedantic about it, it's not that long since I've got up anyway.

The next night we're all in Simba's front room in Stockwell with a quarter of skunk and a bottle or two of Stoli which Toby managed to get duty free from Heathrow, God knows how, when he saw off poor Anna. The bedsheets, when I got up a couple of hours ago, held this faint tang of Parmesan cheese, the ghost of a smell, so I stripped them off the bed and bunged them in the washing machine with a double whack of fabric softener, Domestos and Vecta window cleaner.

Simba's got a weird new boyfriend called Troy who everybody is wary of on account of his hobby. What's he like, Sim, we all asked and she replied well, he's quite cute and really very funny and terribly dignified but he's into this strange new therapy which I haven't heard of before called *involuntary movements*.

Um, what do you mean, Sim?

'Well, like, every now and then he'll sort of twitch or contort his body or writhe, you know?'

We all think about this for a bit and then Sophie asks: 'What, like during sex?'

And Sim goes: 'No . . . no . . . well, I mean, yes, but not only in bed. All the time, like when we were shopping in Muji yesterday and then the day before when we met my mother for lunch at that new Armenian sushi bar in Clerkenwell . . . sort of any time, really. He says it releases harmful energy and allows the body to escape from the straitjacket of muscular conformity, gives the body a moment of autonomy, away from the – what did he say – totalitarian impulse of the brain. He showed me all these Kirlian photographs of people who used the technique as opposed to those who didn't. And the people who do involuntary movements have this really bright orange, blue and purple aura, you know, they really glow.'

'Uh.'

'Oh right.'

'Sure, cool.'

We all say.

And later, when we've finished this vast mount of hummus Simba had left over from her artist's party, the new boyfriend turns up and we're all really welcoming and like, hi, how are *you* and nice to meet you and we make him feel at home. And in fact he's quite good looking, sort of like Jude Law if you screw your eyes up and look from a distance and the first impression is quite favourable but then after about a quarter of an hour, apropos of nothing, he just bellows and starts thrashing around on the floor like a spazz. We all politely move our feet out of the way and cough and don't really know whether it's OK to talk among ourselves whilst this stuff is going on and after about twenty seconds

Troy stops spazzing and climbs to his feet and smiles at us all and sits down next to Simba again.

Really great, Sim.

Hell of a catch.

We all think.

Anyway, the wine is flowing and everything's OK and most of the attention is centred upon weird Troy, which suits me just fine, and then there's a knock at the door and I'm like uh-oh because the knock has got this annoying, confident, Biba tone to it and so far I haven't let on to anyone that I fucked the tramp. God, I wish I could remember how it happened. Some switch gets flicked inside maybe, I don't know. Some switch which should be in a sealed case requiring multiple codewords to become activated, or at least something requiring, you know, thought.

So, sure enough, the door opens and in walks Biba *and* Dominic *and* fucking Radu who immediately sees me and breaks into this big, shit-eating grin and, after glancing at Biba for approval, says slowly and carefully and very loudly: 'Hallo . . . Emily. How . . . are . . . you . . . today?'

And I say fucking terrific, what can I tell you, and everybody is looking at me with their eyes wide as planets and if you took a Kirlian photograph of me right now there'd be no orange, blue and purple aura, there'd be no aura at all, just a thin brown stain.

It later transpires that Radu has actually moved in with Biba and she's going to beg a menial job for him from Saul and Dipak in the bar and she's looking very fucking pleased with herself and magnanimous and she has the gall to wink at me not-that-surreptitiously as Radu inevitably deposits himself down beside me on the floor.

He's all dressed up this evening, in one of Dom's pink Jimmy Heidegger shirts and a pair of grey Marshall MacLuhan cargo trousers and Biba's obviously given him a bath and sprayed him down and so the bread crusts, piss, Parmesan has been replaced by some new scent for boys, Placenta by Jean Lacan, I think. And I mull stuff over to myself and reckon yeah, maybe it wasn't *his* fault last night, sometimes I just lose track, just completely lose it and who can blame a guy, especially a guy like that who is both penniless and foreign, for sort of taking advantage. And I think it's wrong to hold a grudge against Radu, my anger should be directed at Biba and Dominic. I mean, they're meant to be friends, right?

And anyway, clean clothes or not, whatever happens, I won't do it again. Tonight, for once, I leave early and comparatively sober and say goodbye to everyone and Radu gives me this doleful, disappointed look and Dominic just smirks so I kick him on the shin, as if by accident, on my way to the door and leave him yowling and holding his leg and saying clumsy bitch and for once, the journey home on the tube is sort of triumphant apart from a nagging feeling.

Do you ever get this feeling that you're meant to be doing something else? You know, you're out enjoying yourself or maybe just sitting there on a tube train or whatever and there's this weight at the back of your mind nagging away at you but it doesn't actually tell you what it's nagging you about and you try to remember, like, uh, what is it I'm meant to be doing, I'm sure there *was* something but you can't recall it, whatever it was, but the nagging stuff won't go away. No? Oh, OK. Anyway, I got that feeling on the tube. And I had it yesterday, when I was lying in the living room reading *Heat*.

And then there's the night . . .

Night; oh dear.

Night is bad. Maybe I've slept too much already during the last twenty-four hours. I reckon at least nineteen hours have been spent in bed. Maybe that's why night brings back the day in a terrifyingly condensed form, all its iniquities and traumas and acts of gross inappropriate behaviour.

I keep waking up to make sure I'm alone, reaching across the bed expecting to find some fucking homeless person camped out there and then I spin back into sleep and dream of terrapins screaming at me Emily, Emily, what are you doing, you're boiling us alive, except they're not screaming in English but in Romanian, but despite this for some reason I can understand what they're saying, every word, and then the terrapins turn into Nic and he's just laughing saying hey, it's only a joke, chill out, Em, which is what he used to say whenever he'd made me upset or miserable.

There was a dead terrapin nailed to my bedroom door this evening when I got back and a scrawled note from Muppy which said YOU MURDEROUS FUCKING BITCH which I think is just out of order, really over the top, you know? He spends too much time with his aquarium, Muppy, he wants to get some proper human interaction. I bet his Kirlian glow is non-existent.

I slept with him once, when I'd just moved in and was feeling bereft and lonely and insecure and vulnerable and wished to ingratiate myself with my new flatmates and sex seemed to be a sort of suitable means of accomplishing this. Believe me, that was worse than boiling his fucking terrapins. I caught him, mid-fuck, staring intently at his tank to see if Roger the chameleon was catching the flies he had put in a few moments before.

And yeah, sure, now I think about it, I've probably slept with too many people and too often for the wrong reasons. I'm not really sure how many people you're meant to sleep with, or why, or what the rules are. If there's a grand scale of things with Mother Theresa at one end and, oh I don't know, Sophie, I suppose, at the other then I would guess that I'm much nearer the Sophie end. Is that bad? I forget sometimes what the point of it all is, why we do it in the first place. Pleasure, I suppose. Most of the time, the pleasure of feeling a beating heart next to my own. Most of the time. And also, with us, with the gang, there's a strange kind of acquisitiveness about it too. That's truly awful, isn't it? Funny thing is, the worst sex was with Nic. It was this fumbling tentative stuff which left us both rancorous and embarrassed. And then he left me. Maybe that's why he left me, although he said it was because he didn't know where we were going and later I heard from Sophie that he wanted to 'travel'. Travel where? What for? I'd have travelled with him, if he wanted that. I have no particular emotional investment in Balham, to be honest. Thing is, three months later he'd got as far as Wandsworth.

Oh, sleep, please.

I get up for a glass of water, stumbling along the landing past Jamal's failed installations and the huge box within which Muppy keeps Jessica, his Thai Spitting cobra. The box is silent; either the snake is asleep, or out again. Sometimes you open a cupboard up in the kitchen and scream because from between the packets of mung beans and vegetarian rennet and tofu there's this spiteful black head flickering its scarlet tongue hither and thither, its dumb, obsidian eyes regarding you with herpetic loathing. Good job we forced Muppy to get its venom glands removed. Jessica is a Thai Spitting cobra with no spit, a sort of entirely pointless Thai Spitting cobra.

I trudge back to bed with my water and take a few sips and lie back and plead with the terrapins to leave me alone. And they do, they do. Next time I dream, I get Anna's legs instead.

2.

The news from the US, since you asked, is pretty bad.

Anna's in this huge institute in a town called Baton Rouge where they're trying to find out what's going wrong with her and how, maybe, they might reverse the process. Latest thing is they think it's possibly a combination of the time she spent on her sunbed plus this really powerful depilatory gel she used, some sort of awful chemical reaction. But they're not very sure and want to keep her inside for more tests.

Toby is already talking about suing the manu-facturers of the sunbed and the gel too but the doctors say that sadly there's nothing remotely conclusive yet, it's all a bit of a puzzle, to be honest, and they're going to have to keep her there for ages.

Toby says she wants us all to come out for a visit, which is the last thing I'd want if my legs had turned all black and hard and shiny like a beetle's, but there you are. Another friend of Anna's, this rather annoying self-absorbed sort of communist person, Mick, has been over to see her and says she's looking a bit rough but seems to be comfortable enough, although he doesn't trust the doctors. Toby told us all this and says don't worry too much because Mick just hates Americans *per se* so you can't take his analysis of the situation at face value.

So, anyway, I guess we'll all go over if we can raise the money and maybe stay for a few days in New York where Simba's cousin, Astra, has a, you know, loft.

All the gang have now started getting very wary about their personal care products in case they go the same way as Anna. Suddenly, Sophie, for the first time, has hair on her legs. And Biba read this thing which said deodorants give you cancer and the whole deodorant industry is run by three Jews who also, like, have control of the world's armaments, missiles and stuff, and Kentucky Fried Chicken too. And also Kentucky Fried Chicken isn't actually chicken at all, they don't put 'chicken' on the boxes or on the front of the restaurants because they'd fall foul of the trades description acts, because the stuff they sell is actually evil mutant legless blind beakless alien creatures which they keep in a huge vat in total darkness. And these three Jews know all about this but they couldn't give a shit, apparently, and maybe even they're pleased, the Jews, because they don't like us and it's all part of some huge plan and look at what they're doing to Palestine, which is really a disgrace.

And Sophie chipped in saying um, no, it's all about potash, I think, according to this man she knows over in New Cross, the Americans scatter it everywhere deliberately and it gives you cancer and that's probably something to do with the three mysterious Jews too.

And I don't know what to believe, if I'm honest. All this stuff sounds so far-fetched and I know some Jews personally and they seem OK to me, if a bit aloof and geeky. And this other friend, Tabitha, who works in a, you know, art gallery owned by Jews, says they're really polite and don't seem to bear any of us much animosity plus they give five weeks holiday every year and are relaxed about her going to kick boxing lessons on a Friday afternoon. So who knows? Maybe the three mysterious Jews are also responsible for my behaviour on those occasions when I sort of black out and do despicable stuff all over the place.

Anyway, at least they have a name for it now, Anna's illness.

Metastatic keratosis.

Pretty gross, no?

But still, at least poor Anna is away from *this*:

Another night and the usual crowd – Dom, Raj, Biba, Troy, Adie, Simba, Radu, Sophie, Tabitha, Dipak, Bounty, Mick – plus a few more, these people Dominic met on holiday in Guadeloupe last year. Duvalier is thin and sharp with a *recherché* quiff and keeps trying to paw Sophie who is acting all cool and above it all and unfuckable. Twix and Corniche are two very sloaney babes, one of whom Dominic has clearly screwed in the not too distant past, no, I'm not sure which one is which.

We're at Sheepscape, an art gallery-cum-nightclub just off the Wandsworth Road, a venture of Saul's, who is hovering nervously near the bar (or Baaaa, as it's called here).

There are sheep – real, live sheep – wandering unhappily about the dancefloor, which is covered in that fake grass used by greengrocers and old-fashioned fruiterers.

This is, truly, a fucking stupid idea.

Dipak has persuaded us to come – it's like the opening night – and promised hordes of expensive boys and great music and coke and all the alcohol we could drink, which was the clincher. But it's only eleven-thirty and already I wish I was at Rubber Clit or Erewhon, our more regular haunts at this time of the week.

Sheep? I mean, come on, just like, you know, why?

According to Dipak we're meant to interact with the sheep, which seems to me to be an unfair imposition upon the animals, who already look traumatised and borderline litigious.

Anyway, the plan hasn't worked. There's no interaction at all. All the humans are grouped around the bar whilst the sheep are huddled together on the dance floor, showing the early signs of tinnitus. Maybe it just needs someone to wander over and break the ice, I don't know.

Apparently, they're Merino and very expensive.

'My name is Ern and I will pull astern,' goes the song hammering out of the sound system, the only line of vocal in the whole thing, the rest of it this relentless thumping drum'n'bass which is really getting on my nerves and on the nerves of the sheep, by the look of things, this interminable pounding and then on virtually one note this witless refrain 'My name is Ern and I will pull astern.' So, you're Ern! We care? And what's this stuff about pulling astern? Is it just because it rhymes? It's been played all summer in the clubs, this tune, and I really hate it, one day I'm going to find out who the perpetrators are and cause them very bad injuries.

So I'm standing up at the baaaa drinking nice slippery monkeys and damp torpedoes and the music is crashing around my head and everything seems to be conspiring to put me in a worse and worse mood and it's, you know, uh-oh, four more hours to go and I feel this sort of nuzzling in my bottom and look around expecting to see one of those fucking sheep but it's not a sheep, it's only Radu's left hand. He gives me his big Romanian-in-London look and stares across the gallery to the flashing lights and the dancefloor and the truculent, unhappy animals. He shouts into my ear: 'Please, Emily . . . who is Ern?'

And I say search me, Radu, and maybe I'm a little drunk on the monkeys because I sort of ignore him and even sway in time to the music and it feels like I'm doing this for ages but when I look around Radu's still there. He is shaking his head.

'And why these sheep?'

I just shrug and shake my head at this, I can't explain British culture in its entirety to him, some of it doesn't have, you know, an explanation and it gets a bit wearing, really, after a time, this continual request for information like why can't I stand on the left down the escalator and, you know, Oxford *Circus*, so where are the clowns, please, Emily?

But still he doesn't go, probably because another bit of British culture he can't quite get is what girls do when they want you to fuck off and leave them alone for a few minutes, probably in Romania things are a lot clearer in that area, or maybe girls never want men to fuck off in Romania, I don't know.

So still he's right there next to me at the baaaa and I see Troy spazzing on the floor near the door to the chill-out room and Sophie dancing next to Duvalier scattering the sheep across the dancefloor and the rest of the gang are watching this too and then Radu takes hold of my hand and nestles right up to me and says more softly: 'Emily, your friend, Nic. I do not think that he is coming back.'

Which is probably true, sure. A few days ago I got back from helping Simba make another vast batch of guacamole and the little red light was flashing on my ansamachine and the little red light was, as it happened, Nic. He wanted his duvet cover back. After nearly a year. No, hey, Emily, how are you doing what's happening, hope you're well, etc., really missed you, just like can I swing by and pick up my Kenzo duvet cover? Anyway, I listened to his message and then played it back and listened again and the sound of his voice made me feel like I had colitis or something and then Radu came in and unplugged the ansamachine and threw it across the room in a sort of temperamental European gesture of displeasure and I was like, excuse me? And he looks at me and points at the now dismembered ansamachine and says: 'I thought he was the bastard?'

And I say 'a' bastard, Radu, not 'the' bastard. And I add but yeah, sure, true, so what?

But he's right: the boy's gone.

By one o'clock I've *so* had enough of Sheepscape, so I slope off to the toilets intending to chill by myself for a little while and maybe even doze for an hour or two, but when I get there it's impossible because it's so packed with similarly disaffected sheep. They're just standing around in little disconsolate groups bleating to each other. I reckon maybe I should just cut my losses and sneak out, grab a cab and head home, just, you know, leave, when I see in the far corner of the toilets a sheep behaving oddly. It's standing up on its hind legs chopping up a line of coke on the stainless steel counter. I watch transfixed as it lowers its vast nostril to the surface and snorts up about a gram at least and then lifts its blunt fuzzy head and sort of sheepsneezes a couple of times, its eyes wide and open, the pupils swivelled upwards. I guess I'm staring, which is rude, and then this happens: the creature catches my eye and gives me a horrible weird sheepleer and says hey, babe, wanna do a line with me? And I am just like *out* of there, just *out*.

I swear to you that's what happened – and the funny thing is, nobody apart from me either noticed or cared.

Plus there were two other sheep fucking in one of the cubicles and they couldn't even be bothered to close the door.

I climb up the stairs out past the bouncer and stand under the yellow sodium glare of the street light breathing in and out in and out watching the road for taxis and wondering if there's a minicab place nearby or maybe I should just start walking. Saul appears in the doorway of Sheepscape and says thanks for coming, Em, what do you reckon and I tell him yeah, it's terrific, good luck, the sheep really make it, now ring me a minicab, please and he smiles and rings me a cab on his phone and says five minutes and then I have this sudden recollection and say to him oh, and tell Rad that if he wants to come home I'm leaving now and Saul disappears back inside his latest, ludicrous and doomed creative adventure.

So, as I guess you must have gathered, I'm sort of seeing Radu now, which is like OK, I suppose. Trust me about this: he's not the way he was when you first met him. Shaved and scrubbed and de-odorised he's, you know, presentable, this sort of raffish curly black hair and Caramac skin and pale blue eyes the crucial features. Dom said to him a few weeks ago I don't know, there's something of the gypsy about you, Radu, at which point Radu got up and hit him very hard in the mouth, which is very ill-mannered and something we're going to have to work on but then Dominic was ill-mannered also and clearly doesn't know the social demographic of Romania which is something I'm learning about, gradually.

Anyway I'm not entirely sure what's going to come of this relationship, it's another one I've just sort of fallen into without, you know, much in the way of volition and Radu does have these violent moodswings which are worrying but must be something to do with what happened to him back in his own country and why he left but are, as I say, worrying in Balham.

Apparently, right, he was a hospital doctor and really prominent in the opposition which is, like, outlawed? Then one day the secret police came along and beat the shit out of him and did stuff with electrodes and wet towels and Alsatians, all of which he described to me in details, sobbing, and which I cannot, *cannot* repeat right now because it has the same effect on me as poor Anna's legs. Anyway, he told me all this one evening when he was crashing round at my place because Biba had a friend staying, this man called Jochum who's like the very handsome and loaded errant son of a German racing driver and so she didn't want Radu around plus she thought she might have needed the spare room, you can never be entirely sure, can you, and Radu just told me his story in his sad stumbling English – he's much better at it now, by the way – and was crying at the same time, the two of us sitting on the floor in my living room beneath Jamal's huge installation of frozen Findus Chicken and Bacon and Sweetcorn Crispy

Pancakes and me just listening and then shaking my head and crying and saying how could anyone do that to another human being, I don't understand, which made him cry even more. So I put my arms around him and just held him for, God, hours, held him next to me rocking him in my arms like he was, you know, six months old or something which felt good, for me, least. His escape from the police sounded really scary, across all these borders and he had no money and no papers etc., a bit like when I went to Krabi last year, and he dosed on the streets in Dubrovnik and Trieste and Marseilles and Paris and then London, not really knowing what to do and still freaked out, I suppose, by all the wet towel, electrode and Alsatian stuff.

So in the end we sit there with me tiredly stroking his hair and the sobs are sort of spent and it's all very peaceful and then Jessica slithers out from under the sofa and Radu howls like a madman and runs out of the room and I chase after him saying no, no, don't worry, Muppy's had her venom glands removed, it's OK and I let him crash in my room and he doesn't even try to do anything to me, just closes his eyes and falls fast asleep, I don't know, maybe he's scared the cobra will come back if he makes a move or something.

And next day I told Radu he ought to apply to live in this country, like, legally, you know, because it seems to me he's got a really good case but he's worried that if he comes clean to the authorities the secret police will be able to find him – and not surprisingly he's really terrified of them, especially on account of the Alsatians.

What is it with animals, these days? What's got into them? They're all over the place, doing stuff they're not meant to do. Everywhere I look there's some creature acting, you know, strange and un-animalish. Snakes and sheep and dogs and terrapins. Maybe they're becoming more adaptable, sort of accustoming themselves to our way of life and we're merging, us and the animals. Who knows?

Anyway, that was all about a month ago and I sort of decided I'd let him stick around for a while because Jochum's moved into Biba's spare room and seems to be playing a sort of long game with her and I suppose it's no big problem for me, having Radu around, and I don't have a spare room so he has to sleep with me.

He's sort of an ideal boyfriend, in a way, being both solicitous and pathetically grateful when I sleep with him, two good qualities in a man, I find. Plus he's really straightforward about sex, it's just like enough for him to shag me for a bit and then stop, I've slept with him about twenty times and he hasn't once tried to stick his thumb up my bottom or tie me to the radiator, like most men do.

So let's just see how it all works out.

By the way, we're having a sort of party for him round at Biba's next Friday and he feels really honoured and is preparing a speech. What happened was this. Radu's been getting better and better at speaking English even though I still need to correct him about simple words like 'the' and 'a' and tenses and stuff, the improvement's been, you know, incredibly rapid. So a few days ago Troy and Dipak swung by when I was out and they're sitting in my living room and Radu's there and Dipak says, sort of joking, go on Radu, put the kettle on and make some tea, mate, and Radu says, with arms outstretched: 'I'm, like, hello?'

And Dipak cracks up and Troy says: 'Outstanding!' and later tells me what happened and so we're having an 'I'm Like Hello' party to mark Radu's ultimate accession to the gang. The Romanian boys' got the grammar at last.

3.

So once a year I visit my mother, a thing which requires, like, copious amounts of alcohol and class A drugs. I take Radu with me because it's a Saturday and he has nothing better to do other than hide from the imagined secret policemen and complain all the time about how cold it is. Plus, I think, maybe Mum will warm to him, the life he's lived and all that stuff with the Alsatians making him, you know, more interesting than most of the boys I've known before.

We're at Waterloo at, like, eight o'clock in the morning and it's a bright, clear day and everything's cool and we get some nice coffee at Costa Coffee and the train is waiting importantly at platform fourteen, full of people heading to the West Country for the weekend with their kids carrying all these snacks and horrible soft drinks and comics and stuff and my mood's pretty good and I think maybe, when I see Mum this time, I won't end up feeling suicidal or matricidal. But if we're honest, I wouldn't bet on it.

We're in the smoking compartment of the train, settled down facing each other across the table, Radu looking furtively around in case the secret police people have decided similarly to take a break and, like, head for a day out in Devon. Even though he's nicely dressed up people still look at the two of us oddly, maybe on account of the fact that he's a bit older than me and has this perpetually suspicious expression or maybe its his hair which is a tad too long, really, if we're honest, like a cartoon animal's fur and I tell him this is the reason people stare, because they think he should have a good haircut and maybe some styling mousse, nothing more than that and certainly not because they want to do the electrodes, wet towels and dog thing to him.

But he continues to skulk lying low down in his seat, burying himself in a newspaper or keeping his head turned out of the window watching Surrey flash by, all gorse and sprawl.

By the time we reach Basingstoke he's chilled a bit and when the soft green plains and banks of Wiltshire come into view, after Andover, he becomes almost expansive, talking about the countryside in his beloved Romania, which he misses more and more these days, and wondering if he'll ever be able to go back there. When I ask him about his family back home, however, he clams up and an expression of unendurable sadness comes over him, which makes him not that different to most of my previous boyfriends, frankly.

And then we're standing outside the train station at Salisbury waiting for the bus, me and Radu, in a queue with the jabbering American tourists and weird Japanese people and the red double decker turns up and we all clamber aboard and everything, so far, is fine. Radu puts his arm around my shoulders as we head out and up towards the plain and he's quite happy now and he says to me Emily, your mother is good person, yes?

And I look a bit askance at this. And I think and mull it over for a bit and say, well, I've never really thought of it in that way, no – 'good' isn't really the first word that springs to mind when I think about my mother, to be honest. 'Bad' might be nearer the point. Or 'extremely fucking irritating' maybe.

And he looks puzzled at this and says to me but Emily, you love your mother, yes? And I'm like um, run that idea by me again, would you, which provokes him into this long, pompous homily about how sacred a thing it is to love and honour one's mother, come what may, that it is a special bond which can never be broken and is more important even than the special love you have for your country (I'm *sorry?*) and transcends everything and then he stops because I'm tapping him on the shoulder and pointing out of the window at the field just a few hundred yards below the giant standing stones and there, that one on the left, the bright blue one with the moon and the stars on the side and the three-cornered hemp flag fluttering on top, just look . . . that's my mum's teepee.

That shuts him up for a few minutes.

'She is on holiday here, yes?'

Nope, 'fraid not, Radu. I mean yeah, she's probably on holiday, what's new etc., but this is where she, like, lives. All the time.

He goes silent for a bit and his face is distorted with disgust by the time we've climbed down from the bus.

'She is *gypsy?*'

I laugh, which annoys him. No, I say, she's not a gypsy, no. At least there'd be a decent reason for this ludicrous lifestyle if she were a gypsy.

Somewhat unexpectedly, he spits a long stream of phlegm on to the grass verge. I'm not big on spitting, you know? I'm pretty easy-going, by and large – too much so, you might think, sometimes – but spitting is sort of disgusting and just a big *no*.

But Radu's face still has this horrible twist to it.

'Gypsy is fucking *scum*, Emily, is *scum*. We have many gypsy, in Romania. Are thief, all thief. Whore and thief.'

Then, to make things clear, he adds: 'Women is whore; men is thief.' And then: 'They are not washing, gypsy. Not washing ever.'

OK, OK, OK, just cool it, Romanian boy. She's not a fucking gypsy, I say, trust me. She couldn't whittle a fucking clothes peg if her life depended upon it. Now Radu listen to me, I tell him sternly: stop looking at me like that and *never* spit in front of me again, right? My mother, OK, is what we in England call . . . a 'hippy'.

'Hippy?'

'Yeah, a hippy. They also often whore, thief. They also never washing, Rad.'

Strangely, he smiles.

'Ahhh, hippy! Like Grateful Dead band, yes?'

Yeah, I say, sure; exactly like Grateful Dead band.

We climb over a low wooden fence and trudge across the fields through the discarded binliners, used lavatory paper, smashed radios and CD players, engine parts, empty takeaway cartons, hollowed out tubs of synthetic woad, emptied sacks of pulses and lentils, raw sewage and filthy, screeching children.

Radu is wearing a T-shirt which has the stars and stripes across the chest, another of Dom's hand-me-downs, and this filthy little urchin runs up and looks at him and squeaks angrily: 'US Hands Off Chile!' and then disappears into the bushes.

And Radu is, like, excuse me? I shake my head at him, nonplussed, and we walk on. At the first teepee we hear the sounds of furious argument and the second one has all holes in it and seems to be totally uninhabited and third one is my mother's. And across the field comes the sound of that fucking song 'My name is Ern and I will pull astern' except all you can really hear from this distance is the bass drum, but I still recognise it, and we go up to the flap of the teepee but then this man comes out and stops us.

He's wearing this shapeless jerkin made of the sort of stuff they lag pipes with. He's maybe like forty years old, very tall with a rough brown beard and hazy blue eyes and he's looking at us with the spaced-out, vacuous equivalent of suspicion.

'Hello,' he says, 'how can I help you good people?'

I sort of cringe inwardly at the sound of his voice, that disembodied drawl, and I think what would happen if I just punched him and now he's started eyeing the two of us up and down and I force myself to smile and say we're here to see my mum, this is her tent, isn't it?

And he breaks into this big beaming smile and says oh, wow, you're Karen's daughter, that's cool, sure, yes this her teepee. But she's, like, busy?

And I'm like, sorry? Say that again? Busy?

Because here's the truth. If she's busy, it's time for a celebration of sorts. She was last busy in 1976, when she cooked supper. I can still remember the surprise on everyone's face, and then, a little later, the smell, the smoke, the sirens, the flashing lights. It was a hell of an evening, believe me.

But I keep myself calm and say to the man look, just tell her we're here, OK, and he smiles and disappears inside and there's a muffled conversation and then he appears again still grinning like an imbecile and says, OK, you can go inside in ten minutes.

And this just makes me laugh and I say look, it's my mother, we're here now so either we go inside or we go away for another year, which might be no bad thing, frankly, and he shrugs his shoulders still standing in the entrance to the teepee and in the end I just manhandle him out of the way saying sorry, hippy, but we're going *in*.

So I push open the flap of the absurd teepee and gingerly walk inside, Radu right behind me, the bearded roach of a hippy (who *was* he, anyway?) standing helplessly like they always do, outside. It takes some time for my eyes to get used to the musky gloom and I stumble forward smelling this rich sweet smell like vanilla and soaking up the heavy warmth. On one side of the tent there's a big double-bed area filled with heavy, multi-coloured blankets and then a sort of wall hanging echoing the star and moon motif on the outside and then a smaller bed area with bright red blankets and a yellow pillow with a tapestry hippy woman's head on it. Most of this stuff was here last time I visited, but through the gloom and the thick, choking, dopesmog I can see pale yellow candles positioned around the room on the points of a silver star painted on to the blue tarpaulin floor. That's a new development, mum. Lovely. What's more, the candles look pretty risky to me and they stink – but hell, it's not my life, right?

Mother is sitting by the far wall of the tent on another pile of blankets, her head flung back in this slightly annoying manner I remember from when I was a kid. She's got a large joint in one hand and there's a bottle of some evil-looking home-made preparation by her right knee, almost certainly alcoholic, I'd guess. She stays in this apparent reverie for a moment and we stand there in the middle of the tent looking at her and I don't think Radu quite believes it, you know, just thinks it's some sort of elaborate joke being played on him and soon the gang are going to jump out giggling and laughing and saying hi Romanian boy.

Anyway, eventually she looks up and smiles with bovine placidity and says Emily, darling, how lovely, come over here, come over here, have a seat and then suddenly we're embracing in the middle of the tent. She smells of patchouli oil and too many vegetable casseroles but also, somewhere underneath, of my mother.

'Sorry, darling, about suggesting you wait outside,' she says, 'But I was just summoning Pan.'

And she gestures rather grandly to the pentacle on the blue tarpaulin floor.

'Oh, for fuck's sake, Mum,' I say and then look around shaking my head. 'So, did He come, or what? Is He hiding?'

'You caught me in the middle of my summoning,' she says. 'It's a complex operation, Emily. Now sit down and introduce me to your new friend.'

And with this I pull Radu over towards me even though he's looking really apprehensive and may even be about to bolt, like he does sometimes when he's perturbed by something, but I say OK, this is Radu and then mum envelopes him in this big hug and says hello Radu and sort of winks at me and I squirm a bit but it's OK because at least Radu is half-smiling now.

We squat on the blankets and Mum offers round the joint and we both take polite draws on the sweet smoke and it's like some old western when the white people meet the indians and actually, it's a total fucking joke, as always.

So I start to tell her about what I've been doing which, as you might have guessed, doesn't take very long and fill her in a little bit about those of my friends whom she knows or at least has met, like Dom and Biba and poor Anna with her legs. She gets all angry about what's happened to Anna, says we women are poisoning ourselves every day, everything we touch is a sort of poison and it makes her feel she's right to have left the world behind, not many people know but it's all down to these three mysterious Jews and then Radu tells her his story, or sort of the edited highlights, including the towels and Alsatians but for some reason forgetting the electrode stuff and this rather steals the show, as you might well imagine.

Mum does her hippy total empathy thing and cries along with him and holds his hand, leaning across the tarpaulin as he spills out his crazy life story and it's clear she hasn't the faintest idea where Romania is or anything about it and just says stuff like God, how dreadful or I'm so sorry or just darling and occasionally shoots me these incredibly sympathetic glances and I sit back soaking up the dopesmoke and the vanilla smell and just listen to Radu telling the same story he's told now a hundred times.

Then, when Radu is all finished, she stops being the hippy and starts being my mother briefly and says Emily are you really happy and I want to say yeah, no, who knows, what's happy and, more to the point, what are you going to do about it? But instead I just smile and say oh, you know, I'm fine and have you seen Dad recently and she says no but she got a letter with her last cheque in which he signed his name in full as if he were writing to a business rival or a lawyer or the tax people and Mum shrugged and said you know the man, total breadhead.

No, really. She actually used that word. I squirm again, inwardly.

When she left us, back when I was twelve, it seemed to come from nowhere. We were never, you know, deliriously happy as a family, nothing like that, although we had loads of money through Dad, which sort of helped. We just lived in this gentle, affluent, boredom, really. And then it happened. One minute the two of them, Mum and Dad I mean, were the same as usual, not really talking to each other, Dad always at his strange Arab bank just working and sleeping and not really giving a shit what his wife got up to, Mum dippy and hopeless spending her days at art classes and hanging out with weird friends.

Then suddenly she was packing a suitcase, claiming she was suffocated, that she wasn't meant to live like this, it was more of an existence than a life etc. and she was really sorry but she was leaving to live in a *caravan* with a man called *Kestrel*. And she came up to me in the hallway of our house and I was leaning on the bannister-rail playing with my hair and I noticed in the corner of the hall, where the stairs met the floor, a corner of wallpaper, this pale blue vertical abstract pattern a bit like a flower, except not, had peeled away, was coming all loose and I stared at the wallpaper and sort of didn't even look at Mum and Mum said mwwahh love you and see you very soon darling you can come and stay with me look after your Dad I'm really sorry about this and then, and I remember this really clearly, she said: 'Take care, darling, and don't make the same mistakes I've made.'

And with that she was gone.

What mistakes did she mean? The mistake in leaving

or the mistake in not having left before?

Anyway, the whole deal was eventually presented to me as a big improvement in my life, I'd get these really cool holidays spent on the road with Mum and Kestrel (who, like, sculpted) and the rest of the time, during school terms, I'd be at home with Dad and maybe Mum would visit.

But the way it worked out, you know . . . it worked out differently.

For a start, Kestrel left Mum by the end of the first week and she sort of went AWOL for two years, apparently hooked up with a bunch of travellers called Stephen's Children. Nope, no idea who Stephen is. A total twat, I should guess.

Dad, meanwhile, looked after me with increasing ennui and occasional desperation and by the end of week two I was at my grandmother's little house in Dulwich, which is where I stayed for the next six years.

Thinking back, all I remember of the day Mum left was the wallpaper thing and her saying don't make the same mistakes as me and also, on the television, this war thing was happening between us and Argentina, arguing about the Falklands or Malvinas, as Mum called it. I remember watching the TV every night after she'd left and being transfixed by the ships and guns and the general sense of excitement and the flags and I think it's the last time I ever watched a news programme.

We won, didn't we?

I think I was better off with my grandmother, though. She can't stand Mum, or Dad, never could, even though Mum's her, you know, daughter, she always said she was a useless cow, which I suppose is right. I think even Dad was relieved Mum left in the end, although he was embarrassed that it had to be with a man called Kestrel.

And he was certainly relieved to see *me* resettled. He swung by a few times to see how I was. Mum never came.

So, anyway, back in the teepee Mum's telling us both about how good life is just now, it's a big settlement here, nearly fifty people and most of them much younger than her, all doing stuff like painting and sculpture and brass rubbings and various fraudulent new age bollocks with stones they sell at Camden Market and then she tells us about Jeremy, the docile idiot we met outside the tent, and yeah, she's seeing him, he's the one permitted to share that huge mound of foetid blankets.

And she looks at me and says Emily, you're not *really* happy, are you, I can tell, I'm your mother, and I don't disagree so she comes up with this solution which is, like, to join her: both of us. It would be great, we'd be a partnership, she says, you could, like, paint, are you still good at painting, darling?

And at this I nearly go berserk because it's just the last thing I would ever do, just *no*, never, never. And she looks all hurt and says why, what's so wrong with it all and I want to say absolutely, like, everything – but I don't say that, I just shout IT'S THE SQUALOR.

And there's a bit of tension, inside the teepee. Radu shuffles his feet and starts picking at the stitching on the green blanket by his leg.

And after a while Mum says squalor? what's wrong with a bit of mud and I say bit of *mud*? Have you looked out there? And I mean terrapins in the bath has just nothing on this and I lose it a bit and really start in on her, saying partnership, partnership, what sort of fucking partnership did you give me fifteen years ago – you left me for some hippy who binned you in five and a half days and *now* you think I'd want to share this sordid, verminous and *totally* fatuous lifestyle . . . I mean, I'm like, hello? You want me to live with you? OK, fine. Then say sorry and buy a fucking house and wash your clothes. And dump that bearded, witless, gangling oaf Jeremy, too. I mean what's all *that* about?

And another thing . . . burn that absurd book on white majik and sorcery because, mother, you are *so* not a witch . . .

And Mum, who has been listening wide-eyed and mute up until now, breaks in protesting: 'Emily, sweetheart, I'm a qualified High Priestess of Avalon . . .'

And I walk away from her and throw my hands in the air and screech JESUS CHRIST ALMIGHTY and then swing back and screw up my face and shout and what's all this about, this bloody pentacle down here, just rip it up, mother, it doesn't work, the great horned god Pan, he of the pipes and the fucking legs of a fucking goat, has much better things to do than respond to the summons of some fucking clapped out addled old madwoman in a tent on Salisbury Plain . . . and bin the candles, I scream at her, they stink . . . do all that for starters and . . . and . . . I'm really losing it now . . . really losing it, this always happens, it's a yearly exorcism, I suppose, and I'm screaming all these insults and ripping her life to bits when suddenly the flap of the tent is pulled open and a boy comes in, maybe eight or nine years old by the look of him, his face covered in crazy purple fun colours in an Asian warrior design and wearing a ripped basketball shirt and filthy blue jeans and trainers and he walks across and asks Mum something and I've stopped the tirade now and look more closely at him and as I do he seems to see me for, like, the first time and his expression is one of mild surprise, just mild surprise really, no big deal, he's not, you know, fazed at all and he just smiles at me slightly, his head on one side, this expression I would recognise even if I'd never seen it before and he says to me: 'Oh. Hi, Mum.'

The tension inside the teepee, which I think I mentioned earlier had been firmly established, now mounts a little, you know?

I can't move for a moment, my legs have sort of gone from me and my stomach feels really light and frothy. There's this awkward silence and Mum is looking at me with eyebrows raised, nodding her head as if to say yeah, you feel morally well placed to carry on that little attack of yours, what do you reckon? And I look at this kid with the face paint and the filth . . . but it's the same hair cropped loosely over his eyes and the same way he has of standing when he's, like, embarrassed (which, uh, I guess he is now), slightly stooped, it's something I do too and I can't think of what to say so I take a deep breath and my voice comes out all high and cracked.

'Hello, Jack,' is all I can manage.

Mum sort of snorts and says hey, Emily, long time no see, hmm?

My legs still feel far off and useless as I stand there, stupidly smiling at the child. Yeah, four years is a long time, she's right, a very long time in the life of a little boy. Jack, though, seems less affected than any of us.

'Thanks for the present, Mum. I was going to write but . . .' His voice trails off and he shrugs and smiles. I'd

sent him a football shirt on his birthday, back in
November. November 12, in fact. He was just getting
into football in a big way. He supports, you know,
Manchester United.

'That's OK, Jack,' I say trying very hard to keep a
grip of all this and feeling my heart pounding harder
and harder and harder, 'you didn't have to write
anything. What are you doing here, though?'

He grins this big grin.

'Greatgran's gone completely doolally and they've
taken her away!' Jack pulls this face which I guess must
signify senile dementia, his jaw wide open and drool
dribbling down his chin.

'Not *quite* true, young man,' says Mum and then
adds for my benefit, 'she was feeling tired, that's all.
She'd just had enough, I think. Checked herself into a
sort of rest place for three weeks. She's back out next
Monday. She's getting on, you know? Nearly eighty-
three? Said to me when she dropped him off that she
had this vision of, you know, being saddled with Jack's
kids too, that it was this neverending thing, that she
wouldn't be allowed even to die.'

'Can't imagine her dying,' I mumble. 'She seems so
strong, you know?'

And now Mum and me are suddenly united on the
same side, two people who have made a vital, long-
lasting contribution to the art of parenting.

So, anyway, then, Jack turns to Mum and says he
wants to go up to the stones is that OK and Mum says
yeah sure but don't climb on them and he says 'course
not and he says a quick g'bye to me and turns to go and
I say hey, Jack, how about a hug for Mum and he stops
and looks at his grandmother and then back at me and
he walks over and there's suddenly this slightly sour-

smelling bag of skin and bones in my arms, this scarcely believable lump of boy, a big boy now and I hold on to him for a moment and feel his resistance stiffen so I let him go and he's just, like, out of there.

When he's left we all stand around not really knowing what to do. Radu is sort of immobilised and totally speechless which, in the circumstances, I guess, is a reaction I understand and the air in the teepee is all full of the quarrel between me and Mum and then thickened by Jack's arrival.

I think maybe it's time to go so I say thanks, Mum, we'd better be on our way and turn down her kind offer of tea made from dried bark or the skin of a weasel or something and she's like, uh, fine, come again soon, it doesn't have to be just once a year, you know, and bye, Radu – and she gives him this hug – really lovely to meet you etc. And this smell of embarrassment lingers, on both sides.

We walk outside and I ask Radu if he wants to see the stones because they're a national monument, even though actually they're quite boring, and he's like yeah, why not, so we traipse up the littered field in silence, Jack miles ahead of us running across the plain, and I'm feeling a bit, you know, mixed up? And I'm thinking to myself maybe I should get to know Jack a bit better, it's not too late and he's sort of my responsibility, really, so the least I could do is put some time aside to see him maybe once a week at first and this fantasy starts to build up in my head where he's living with me in this small house and we're both sort of happy and in the background of this fantasy there's the shadowy, unseen presence of a man but I can't fill in the picture to make it a real man.

And we're halfway up to the stones and Radu puts his arm around my shoulders and says Emily are you OK and I say yeah, sure, and then he says to me you know I have child, too, in Romania.

And I'm like, uh, surprise me.

And he says: 'He is boy as well. Twelve years. We call him Gheorghe. He is with mother in Cluj. Big, big boy, with the hair,' and he holds up a tuft of his hair and laughs. Then he says: 'I miss him, Gheorghe. Maybe you meet him one day.'

And yeah, I think, why not.

And we give up on going all the way to the stones because I'm tired with the walking, I don't really do walking and before we turn back I look up at the stones and there's this boy halfway up one of them, clambering up by a rope, the sun shining across his back and the boy tiny, clinging on to the side of this huge, huge stone, silhouetted by the sun, the boy and the stone.

He swings free on the rope and sees us and gives this little half-wave and I wave back and then he swings round and climbs and climbs all the way up.

We don't talk much on the journey back, though I gave Radu a brief version of what happened with Jack all those years ago and why he's been living with his great-grandmother.

Jack wasn't, you know, planned? It was just a university thing, you know? Just this thing that happened? I was all set for a termination, an abortion, which would have sorted it out and I don't have any like ethical objection but I just . . . I just *forgot*. I know that sounds ridiculous. But I decided that's what I'd do and when I'd do it but other stuff kept getting in the way and I kept putting it off and saying yeah I'll go for the consultancy next week but then there were, you know, exams or holidays or whatever . . . and then as things turned out I just had the baby. It was a, you know, shock? In a strange way I didn't really expect it to happen at all, even though I got bigger and heavier every month, it never really registered with me.

And then of course I couldn't keep him while I was studying so he went to gran, just like I did, except in Jack's case rather earlier in life. After two months of horrid breast-feeding, in fact.

I still swung by quite regularly in that first year but then I suppose the visits just sort of dwindled, just got more and more spaced out and eventually, you know, stopped altogether. It became this thing I didn't like to think about and I guess I avoided seeing Jack – and by extension, Gran – because it reminded me of this horrible mistake I'd made, even though he was always a sweet kid with his flop of hair and strangely adult mannerisms.

And, by the way, in case you were thinking of enquiring: staying with Jack's father was just so not on, you know? He was called *Terry* and he came from S*toke*, I mean hello?

Still, no use beating yourself up about stuff like that, is it? Can't just carry things around with you, you'd go mad. But, I don't know, maybe I'm at the right stage now to, like, take an active part in his upbringing again? Seeing him gave me this weird tugging feeling and I'm not sure if it was just, like, guilt or something like maternal instinct or even, you know, love.

But there was something, anyway . . . so I'm thinking to myself, as the train speeds back through the scattered woods and pale fields of Hampshire, maybe I should make this plan and put aside time to see him, like, once a week at first? Get to know him, give his great-gran a break maybe during the week. I mean it's not as if I'm doing much, is it?

Plus I want to know why Gran thought he'd be better off with Mum than with me: I mean what's all that about? When we get back home I'm going to ring her and find out and I'll write to Jack and tell him, you know, like, sorry, Mum's back. If you want her.

Radu meanwhile has gone all furtive and pensive, huddled up in his window seat hardly talking, probably thinking about George or whatever his son's called, I guess.

OK, so later I'm in another wine bar on Battersea Rise consoling Saul and Dipak because the Animal Liberation Front has firebombed Sheepscape on account of the, you know, sheep. The nightclub lasted two weeks before the council stepped in to rescue the animals. They took them away and examined them and found they were distressed and traumatised and in danger of suffering permanent ear damage from the My name is Ern etc. music. I say they should have examined the fucking humans.

So, first the nightclub gets closed down and then the nightclub gets firebombed and even that isn't enough for these crazy animal lib people and they track Saul and Dipak down to their old wine bar and firebomb that *too*. Saul has received, you know, death threats and his name is on this really hostile website and someone posted catshit through his letterbox and daubed his windows with blood, the origins of which remain a mystery.

By and large, everyone's agreed, the sheep were a bad idea.

Saul's sitting in a corner sipping a glass of Sancerre and listening to Dipak plan the next venture which Saul is adamant must contain no live fauna, like not even silverfish. Dipak's going to borrow some more money from his dad who is like a big military something in, you know, Pakistan or India or somewhere and bails him out every six months or so with vast cheques.

We're all getting drunk in a suitably sombre way except for Radu who is looking censorious and eastern European in a cheap two-piece suit from River Island.

It's the day after our trip to see Mum and I still haven't finished the letter to Jack, it's harder than I thought it would be to write stuff down and I can't quite get the tone right, you know?

I rang Gran though and asked her how she was and why Jack was left with Mum rather than me and she said well, Emily, I wondered should I send him to live with Karen in that foetid, stinking teepee, surrounded by raw sewage and filthy, drug-addled hippies or should I leave him with you in London and there was no contest, really. And I tell her I'm going to start seeing Jack more – well, like, at all, really – and maybe I'll end up looking after him and she's yeah, yeah, yeah, right, sure, whatever. So I suppose she doesn't believe me when I tell her I'll be back for Jack. But I will, I will. Trust me.

Radu's beginning to annoy me at the moment, since we got back from Wiltshire, being all non-communicative and surly and even more terrified of the secret police coming to get him. He's also being more and more disparaging of London which he says is a toilet, a really disgusting place, he hates it and wishes he could leave. We had this strange row this morning which I still can't make head nor tail of, to tell you the truth. There was me and Muppy drinking tea in the kitchen when Radu storms out of the bathroom, his face dripping wet, clearly highly antagonised, you know? So we sit there looking at him and he shakes his head in rage and shouts: 'This is not civilised country!'

And we both keep looking and aren't really sure what to say and then Radu says: 'This is *not* civilised country. In civilised country there are *mixer taps*.'

And, right, we think he's joking at first and then we realise he isn't and Muppy screws up his face in puzzlement and goes, mixer taps, Radu, what do you mean? And Radu goes: 'MIXER TAPS! Is simple: mixer taps. Here,' he says, miming the action of turning on a tap, 'you have two taps. You have hot tap. You have cold tap. You either too hot or too cold! In a civilised country, they have mixer taps . . .'

And we're like, uh-oh, he's furious, furious about taps. Muppy sort of swallows a laugh and Radu looks down at him and points a finger and says more calmly: 'I tell you, there are mixer taps. And I tell you another thing. In a civilised country they know what is right and they know what is wrong! This is the case in Romania.'

And Muppy furrows his brow and goes: 'What, you mean right and wrong in a bathroom fittings sense?'

And Radu nods and says: 'Yes, and in every sense.'

And he goes back into the bathroom, his point apparently made. Muppy stands up and shouts after him: 'You're meant to mix the hot and cold water in the bowl, Radu.'

But there's just silence from the bathroom.

Muppy says to me: 'Well, I was just trying to be helpful.'

★

So this bizarre outburst occurred this morning and since then he's been all sulky and resentful. Plus, as I say, he's even more worried and furtive than usual and didn't really want to go out to see Saul and Dipak in the first place. He thinks two members of the secret police have tracked him down and are just waiting for a moment to pounce. It's true that Biba saw a couple of evil-looking guys in raincoats hanging round the corner of our street but then, this is, like, Balham, you know? Whatever, Radu thinks his card is marked and won't go out unless Muppy or someone has scouted up and down the high street looking for dubious Mediterranean-looking men.

And even then he doesn't like going out very much; as I say, he hates London. Says it's decadent.

I don't know, he was quite sweet to me in Wiltshire but I can tell things have cooled between us. It's more than a week since we had sex and he used to wake me every morning with this big grateful Romanian smile and hallo Emily but now he just farts, turns over and snores.

So right now he's hunched up in one corner of this wine bar and Saul's hunched in the other and we're all somewhere in between. Toby sidles up to me at one point and tells me he saw Nic last week and the boy's looking well and has a girlfriend called Astra or something who owns like racehorses and he's very happy. I'm about to ask if he mentioned me at all when we're all disturbed by this ruckus in the third corner of the bar and shouting and stuff and we think oh no it's animal lib people again but it isn't it's only Troy spazzing out on the floor and people near him getting upset about their drinks being knocked over and stuff. Simba is also getting weary of her man. The spazzing was sort of interesting at first but is now just a, you know, bore. Maybe it's all change for the gang once again, you know?

And Biba comes up and tells me Dom has a new girlfriend called Loris, which according to Biba's dictionary is an indolent, bear-like creature with poisonous skin. Sounds about right for Dom, I reckon, and Biba laughs and I say what's she really like and Biba says: 'Well, for a start, she's black.'

And I say: 'What, Indian or Pakistani or is she, you know, fully blown?'

And Biba says definitely fully blown and raises her eyebrows and says the great fascist Dom, huh. Who'd have thought it?

And then Biba says that Saul said that there was a, like, election or something last week and the whole government's just changed and everything's going to be different from now on and I ask Biba in what way different and she said she wasn't sure, really, and I wonder why I didn't hear about the election and wander across and ask Saul what happened and he says simply: 'We lost.'

And then I'm drinking vodka and slimline and thinking to myself maybe I should split, go home, finish that letter to Jack, but I can't afford the cab fare on my own so instead I wander up to the bar and order another drink and sit down with my glass and think about stuff.

So I sit there, looking around at this familiar scene in front of me and wonder if this strange hole inside is simply a lack of Nic. And I wonder what Astra's like and hope Nic is really happy.

OK. So sometimes I lie.

4.

So now it's time to go out to see Anna, all of us hoping the spectacle won't be too gross but not very convinced of this because last we heard was Toby saying she's begun to stridulate.

I did a line of coke before getting on the plane and I think my sinuses are going to burst open. We're climbing, climbing high above a drenched grey London and I feel nostalgic for the place even now and hold tight on to Toby's hand and my palms are damp with fear. I don't like flying. Toby bought me the ticket or at least loaned me the money which means his name gets added to a growing angry band of creditors which now include pretty much all of my friends except for Radu, of course. The terrifying prospect of getting a job is looming ever closer and there's a problem here because there's nothing I can do, I can't even stand up properly, sometimes. I thought I was going to get money from Simba for helping her with the guacamole but when I asked she got all sniffy and said she thought I *wanted* to spend the entire day cutting up avocados and squeezing lemons. I mean, hello?

So that was thirty quid I thought was mine just taken away, sort of.

Plus this was the weekend I was going to swing by and see Jack but we had to fly today because otherwise the plane tickets would have been, you know, twice the price and we're all seriously broke. Still, I have my letter to Jack with me and I'm going to finish it on the flight. It's two weeks since I saw him and there's so much to say, too much maybe.

We'll be cruising at thirty-five thousand feet says the pilot.

Yeah, sure, I think. So what's new?

Anyway there's me and Biba and Toby and Sophie and that's it. Radu wouldn't come because he didn't have the plane money plus he hates America even more than London plus he thought they might not let him in or indeed let him *back* in when he tried to return.

Dominic wouldn't come because Sophie's here plus he's got this new girlfriend, Loris, and Troy didn't know Anna well enough plus we thought there'd be problems with him on the plane on account of the involuntary movements stuff. Jochum is house-sitting for Biba and Saul and Dipak are busy on their next venture which they won't tell anybody about.

We change at New York and fly down to this godforsaken place called Baton Rouge where Anna is in this scary research establishment run by the military. And the plane is jumping around high above the Atlantic and I look out of the window and there's just this cold grey blue steel world and nothing out there for hundreds and hundreds of miles and the outer space feeling creeps up on me again and I'm sitting there still holding Toby's hand and I hope, I just hope, they don't make me look at her legs.

Except now it's not just her legs.

We're all holed up in this motel ten miles or so away from the research institute on the edge of a huge swamp which stretches back as far as you can see. It's midnight and we're all pretty upset and dying for a smoke but of course nobody's got anything and Biba is grinding up all these Tylenol and mixing it with her bourbon and holding forth in this totally hysterical way about how this is the last time any of us will ever see

Anna alive and she doesn't trust the research institute and maybe we should, you know, spring her from there and carry her home to London, I mean how much worse off would she be? And for once I half agree with her, I'm sitting there on the edge of this bright orange bed watching huge insects get zapped by this electric thing by the window on the wall of our room and this has me, like, mesmerised and Toby is silent crashed out at my feet, he took it really badly, and Sophie's lying full out on the bed and the nylon sparks every time she turns over or just moves a little. We're all a bit crazed and frightened and there are these spooky animal sounds from the huge swamp and also from the scummy rooms all around us and we don't know what to do, really.

The research institute was like twenty miles from this town, Baton Rouge, and full of top secret signs and do not enter and danger and go away and Biohazard! Stuff like that, real fuck off and die signs, like they have at scary nuke centres or anywhere you're not meant to be.

It was guarded by soldiers with machine guns and the staff were strange, not like doctors and nurses at all, really, from my experience. I mean, I knew it was run by the military but I thought it would be, like, an army hospital?

Anyway, we all roll up at the front door and there's problems immediately because of ID verification and we're kept there for ages and ages and then the signal comes through that we can proceed but only after they've confiscated Sophie's camera and rummaged through our hand luggage and everything.

Then we're walked for what seems like miles by this uniformed guard carrying a fucking sub-machinegun, past half-buried concrete bunkers and strange metal constructions which look like that chemical plant near the start of the Blackwall Tunnel. The lights are on in some of these places and thin grey smoke leaking from the chimneys and we all wonder what the fuck they're up to in there except we don't really want to know, if we're honest.

Eventually we get to what must be the main bit of the institute, this long, low-slung white-painted building with tiny windows all down one side and then we're met by this slick, over-familiar, bald-headed American man called Frank whom everybody wants to hit, like, immediately. He tells us that Anna's in this room by herself and we've got to put masks on to go in and we're not allowed to see her unaccompanied. And Frank walks with us down these deserted antiseptic corridors our nostrils filled with the stink of carbolic and he's telling us all the time, look, this is going to be real depressing for you I think, the disease has gotten worse, really sorry, etc., there's not much we can do and I'm like uh-oh, don't know if I can cope with this and then the gauze masks are taped to our faces because we're outside this room and the sign on the door says it's Anna's room. And, one by one, with trepidation, all of us shaking, we go in.

Inside it's dark, really dark, just this dull red light from the ceiling, sort of really hard to see anything at all but even so, when we gather around her bed we're just like, hello, what the fuck is going on here? Her entire body seems encased in this horrible, corrugated black-brown armour plating, right up to her breasts, which are still sort of normal except for the nipples, which are jet black. In addition there's these sort of small, brown spines sticking out all over her stomach and her legs with hairs growing from the end. Her face is pretty much OK except her eyes look like she's been tripping on something incredible, really deep violet and like dilated and when we look closer we can see the skin on her arms is beginning to go crinkly brown, too. She's hooked up to these two machines, one draining a thick, off-white liquid like McDonald's vanilla milkshake from her ribcage and the other monitoring something and going beep beep beep, maybe it's her heartbeat or something.

And how gross is this? At first I think her head is wired up to something too but I look closer and closer and don't quite believe it because it's not wired up to anything it's actually *antennae*.

There's a smell of disinfectant and decaying vegetable matter and I think I'm going to gag. As we all stand there totally traumatised Anna looks up with this astonishingly serene expression and then smiles at Toby who, like, takes her hand.

'Long way to come,' she says at last, 'thank you.'

We sort of murmur a bit still transfixed at what's happened to her body and I can hear Biba already snuffling next to me so I dig her in the ribs and take hold of Anna's other hand and then notice how hot it is, the room and her hand.

Anna smiles again and says: 'So, guys. Who's fucking who these days?'

And as she speaks her antennae wave about in the air.

But at least this breaks the ice, the who is fucking who bit, because that's sort of the old Anna, the Anna we all know and love etc. and Biba starts off on this long anecdote about me and Radu which I grin sheepishly through and then tells Anna about Troy and Simba and the spazzing business and then she sort of just dries up and stops and there's, like, silence in the room again except for the beep beep beep of one machine and a slight gurgling sound from the other.

My eyes are straining to see in the gloom and Anna notices me squinting and says she can't take bright light any more, her eyes are too weak and she says she's really sorry and everything. And we've only been there for about ten minutes when Frank comes forward and says time to go and Anna doesn't complain so we just deposit loads of books, magazines and chocolates with her and ask if there's anything we can get for her and she's, like, no, don't worry, everything's cool, take care, see you soon. And we say goodbye and kiss her and say we'll be back very soon and we make for the door, utterly shattered, and as we're about to leave there's this totally whacko noise coming from the bed and we turn and look around and it's Anna, she's stridulating.

Outside in the corridor Biba immediately throws up all over Frank who is quite sweet about it really and there's Toby standing with his head pressed against the wall, totally freaked out and just hyperventilating and everything and Frank presses a buzzer and some black women wearing overalls turn up and one of them starts clearing up the puke and the others help Biba and Toby along to a special room full of soft furnishings and soothing, pastel-coloured paintings and me, I feel really numb and Sophie's asking if it's okay to smoke and no, it isn't.

So we're all in this room and Biba's crying and Toby's out of it entirely and this other doctor appears in the doorway, dressed in a smart suit and a tie rather than a white coat or overalls like everybody else in this place. He's got short, wiry black hair and steel-rimmed glasses and he gives us all a rueful smile and says hi, I'm Lieutenant Angstbeisser and I'd like to say a few words to all you folks and then he crouches in the room and starts speaking: 'Look, I know this is terribly traumatic for you. I know that seeing a friend, a close friend, become entombed in her own skin must be the most dreadful thing to experience. But the situation might not be quite as bad as it may seem to you now. You have to leave here knowing that in the US Army First Medical Research Institute, Louisiana, your friend is getting the best possible treatment money can buy. No expense has been spared. There are, for example, three consultants detailed to her case alone. She has five-star, gourmet food, if she wants it and superb in-room entertainment: plasma screen television, DVD, Internet access. She is getting exactly the sort of care you might imagine from the most powerful military machine on God's earth. She is in *great* hands, believe me.'

Toby looks at him open-mouthed and shakes his head. 'She's *dying*.'

Lieutenant Angstbeisser considers this concept for a while and then extends his hand to Toby. 'Hi,' he says, 'you are?'

'Toby du Noy,' mumbles Toby.

'Well, now, Toby, we just don't know that. We just don't know. I'm not going to kid you that her condition isn't serious – it's very serious. She's a pretty sick girl and I guess it must look bad from where you're standing. But maybe we'll beat this thing yet –'

'Are you *kidding*?' Toby shouts at him. 'Since she's been here the rate of her illness has speeded up –'

'Ahh,' says Angstbeisser, 'but we don't know that

she's dying. It may be true that she is on the way to becoming a very different person from the one you all remember. That may well be true. Not necessarily a worse person, either, for that matter. And certainly, physically speaking, a much stronger person, in certain environmental conditions. You've got to have faith, Toby . . .'

'Faith?' says Biba suddenly. 'All she wanted to do was lose some hair from her legs.'

'I know, I know,' says Angstbeisser, shaking his head sadly. 'But we still have to have faith. Faith in her ability to fight this thing – or, perhaps, in the end, adapt to it – and faith in our technology, which I have to say is the very best in the world. Can I ask your name please?'

'Fuck my name,' snaps Biba and stands, looking around at the rest of us. Toby gets to his feet too and says to Angstbeisser: 'Look, there's another thing which has been worrying us. We know all about the cost of medical treatment in America and we know, from what you're saying, that this can't be cheap . . .'

'Whhhhhhhooooooh . . . an understatement, if I may say so, Toby.'

'. . . yeah, well, her parents aren't rich, you know? They're just like, normal? I want to know that she's not going to be turfed out of here as soon as the money runs dry, maybe when she's halfway through whatever treatment you're giving her.'

Angstbeisser looks mildly surprised, then nods his head. 'Think that's one for you, Frank . . .'

Frank steps forward looking dead serious. 'No question of that, sir. Just no question. Here at the US Army First Medical Research Institute we accept no paying patients at all. The US Government foots the bill. Indeed, in your friend's case, we have agreed to pay her father and mother a fairly substantial monthly sum, in order to compensate for the fact that she is being cared for so many miles from home.'

It takes, sort of, a moment or so for this to sink in and then we're like: '*what*?'

'You're paying *them*?'

'Are you, like, joking . . .?'

And Frank breaks in, all synthetic outrage and anger. 'Hey! Hold on! Let's not all get the wrong idea about this! There is no question, no question, but that Anna is getting the best treatment she could get anywhere in the world. The best. Nobody, but nobody, has done such advanced research into MK. And the fact is this: maybe we can help Anna *and*, at the same time, discover a few remarkable facts which might genuinely enable mankind to progress. Especially in a military sense.'

We're all just stricken. Toby is shaking, virtually frothing at the mouth. 'I . . . WANT . . . HER . . . OUT!'

Frank spreads his arms wide open and looks around at us all. 'Well, sure, if that's what you want. This is the United States of America; we're a democracy. Everything we do is accountable. Now, Anna's parents are down on the admission form as her guardians. All they gotta do is sign a release form and whammo, the girl's out of here, discharged. But understand – she's getting quality treatment here.'

'And maybe,' Angstbeisser puts in, 'just maybe her parents are looking at the broader picture, you know? Maybe they understand that Anna is even more valuable than they had thought she would be. Valuable to the world.'

★

So now we're lounging in this Louisiana motel, dopeless and feeling impotent. Toby tried to call up Anna's parents on his mobile but it didn't work out here. So he rang from the motel lobby, slamming dimes in the phone and Anna's parents were just really evasive and non-committal and they said they didn't want to do anything about it just yet, just see how the treatment progresses and when they'd last seen Anna she seemed to be comfortable and happy, etc.

And we lie there whacked out and Biba says again: 'She only wanted to lose some hair from her legs, you know?' and Sophie's like shaking her head really sadly and saying: 'She should have waxed.'

And I just want to go home now, though Sophie's still talking about crashing at Astra's loft for a few days and Biba's all for launching an armed assault on the US Army First Medical Research Institute and taking poor Anna away, somewhere, anywhere.

I drag myself off the bed and take a walk outside. I cross the parking lot in this thick, hot air and my shirt is soon damp but that feels OK and I stand at the edge of the motel compound where the swamps begin and listen to the big insect noises, like static on a cheap radio, and every now and then a strange bird shrieks out and I stay like that for ages, watching the swamp and thinking about poor Anna.

5.

Back home things are getting worse, closing in, all these separate things like acting together and I just don't know what to do. Still haven't finished my letter to Jack and half of me is wondering if it's, you know, such a good idea to write? Not sure what use I am to him, in all honesty. I sit down at the table in the kitchen with his letter in front of me and I don't know what to write. All I've got so far is Dear Jack it was good to see you yesterday. Except now, it's like a month ago.

And there's more trouble with Radu, too. I'm just not sure it's working out, you know? Sometimes I think I might even love him but then I think no, how wrong can you be etc. And I think actually he's really irritating sometimes, especially when he's sulking and resentful, but part of me thinks I should just give it more time.

And then this happens.

He's become pretty much totally reclusive, locked away in my room and refuses to come out most of the time or even open the door for anyone except me. He's been ranting about black people and decadence again and about God and also Muppy leaving wet towels in the lounge and Muppy's getting pretty sick of him, to tell you the truth.

There's me and Biba and Jochum and Muppy and Dominic in Biba's house and Muppy's saying he should be allowed to leave wet towels wherever he likes as *he's* here legally at least and I say you've got to understand, Muppy, wet towels have a very real significance in Radu's life i.e. he was tortured with one.

And Dominic gives one of his smug upper-class titters and says oh, really, do you think so, Emily?

And I say yes, he told me all about it, what do you mean and Dominic looks at Biba and Biba looks back at Dominic and then Dominic speaks.

'Well, OK, Emily,' he says. 'You know those two

guys who Radu said were the secret police? I spoke to them the day before yesterday. I was getting sick of Radu going psycho every time he saw them and whilst you were away they've been hanging round quite a lot more. So I thought I'd tell them to fuck off, you know? Maybe threaten them with the police or something . . .'

'Yes,' I say, 'and . . .?'

'Well, I go up to these two guys and say, you know, who are you and why are you hanging around here and they say straight away, do you know this man? And they produce a page from a Romanian newspaper which has a picture of your Radu right in the middle of it and I say, like, yeah, what if I do?'

And I'm furious, I say you said *what*? They're the fucking secret police how could you just give him away like that and Biba is saying shush, shush, be quiet Emily, just listen, and Dom goes on: 'Anyway, these two men say well, he's like wanted for a number of crimes back in Romania, stuff dating back more than ten years when he was like some henchman of the ruler, this man called Ceausescu. And this man Ceausescu was just a total cunt and the people of Romania all got together and like killed him and tried to kill all his friends and allies too, of which Radu, they said, was one of the more prominent.'

And I don't say anything to this. I just feel my stomach start to slip away inside me.

'Sssso,' Dom goes on, 'I look at this newspaper cutting and I can't really understand it because it's in Romanian and they tell me that Radu's wanted for stuff like rape and murder and torturing people and crimes against humanity. And genocide. And fraud. But I'm pretty disbelieving and I tell them to get the fuck out of here anyway before I call the cops and if the truth be told they're from the Romanian secret police illegally hunting a member of the underground.

'And they sort of really laugh at this, you know? And I ask them what's so fucking funny and they say *we're* not the fucking secret police, we're from a human rights organisation in Bucharest and they show me these little ID cards and they say Radu is the one who was in the secret police. That was his job. He was a secret policeman, and they say he was like in the Romanian equivalent of the KGB. And then they start filling me in on the rather startling details of his crimes.'

Dominic's sitting there looking really smug and Biba's looking very knowing, which is a fucking liberty considering she's the one who found Radu in the first place and I try to speak but my mouth's gone all dry and cracked and broken. But I pull myself together and say in this thin hopeless voice: 'No reason to believe them, is there? I mean, they wouldn't tell you if they were the secret police, would they? It doesn't add up, does it? Why would Radu come here of all places?'

And Dominic says: 'Why wouldn't he come here? These men said his crimes were so grotesque that every country in Europe knows all about him – that's why he had to leave Dubrovnik and Paris and all those other places he was staying. Sooner or later he gets found out and has to make a run for it.

'Oh, I don't know what to believe, Em. But Radu's story is a bit odd, when you think about it. He'd have a brilliant case for asylum in any western country if he was who he says he was – but he just hides, hides. And these men said that Romania's a democracy now, just like here, so he wouldn't have anything to fear if he hadn't committed all these terrible crimes.'

I think about all this, my head spinning. 'What did you tell them, in the end?'

'Nothing conclusive, really. It's up to you, isn't it? They gave me a phone number to ring.'

Dominic passes me a scrap of paper with a mobile telephone number on it. I stare at the figures and say: 'He's, like, charged with rape?'

'Yes, of old people mostly. And murder. And genocide, or something.'

'But we don't know for sure if that's all true, do we?'

'No, Em. I guess we don't know for sure.'

I mean, what would you do?

Mostly with boys you have to put up with worries that they're like screwing someone else and it's a doubt you either live with or you bin them, depending upon what you feel for them versus the, you know, nature of the allegations. And the weight of the evidence.

Except here we have a case where my current boyfriend stands accused of stuff like crimes against humanity plus rape plus murder plus fraud and all I can think about immediately is how he cried that night when he told me about what had happened to him. Projection, is what Dominic says. He's feeling guilty about being a totally fucking psychotic madman and feels the need to tell somebody about it except he can't really tell them so he says it happened to him instead. Plausible?

Maybe, sure, yeah.

And then I think how sweet he can be sometimes, especially when we're screwing and his lost-in-London look and the cute fractured English and I reckon you must be able to tell these things; something, surely, must mark you out? Aren't you one thing or another?

A whacko or someone normal? And if you're a whacko surely you don't wake up in the middle of the night crying and then with this huge tenderness and humility ask your girlfriend to hold you because you're scared and then fall asleep in her arms . . . do you? Is that what psychos do?

I don't know. I thought I was getting near the end with Radu and should maybe just finish it completely and then this new information comes along and part of me thinks um, I guess that should be the clincher. And another part isn't very sure.

I'm, like, so tired of forever ending relationships on some pretext or another, you know? I just get exhausted at the prospect of it. Sssssoo tired. Those horrible conversations and then the pleading and then having to sort out minicabs to take all the stuff away and then phone calls and not really ever knowing if it was the right decision in the first place.

And then having to be with someone new and probably, if we're honest, worse.

And with Radu I think, well, maybe I should bin him anyway because it was like not working out and I won't even have to mention the mass murder stuff and maybe I should just do that and not get too closely involved. There's too much going on, too much to think about. And I'm sort of ultra worried about money right now, too, and have taken a part-time job with Simba making dips and that's taking up quite a lot of my time.

And then there's the thing with Jack. I really have to finish that letter. It's just a matter of getting my head clear for a bit, time to think about what to write, what to tell him.

So when I get home Radu the genocidalist is slumped in front of the television watching *Robot*

Wars and drinking from a carton of orange juice, Jessica wrapped around his feet snoozing comfortably. I let them both lie there. What's the point of confronting him about it all? He'll still argue that those men at the bottom of the street are from the secret police and just telling everybody lies and really want to do the Alsatians, wet towels and electrodes thing to him again.

I mean, he's not going to say fuck me, Emily, you've got me bang to rights on this one, is he?

So instead of saying hello are you a mass murderer? I just say hi Radu d'you have a good day and later sleep with him and frankly it's a bit better than usual, the sex.

And then, next morning, I think, hang on . . . maybe I don't have to confront him about anything? Maybe this time that inevitable progression of horrid events, the sort of thing that happens every time you break up with someone, can be averted, pretty much painlessly. And this thought lodges itself deep inside my brain and I know it's not a good thing to think but it's, you know, an obvious and easy answer and once the Radu stuff gets sorted out maybe I can concentrate on seeing Jack. Or at least finishing that letter.

6.

All Anna wanted was to lose some hair from her legs. There was never any intention, on her part, to become transformed into a giant locust. They say she's happy, out there, eating grain and rubbing her legs together. But it's not the sort of life I'd have chosen. Not that we always have a choice . . .

This morning I crept out of my room early, kicking

Jessica, who was swallowing a mouse, away from the front door and went for a short walk along Balham High Street, just to clear my mind. Then I went home and told Radu I was heading off to Biba's and arranged to meet him later at Rebatos in Stockwell.

Then I rang the number Dominic gave me.

I sat in a little coffee shop opposite Rebatos and watched silently, sipping my coffee, as the two men bundled Radu into a grey Vauxhall Astra and sped off, towards Kennington. I think he saw me as the men pounced, this expression of vague confusion flickered across his face, confusion and maybe, you know, a little bit of consternation and then the two men jumped out from nowhere and were on him, putting a coat over his head and bundling him into the back of their car.

And just for a moment I thought to myself go on, Radu, fight them, fight them off, run away, but he scarcely put up a struggle at all, just sort of slumped quietly back in the car and was gone.

What did I feel? Nothing much, to be honest. Just tiredness; tiredness and the thought that I turned him in not because he's a mass murderer, rapist, fraudster etc. but because he had become really, you know, irritating in the last few weeks and that I didn't really like him very much as a person, once the interesting language and cultural differences had been, you know, eradicated.

I guess that's awful.

And even then, as I sat in the coffee shop, this thought went through my head about how useful it would be if you could always get rid of boyfriends so easily and efficiently and painlessly, someone else doing the hard work.

★

I ask the girl behind the counter for another cappuccino except with a double shot of coffee; they skimp, these days, on the coffee, all you get is this frothy hot milk with the faintest flavour of coffee, I think I preferred it before there were all these coffee shops everywhere and when coffee was like this dark brown gunge but at least you could taste the stuff.

Ring, Ring, Goes the Bell

Ms McCall gazed down at Pfister through his office window. She looked sort of surprised at what she was seeing.

And Pfister was at last sufficiently spooked to rise from behind his desk and draw shut the vinyl blinds. All morning she'd been staring at him, the eyes bearing down, maybe accusatorily, the expression unchanging, like a sort of ironic, post-modern basilisk, as third-formers hooted and screamed and howled with laughter forty feet below.

Even now, as he pulled on the nylon cord, several of them looked round and jeered at him, pointing at McCall and sniggering. One boy formed his hand into a loose fist and began to move it rapidly up and down, a familiar gesture for Pfister. Pfister was not, it seemed a name sufficiently obscene or offensive by itself and so the headmaster's pseudonym amongst his 1,700 children was the rather simpler and more direct 'wanker'.

He rapped on the window and the children slowly dispersed, still cackling, and Pfister was left just staring at McCall staring back at him. Stop staring like that, woman, he thought to himself. He drew the blind and sighed and returned to his big pine desk, strewn with a multitude of timesheets and reports and assessments, all of which should have been dealt with by now.

But he couldn't work. Ms McCall, he knew, was still

staring at him, even though the blinds were shut.

He shifted in his seat. He counted the loose change in the little grey plastic tray in the top drawer of his desk. With a disassembled paper clip he picked his teeth free of the remains of his hasty and inadequate lunch.

And then he checked the time again: 14.43. With another slow sigh of resignation he punched the speakerphone button. 'Where's Daryl Haste, Jenny?'

There was some static-induced crackling as his PA fiddled with the extension cord in the reception room next door.

'He was doing double physics, but said he'd swing by as soon as he could. Um . . . let me see . . . that was at ten. Do you want me to chase him up?'

'Yes. I think five hours is long enough leeway. And I am dubious about the 'physics' excuse, if you want the truth. And, further, it is time somebody did something about Ms McCall. She's getting my bloody goat, up there. Please sort it out.'

'Yes, boss.'

But it was another forty-five minutes before the speakerphone at last announced the arrival of Daryl Haste. Almost simultaneously, the door swung open, unheralded by an enquiring knock, and a shaven-headed fourth former slunk into the office and stood a few yards from Pfister's desk, an expression of outrageous tedium on his pasty face, and traces of blood on his shirt. The headmaster sighed a little and extracted a pale blue 'incident sheet' from his drawer and then unsheathed his fountain pen, a gift from the Board of Governors to mark his fifth benighted year as Principal of the Daniel Ortega Community School.

'Daryl, thank you for coming. Please take a seat.'

Pfister's voice was neutral, conveying neither

familiarity nor opprobrium. It was how, in situations like these, one was trained to speak.

The teenager lowered himself sulkily into a chair and began to worry at a gargantuan spot on his forehead. The spot was a swollen, angry red but not yet ripe enough to be successfully excavated without taking most of the rest of his head with it. The thing must be painful and distracting for the boy.

Pfister stared at him in silence for some moments.

Eventually Daryl Haste concluded his facial examination and deigned to look back at Pfister. 'What *now*?' he said, with a degree of impatience and resignation.

Pfister wondered how best to broach the subject. A spurt of the most unprofessional loathing seared through his bloodstream. One really shouldn't get involved, on a personal level, he silently reprimanded himself.

But this time, he thought – fuck it: I really *want* the little bastard. Except how? These things were so difficult to judge. And a lot rested on the tone of this initial encounter. Let's keep it calm and direct, thought Pfister, for a start.

'Daryl. Why did you kill Ms McCall and mount her head on a forty foot pole?'

Daryl clicked his teeth irritably. 'Dunno, really, do I? I think I felt excluded, and brutalised, at the time, probably. But I am very sorry. I've already said so, haven't I? And I do feel . . . remorse.'

Daryl then gave the headmaster a sort of ghastly half smile. 'And I am much better now,' he added, 'and feel able to pursue my studies without posing a further threat to any pupil or member of staff.'

What annoyed Pfister was how pat Daryl was, how

easily these phrases – learned by rote from the plethora of parole officers and social workers and psychologists – glided so smoothly from his tongue. Particularly as, for the rest of the time, Daryl Haste was almost wholly inarticulate. Pfister made a cursory jotting on the blue form. 'I need to ask you this, Daryl, for the record,' he said, tapping his incident sheet. 'Did you sexually assault Ms McCall?'

'Dunno. Can't remember. I was depressed at the time.'

'Look. I am asking you because I need the full details. But the police will soon begin their various tests and investigations and then it will be –'

'Yes, yes, yes, all right! I fucked her up the arse.'

'When she was already dead, or whilst she was still alive?'

'Oh, for fuck's sake, I can't remember.'

He paused in rumination. 'I think it was when she was dying.'

Pfister nodded and scribbled some more. 'So after you first stabbed her, but before you removed her head?'

'Um. Yes. Well, bit of both, really.'

'OK. Now, how did you sever the head from the body?'

Daryl reached inside his blazer pocket and produced a long kitchen knife. He threw it across the desk. 'With this.'

Pfister looked at the implement – upon which the blood had not yet completely congealed – and left it where it was, describing it briefly on his form. 'Large wooden-handled serrated knife, possibly intended for cutting bread,' he wrote.

'And was this the weapon used to actually kill Ms McCall?'

'Yes, *obviously*. But I punched her in the throat a couple of times, too, when she started to scream.'

'And what, may I ask, was the provocation for this attack of yours?'

'She was on my fucking back all the time, do this, do that, then she had a go at me for stabbing Dalgetti and I just lost it. I felt excluded and bru −'

'Dalgetti? You stabbed him? How is he?' Nobody had told the headmaster about this comparatively minor incident.

'Oh, he's fine, I didn't even stab him, really, just slashed him a bit, round the neck. He's got a bandage.'

'Daryl, listen to me. This time you're in big trouble. This is going to mean, at the very least, fairly detailed psychiatric reports and assessments and in the end, I would have thought, a change of school.'

The boy leaned forward in his seat and clenched his fists on his knees. 'That's the sort of shit that made me do it in the first place,' he whined. 'I always end up feeling excluded and brutalised cos people keep getting in my face all the time. And anyway, as I've told you, I really feel remorse for Ms McCall. Honest.'

'Yes, I'm sure you do. But it's not the first time, is it?'

'What do you fucking mean by that?'

'Well, there was the regrettable deracination of Mr Sparks, for example . . .'

'Fuck off! That wasn't me, that was Flaubert from 4R, you total fucking moron!'

'Oh. Was it?' Pfister searched back through his memory which, these days, he admitted, had become a little permeable. 'I'm sorry, very sorry. I didn't mean to accuse you erroneously. Please accept my apologies. But, Daryl, help me out here − there was something else awful with you, I'm certain. I've got it here on file somewhere . . .' Pfister began to rummage in his file draw.

Daryl Haste clicked his teeth in annoyance again. 'I stabbed Mr Gibson in the face last year during Life Sciences class but he fucking asked for it, everybody said so, even the social worker, plus afterwards they made me do loads of those stupid psycho tests even though I made it clear I was sorry and remorseful etcetera, and would have said sorry to Mr Gibson if he hadn't left the fucking school, so I don't know why you're bringing this up now . . .'

Ah, yes, that was it. Pfister remembered. Upon recommendation from the local education committee and its ambitious young chairman, Dave Shibboleth, Daryl had not been excluded from school for this regrettable incident. The successful argument against expulsion was simple but devastating: Haste's violent tendencies were proven to have extended only to his science teacher, Mr Gibson and it was accepted that a degree of personal animus, if not actual physical violence, was in turn reciprocated. Since Mr Gibson had voluntarily left Ortega there was nobody in the school to whom Daryl posed a threat. Pfister realised that the same argument might well be made now. Serena McCall was dead – i.e., no longer in a position to suffer Haste's violent or, indeed, amorous attentions.

The important thing was not to lose your cool, Pfister knew. But one could only take so much of this terrible glibness, this whining, and above all, the palpable unfairness of the whole thing. He had quite liked Serena McCall – a promising teacher who was more than averagely popular with the student body – or at least for those not congenitally disposed to the acts of rape and murder. She should surely not have departed this life with a juvenile penis wedged up her arse and her head stuck on a pole. Pfister was resolved about this: McCall's death must be marked by something more significant than another round of psychiatric tests and the likely transfer of Haste to a school where the perimeter fence was maybe at most a few inches higher. Because that was the likely scenario, as both of them well knew. Haste's close acquaintance and familiarity with the pseudo-legal process, plus his undeniably deprived background – social, economic and familial – would ensure that society exacted the minimum amount of retribution, if any at all.

But he wanted him, this time, he really, really, wanted him. Everything about the little shit called for a more rigorous form of censure than that which would normally occur. Those dumb vacant eyes, the aggressive swagger, the bored body language, the thin whine of complaint when he spoke, the reflexive insolence, the clear conviction that he was the victim in all of this and, concomitantly, his terrible lack of empathy.

Not to mention, of course, his penchant for killing, maiming or raping members of staff during bursts of psychotic aggression. I want retribution, Pfister thought. I want retribution and I want it in spades. And that very phrase must have been delivered unto his head from a similarly vengeful deity because, suddenly, repeating it to himself, he conceived the germ of an idea.

Pfister mulled the notion over for a moment or so. This will be tricky, he thought, but it might just work. Play it long, he thought. Play it long and get him on your side. Then when he's off guard, throw him a beamer. And maybe, just maybe . . .

He sat back in his chair and put his fountain pen to one side. 'We haven't served you very well here, have we, Daryl?'

The kid looked back suspiciously. 'What do you mean?'

'Well, you'll be leaving with virtually no qualifications. You've been in trouble continually since you arrived here. It can't have been a happy time for you.'

'Yeah, well, used to it by now,' he murmured, the self-pity oozing like pus. 'Had a really fucking bad time at home, too, cos my dad fucked off.'

'I know, I know, Daryl. How could we have helped you more? What could we have done?'

'Just, whatever. Stop stuff like this, you know? Get off my fucking back a bit?'

'Yeah, I know. Just rules, isn't it?'

'Yeah, stupid rules. People just don't know what I've been through.'

'I'm sorry, Daryl. It's clear to me we should have listened to you a little more, in the early days. It's funny, isn't it, but I only ever see you when you're in trouble? What a dreadful indictment of our school. That's no way for us to form a good relationship, is it?'

Daryl nodded his head slowly. 'If I could have talked things through a bit more maybe, I don't know, all this might not have happened, this stuff where I just, you know, lose it . . .'

'. . . I know, I know. I see that now. Is there anything at all you've enjoyed here at school?'

Haste sat back in his chair and thought for a moment. 'Don't think so, no.'

'Sport?'

'Uh-oh. I mean, football's OK, s'pose. Quite like woodwork except Mr Marshall's a cunt, isn't he?'

'Yes, Daryl. He's a total and utter cunt.'

The boy exploded with laughter.

'Hey! You said a teacher was a cunt! Ha ha ha ha ha. You can't say that!'

'Cunt! cunt! cunt! cunt! cunt! cunt! cunt! Mr Marshall is a grade A cunt!' shouted Pfister.

Daryl yelped and whinnied with delight.

'You see, Daryl, there are probably quite a few things we could agree upon. For example, Mr Dougan: tosser, or what?'

'Fucking *right* tosser, total fucking cunt.'

'And Mr Vachery, what about him?'

'Cunt!'

'Yes, and he probably fiddles with the kiddies.'

Daryl convulsed again, his face wreathed in happiness.

The speaker phone buzzed. It was Jenny. 'Everything OK in there, sir?'

'Yes, all absolutely fine, thank you, Jenny.'

Daryl ignored the intrusion. He leaned forward in his chair and said, surreptitiously: 'You know who I hate most, sir?'

'Who, Daryl?'

'Gillette. He looks like a fucking pig, a great fat sweaty pig. And he's a cunt. And an arsehole.'

'Do you know, Daryl, I'm tempted to agree with you.'

The boy grinned at him.

'Look Daryl,' said Pfister, putting the pale blue form away in a drawer, 'let's say no more about this latest business, shall we?'

'Yes! OK, sir!'

'The police will want a few words, I suspect. But next time we meet let it be to discuss which other useless members of my teaching staff are complete and utter cunts, OK?'

'Yes, sure, no problem with that, sir. I've got a fucking huge list of them!'

'I bet you have. Well, for now, why don't you go back to your class and we'll meet again under more friendly circumstances.'

Daryl rose from his chair, smiling happily.

'OK, sir. Better get along. Got double French with that lice-ridden frog *whore* Ms Chevenement!'

'Ha ha ha, indeed. Sad cow! Just one more thing before you go . . .'

Pfister had baited the trap. It wasn't, in the end, that difficult at all. It wasn't in the end remotely difficult.

'What, sir?'

Affably and as if it didn't really matter and quite possibly as if Pfister himself would agree with whatever answer was forthcoming, he asked: 'Why did you pick on Ms McCall?'

Daryl, still grinning broadly, couldn't stop himself. 'Told you. She was on my fucking back all the time. And . . .'

'And . . .?'

'Can't fucking stand the stupid black nigger bitch . . .'

And then, knowing the rules of the game and suddenly realising that he had, very briefly but very, very, definitely transgressed them, he froze.

And for the first time there was the glimmer of real panic in those vacant eyes.

And Pfister felt his whole body relax and allowed himself just the ghost of a sweet smile. 'Ahhh, Daryl, Daryl, Daryl . . .' he said to the trembling school-boy. 'I think you'd better sit yourself back down. I believe we have some very serious business to discuss.'

And he took from his drawer another form – except this one was red, not blue.

The Lost Honour of Engin Hassan

Engin Hassan has been wrestling with a tricky little problem all morning. Is it all right, he wonders, to use the bus and taxi lane on his way to blow up the filthy Jew art gallery and attached brasserie, or will it cause more problems than it solves? Even now, as he sits in his car at the traffic lights, coated in a thin sheen of sweat, his hands drumming nervously on the steering wheel, he cannot make up his mind. On the one hand, he would be delivered to heaven more rapidly, without doubt. And he might even make good the designated time of arrival at the gallery as well – an important thing, because the crowds dwindle very quickly indeed after the lunchtime rush. On the other hand, he would be breaking the law and therefore runs the risk of being stopped by a policeman – something which would seriously threaten the success of the entire operation. What would Tariq do? Ah, but that's the trouble – Tariq isn't here. He's on his own now.

During his dry run yesterday he drove legally the whole way, but the traffic was, inexplicably, a lot lighter. You just can't tell with traffic in this city, he thinks. It is as unpredictable as the English weather.

The car radio is tuned to a popular music station. Engin's concentration starts to drift as he finds himself singing along with Ronan Keating cheerfully, if a little out of key, 'life is a roller coaster, you gotta ride it.' It is a philosophy with which Engin entirely concurs.

The lights change and the cars in front of him nudge forward at about three miles per hour. Engin sees the problem: a supermarket delivery lorry has jack-knifed across the outside lanes in its attempt to make a tight left turn. He grunts and swings his car out to the left – into the forbidden channel – and puts his foot to the floor. Sod it, he says to himself. May as well be killed for a sheep as a lamb. Allah will surely not be censorious about such a minor traffic violation, not when it's in such an exemplary cause. Traffic laws are man made, are they not? Stop me if I'm wrong, he says to himself, but there is nothing in the Koran about bus and taxi lanes.

He speeds along the wide central boulevard and at last . . . there it is! He can see up ahead, beyond the parade of expensive shops, the gallery restaurant; must be less than a quarter of a mile away. He has obviously made a wise decision. Not only will he hit his target on time, but the traffic is moving so slowly in the centre lanes that he doubts he would have been afforded sufficient build-up of speed to break through the front door and carry on through the reception area to the opening of the main gallery at the rear. They were very insistent about that. The restaurant is on the first floor in a kind of atrium, set well back from the front of the building. No use just blowing the reception area to hell. Pig-faced criminal Jewish dog casualties would, in that case, be regrettably minimal.

Three hundred yards to go. Driving with one hand, he opens the glove box and removes the small matt-black metal remote controlled detonator and places it on his lap. It's a brand new Czech model, this detonator, with a range of 5.5 miles. But it won't be tested to the full on this occasion. His plastic explosives are packed securely in the boot, about 5.5 feet away. No chance of a mishap there!

What glory awaits him, just the other side of that blond timber and distressed metal carnival of obscene US–Zionist decadence! Seventy-two virgins, for a start. Imagine, to bury one's face for ever in the silky, unpolluted minge of a celestial virgin! And then he frowns. He hopes that they are virgins as a result of their own modesty, Godliness and self-restraint. Rather than because nobody previously has wanted to relieve them of their virginity. It seems only right and fair that, after all this effort, they should be pretty fit virgins. Seventy-two virgins who look a bit like Cassie, the nice petite Indian girl who works in his local dry cleaner's, would do very nicely, thank you, Allah.

But then he's worried about this mystical number seventy-two, as well. It may seem a lot down here on earth – but to last an eternity? What happens when he's used them all up? Or maybe it's simply that every time he wishes to express his essential manhood Allah makes provision of a whole new bunch of seventy-two virgins from which to choose. That would be much more conducive and would save him the bother of rationing the virgins across the unending millennia. And if this *is* the case can he therefore have two at once? Or three? Or all seventy-two?

Trouble is, none of this was really explained in detail. And he didn't like to ask: it seemed impertinent and, in any case, not the sort of thing he could talk about to Tariq, who can be awfully impatient and severe.

Ah well, he'll find out soon enough.

One hundred yards. He notices his heart is beating a little faster and despite the air conditioning the sweat is welling up through his shirt. He will have to pull out a little into the right hand lane in order to improve the angle of impact with the front doors of the gallery; but that's OK, there's a small gap between two dawdling cars just ahead . . .

At fifty yards he recites a sura from the Koran, takes a big gulp of air and, swinging sharply to the right, puts his foot down.

Vvvvrrroooommmmmmmm!

Is it permissible to put one's middle finger up a celestial virgin's bottom? He is not sure about this at all. It's something he would quite like to do but suspects that, up there, with Allah watching, it's not on, really.

But it is not a subject over which, sadly, there is very much time for intense contemplation.

He honks his horn to scatter the pedestrians and swings back to the left, mounts the pavement almost imperceptibly and smashes through the front doors of the gallery almost head on. Perfect positioning! The blond wood supports are ripped in two, glass scything through the air in cruel, lethal shards. He is vaguely aware of all these people screaming but he drives on, crushing the steel edge of the front desk and sending the receptionist hurtling over the car behind him, her infidel whore face stretched open in this rictus of incredulity and terror. He slams on the brakes and skids the final forty yards and then, with a soft crunch, he hits the exposed concrete wall which marks the entrance to the gallery proper. Above him he sees mayhem as diners on the brasserie balcony dive under their seats for cover – but too bad guys, sorry, he thinks, far too late for that. The car is now stationary exactly where he was instructed to put it.

He thanks God with brief profusion and screws his eyes shut and presses the red button in the centre of the detonator.

He wonders what the point of shutting his eyes was.

And then, he wonders how come he's able to wonder what the point of shutting his eyes was.

'Ten minutes, Mr Hassan!'

The runner's voice barking outside his door shakes Engin from a deeply troubled reverie. Oh dear me, he frets, quickly cramming a Chinese spring roll into his mouth from the tray of canapés delivered to his dressing room only, he thinks, a few moments ago. Did he fall asleep? Ten minutes to go and he hasn't even been through make-up yet! Nor has he started on the prawn won-tons or the large bowl of exotic fruit or the selection of soft drinks kindly provided for his delectation. These days, he muses, there is never enough time. Hurry, hurry, hurry, every hour that God sends.

But it was nice of Parky to drop by his room and say hello, earlier on. Not every television host takes the trouble to meet his or her guests before the programme starts. And Parky is by far the most famous host of them all.

'Hello there, Engin,' Parky had said, poking his head around the door. 'You being nicely catered for, then?'

Yes, yes, yes, Mr Parkinson, everything's lovely, Engin found himself burbling. And then, for want of a conversation, he had asked for the names of the other guests on the programme – even though he knew already who they were, not least because their dressing rooms were next to his.

Parky filled him in, with a few wry Yorkshire wisecracks thrown around here and there. What a nice man! The best chatshow hosts have the ability to make you feel totally at ease even before you're blinking in the television lights, doing your stuff. That ignorant pig Frank Skinner didn't even shake his hand or say goodbye afterwards – and the interview was a waste of time, too, being just a platform for a sorry ensemble of Skinner's witless, childish jokes. Why have him on at all? Why not just put a cardboard cut-out of Engin Hassan in the chair and let Frank make all those jokes just the same?

Engin sighs and hoists himself to his feet, grabs a can of Sprite from the freezer bowl, checks that he's got everything, straightens his Boss jacket around himself and heads out of the door, to the make-up room.

Up and down the corridor, producers and researchers and runners are immersed in that pointlessly feverish panic peculiar to the medium of television. The show has now begun and Parky is out on the set, interviewing his first guest – a lady with Down's Syndrome who has nonetheless been selected to stand as the Conservative Candidate for Mole Valley (wherever *that* is). Engin said hello to her earlier on as she stood in the foyer – the poor woman all in a sweet dither, not quite knowing why she was here.

The make-up lady is very attractive indeed, thinks Engin as he slurps his sugary soft drink. She is another version of how he used to want Allah's virgins to be, back when he was always trying to blow people up. She has a cascade of bronze hair falling way down her back and a wickedly malleable mouth. She sits him in the chair and drapes a cloth around his neck.

'This your first time on telly then, Mr Hassan?'

Engin laughs indulgently. 'No, no – far from it. These days I seem to be on television all the time, although I'm not sure why, ha ha ha. Can't think why people would want to hear what I've got to say. But I've become a bit of a trouper!'

The woman dabs a swathe of dark brown foundation across Engin's face. 'That's nice,' she trills. 'What were you on last, then?'

Engin has to think for a moment. These shows come to seem, after a time, to merge with one another. 'Ummm . . . it was *Celebrity the Weakest Link*, or *This is Your Life* – I can't really remember.'

'Oooh, I think I saw *The Weakest Link*. Was it fun?'

He had not enjoyed *The Weakest Link* at all, to be honest – what with that hideous rude woman asking him questions which he had not the faintest glimmer of a chance of answering. He was the first contestant that week to be binned. How the hell was he to know who Hamlet's brother was? If only they'd asked him something from the glorious annals of Islamic literature! They are very culturally biased, these quiz programmes. But *This is Your Life* was lovely and it brought a lump to his throat when they presented to him an ancient but still sprightly Mrs Badareyev, a neighbour for whom he had run countless errands as a little boy living by the dusty shores of Lake Van. He had gasped in genuine disbelief and held his head in his hands when she was announced on stage. And then the old cow had gone and spoilt it by saying through an interpreter, in her peasant's, phlegm-throttled croak: 'Even back then, we all used to say to each other – Engin, well, he is a very, very stupid child. We all chuckled amongst ourselves whenever he appeared and said: nothing good will come of that fat boy, believe me, nothing good at all!'

How the audience laughed! And how annoying then, after such an unfair and spiteful calumny, to have to embrace the treacherous crone in front of all those millions of people. Ignorant, ungrateful hag!

Still, the television people had done their research extremely well, to the extent that Engin was worried at one point that they might even have Tariq on a video link from a cave somewhere in the Hindu Kush. Every teasing introduction made by the host had him sweating nervously and glancing at the video screen. There seems to be nothing they cannot do, these clever TV people, when they put a mind to it. Everybody, it seems, bends to their will.

'Oh yes,' he says to the make up girl, '*The Weakest Link* was wonderful fun! That Anne Robinson, dear me! What a stern lady!'

And then he asks ingratiatingly, as she's splashing powder over his forehead: 'So, did you do the make-up for a certain Mr Robbie Williams?'

Robbie's the main guest on the show, the real star attraction. There were about 2,000 teenage girls screaming and wetting their pants outside the studios. He saw them as he came in, and watched their faces wreathe in disappointment as it was him, Engin, who was discharged from the black Mercedes, rather than their idol. Robbie was polite enough to say hello to Engin just after he arrived. In fact, he said, affably, with that famous simian grin: 'Hello, mate, how's it going?' And then he disappeared into his rather larger dressing room.

'Yes! He's *so* sweet,' says the make-up infidel whore. 'Not the least bit up himself, know'mean? Chattin' away he was, like I was his best friend!'

'A very talented entertainer, to be sure,' says Engin and starts singing to her: 'she's tha onnnne'.

'Did you know,' he says to the make up girl, 'that "She's the One" was written about Princess Diana?'

'Oooh, no, I never. I thought it was about Robbie's ex-girlfriend. You know, the pretty one who had the abortion.'

'No, no. It was written by a man called Karl Wallinger and . . .'

But he does not have time to explain because the runner has come back, panting and frantic, and he's due on set *now*.

Having been fitted with his little microphone, he waits patiently behind thick blue curtains backstage, the floor manager standing by ready to give him the signal to march on. But Parky is having trouble finishing off with the Down's Syndrome lady – she doesn't seem to want to leave and all the producers are casting anxious glances at each other. Eventually, a stage hand manually drags her from her seat – the cameras pan discreetly away at this point – and then Parky relaxes, says a smooth thank you, and begins his preamble for Engin.

How many programmes has he done now, Engin? Good lord, it must be nearly one hundred. It wasn't quite what he thought would happen to him, when he was pushed out of the gates of Belmarsh Prison by a warder who said to him, not unpleasantly, go on, you useless fucking raghead, fuck off home. He'd thought then, mulling over his various options, that if the media people wanted him for anything it would be as a pundit on terrorism, a ready-made expert who could say who was trying to blow up who and why they were doing it and what their state of mind was during the operation. But no, they didn't want that at all. And, when you think about it, why on earth would they? He had proved that, effectively, he was less qualified than almost anybody in the world to talk about successful acts of terrorism.

Instead, the quality they sought in him was summed up most pithily and accurately by that very prison warder: fucking useless. Absolutely fucking useless. And being fucking useless was, unquestionably – although, to Engin, puzzlingly – a valuable commodity for the television people. 'People just lap up failure,' his grinning agent, Mr Sternberg, told him, 'they love it. Go and fail for them and keep a cheerful face and trust me, you'll be adored by one and all.' Oh, if only his two visitors this morning could have been made to understand! Where's the harm? Where's the harm?

Still, no time for that now; here we are. Prepare yourself Engin! Get ready for that special television swagger and try not to trip over your feet like you did on Jonathan Ross! Deep, deep breath now . . . it's time!

Has he got everything? He is, for a second, sweatingly unsure . . . but it's too late, anyway. Because Parky has finished his introduction with the words: 'Ladies and gentlemen . . . a warm welcome please for Engin Hassan . . . the useless terrorist!'

And, as instructed by the floor manager, the audience goes wild and the famous music starts and, having fixed on his fat face a suitably humble, self-deprecatory smile, Engin strides out in front of the cameras.

★

Slowly, then, Engin opens his eyes. There are no virgins anywhere to be seen. He's still in the car, surrounded by debris and screaming people, a big white wall up in front of him. Doesn't look like heaven. Looks a lot more like he's still in the filthy Jew art gallery.

He gazes down at his lap: there's the black metal detonator. He can't quite believe it, after all that Tariq and the firearms expert – that sinister Sudanese man, what was it, Ibrahim? – assured him, but it seems not to have worked. He screws his eyes shut and presses the red button once more, this time with a little less religious fervour.

Nothing! Nothing at all!

Has he done something wrong? Is it out of batteries?

He pushes the button again, this time with his eyes open.

And then again, and again, and again.

Still nothing! Surely, God, he cannot have fucked it up again?

Engin becomes aware of a gentle tapping at his side window. He looks around and – oh dear me no, this is all he needs – it's one of those special Jews, with the big black Victorian hats and the long curly sideburns.

'Unnngh,' Engin grimaces, and hammers away again at the little red button.

'Are you all right, sir?' asks the Jewish man.

Engin flings the detonator to the floor in disgust. He winds down the window.

'I think my detonator's broken,' he says – lost, really, for any other feasible explanation in his unfortunate predicament.

'Oh, I see. You *are* a suicide bomber, after all,' says the Jewish man. The screaming has stopped and a number of other people are beginning to converge upon the car. 'Can I have a look?'

'What?' says Engin.

'Can I have a look at the detonator? I might be able to fix it. I've had a bit of experience in electronic micro-circuitry.'

'Ummm . . . sure.' Engin hands over the little black box. The Jewish man takes a tiny screwdriver out of a pocket in his black frock coat and pokes around with it for a minute or so. Then he hands the detonator back.

'Try it now,' he says.

Engin pushes the little red button once more, noticing as he does so that the Jewish man has put his hands over his ears. What good would that do you, you ass, Engin thinks to himself.

But still there's nothing.

A youngish white woman has joined the Jew by the window, brushing herself down from the dust and the tiny bits of smashed glass from the front of the gallery. A small piece of woodchip is lodged in her long hair and she has a graze on her forehead. The Jew explains to her, very succinctly, what the problem is.

'Oh dear me,' she says. 'What a mess.'

'Yes,' says Engin, sadly. 'Some people are going to be very cross with me.'

'I daresay. Are you sure it's not a problem with the explosives themselves?' she asks.

Engin thinks for a moment and then shakes his head. 'I wouldn't have thought so for a moment, no. It's all good quality stuff.'

The woman nods. 'Are you sure you packed them, though?'

A horrible sliver of doubt suddenly becomes embedded in Engin's troubled mind. 'Umm . . . yes, yes, I think so,' he says.

'Where are they, then?'

'In the boot, wrapped up in greaseproof paper.'

'Shall we have a look?' says the young woman.

'Seems like a sensible thing to do, at this stage,' admonishes the Jew.

'Yeah,' says Engin, unbuckling his safety belt and opening the car door. 'May as well, I suppose.'

Together they walk around to the back of the car. A couple of other bystanders join them as Engin fiddles about trying to find the right key for the boot, always a problem. He should mark it with a piece of Sellotape or something, he thinks. And then he's thinking to himself please, please, please don't let me have forgotten to pack the damned Semtex.

But no, he definitely remembers packing it! He had to wedge it safely in place, up against the spare wheel, it was quite a delicate operation.

Engin triumphantly brandishes the requisite key to his growing audience. 'Aha! Found it at last!' he says and unlocks the boot.

And sure enough, next to the spare wheel, there's a rectangular package covered in grey greaseproof paper. 'There!' Engin exclaims. 'I *knew* I'd packed it.'

The young woman looks doubtful, though.

'Doesn't look big enough for a bomb, to me,' she confesses.

'Well I can assure you, young la . . .' Engin stops suddenly because the Jewish man is leaning over the opened boot and intently sniffing its contents. 'Excuse me, sir? Can I help you?' Engin addresses him, slightly affronted by this somewhat rude behaviour.

'I'm sorry, but it doesn't smell like explosives to me . . .'

'Oh, really. What does it smell of, then?'

The Jew raises his nose to the air. 'Smells of fish,' he says, 'possibly mackerel. Or maybe even gurnard. Hard to tell.'

Engin gulps and closes his eyes in torment. Please no, he thinks. Please not this.

'I think you should have a look inside,' says the rather pushy young woman, exchanging knowing glances with the Jew.

Engin sighs and takes out a small pocket knife with which he begins to hack away at the string binding the parcel together. He unwraps the greaseproof paper and then pulls apart the plastic carrier bag inside. He cannot adequately express his dismay. His audience exclaims, as one: 'Oho!'

'There's your problem!'

'Not going to make much of a bang with that, are you?'

'Could leave it on the radiator for a few days and stink us all to death, ha, ha, ha.'

But Engin has collapsed to his knees, holding his head in his hands, rocking backwards and forwards.

'What have I done, what have I done, what have I done?' he wails.

'You've attempted to vaporise us all with a pound of fish, sir. That's what you've done.'

And then everybody goes quiet because Engin is still on his knees, rocking and sobbing, rocking and sobbing. The crowd shuffles its feet embarrassedly.

'How did that happen, then?' asks the young woman, rather accusatorily.

Engin remembers and sobs disconsolately. 'It was

first thing this morning,' he explains, his voice wet with tears. 'I promised Mrs Aziz that I would collect some halibut for her from the fishmonger's. I met her at an Islamic Jihad Cultural Night, a few months back. She lives about four blocks down and can't get out as much as she used to. I think it's her sciatica. She's nearly eighty now, you know, but she likes a nice bit of fish. I said I'd get the halibut and obviously, obviously,' he laments, 'it was a stupid thing to have offered to do because I was so preoccupied with all this suicide-bomb business.'

'Um' and 'Oh dear,' everybody says.

'Well,' remarks the Jew. 'If that's Mrs Aziz's halibut, where are your explosives?'

There's another thoughtful and rather painful silence. 'I'm afraid,' says Engin very quietly indeed, 'that I must have left them outside Mrs Aziz's front door.'

'Oh,' says the young woman.

'Tttssssshhhhh. Bad, bad news,' says the Jew.

'Yes,' Engin agrees. 'Dreadful, awful, news. Poor, poor, Mrs Aziz. She deserved better.'

'I suppose she's rather saved our bacon, though, hasn't she?' says one rather thoughtless chap at the back of the throng around the car.

Nobody replies. Everybody treats this observation with the contempt it deserves.

Then the pushy young woman cups a hand to her ear and says: 'Uh-oh. More trouble. Sounds like the police are on their way.'

And sure enough, there comes the noise of sirens from the middle distance, the sound of a swarm of deranged and angry infidel bees. What to do?

Engin staggers to his feet and wipes his eyes with the back of his hand. 'Oh dear me yes, the police. I'd forgotten about them, too,' he says. 'I'd better make haste, if you don't mind . . .'

And without further ado he pelts out past the wrecked front desk, leaps over the dead receptionist, dodges through the debris surrounding the shattered front door and tears into the street, running like a fat and not very agile mountain hare.

'Hey! Hey!' shouts the Jew. 'Come back! What about your fish?'

Wubble wubble wubble wubble wubble, goes Engin as he lies in his tepid, stagnant bath in the Kensington Hilton Hotel in west London. Relaxed, but bored, he is reduced to placing his mouth level with the top of the scummy, sudsy water and blowing repeatedly. Wubble wubble, he goes again. What fun and what luxury, really. Certainly more luxury than he has known before. This hotel will do anything for you; it's all ready, waiting, at the flick of a switch or the barked command down a telephone. There were even whores hanging around the lobby. Proper whore-whores, rather than simply your run of the mill normal infidel western women whores. He could have had them, if he'd wanted, too. Apparently, there's no trouble sticking your middle finger up *their* bottoms.

Aaaah, how nice it is, he thinks, waving the water around with a pudgy arm, to have people doing things for you. It was not always like this for Engin. And nor was Belmarsh Prison the worst of his previous experiences, either. That, he thinks grimly, would have to be Chechnya. Another horribly botched job, too. He quickly banishes from his mind the awful time he spent in Grozny. Think of the nice things in life, instead, Engin, he silently admonishes himself.

Rap rap! There's a sharp knock at the door to his suite.

'Room service, Mr Hassan!'

Room service! Imagine!

Engin drags himself from his murky swamp. He shakes himself down and wraps a huge bath towel around his burgeoning gut and opens the door to the corridor. Unfortunately, immediately he does so he is felled by a thick, heavy blow to the front of his head. His legs give way beneath him and four strong arms grab hold of his shoulders and his neck and his feet. And then he feels himself being swung backwards and forwards, backwards and forwards and flying though the air as if propelled by one of those SAM ground-to-air missile launchers. He lands, with a dull, muffled explosion, face down on his bed.

'Stay there, face down. Don't move,' says a thin, nasty-sounding voice with a Pakistani accent.

'Gnnng,' Engin groans.

Another voice comes from behind him. It is a voice he would know from anywhere. He is not very happy to hear it now, to tell the truth.

'Did you call room service, Engin?' asks the voice.

'Unnng,' he groans. 'No.'

'Then why would you expect them to come?'

Engin ponders this for a moment. 'Um, I thought they might have decided to bring me something of their own volition,' is what he comes up with.

'Oh, Engin, Engin,' sighs the voice. 'You are still utterly fucking useless, aren't you?'

'Yes,' he replies, his voice muffled by the pillow, 'I suppose so, Tariq.'

'Engin, you can sit up now.'

Engin's head throbs with a raw, pulsing violence.

With great difficulty, he hoists himself up and around into an uncomfortable half-sitting, half-recumbent position, his bath towel gaping open, to face his two assailants.

Ahh, Tariq. So long it's been! His former boss's face is a little more lined and the hair a little thinner, but he is no less handsome, or imposing, or worrying, than in the old days. But compared to the man sitting next to him – glowering beneath a turban, his extravagant grey beard stretching well beyond his waist and dressed in the suffocating grey robes of the Peshwari tradition, little black eyes like tiny nuggets of cheap, imported Polish anthracite betraying not a glimmer of humour.

'Hello again, Engin,' says Tariq, affably enough. 'Please let me introduce my friend and colleague, Dr Abu Afshin al Anwar Mohammed, Professor of Applied Literal Koranic Absurdities at the Central Polytechnic of Islamabad – and, of course, a brother in our glorious and eternal struggle.'

'Um,' says Engin. 'Enchanté.'

Dr Abu Afshin al Anwar Mohammed does not return the greeting. He sits utterly still on his chair with his thin lips closed tight in a gesture of distaste.

Engin claps his hands together and smiles at them both.

'Well,' he says, 'would anyone like a drink?'

I ought to point out, at this stage, that this is not a story which seeks to draw parallels between appearing on stupid television programmes and maiming innocent people in a suicide bomb. It is just a story about an idiot, a story about one man. It may be true that murdering people with high explosives and performing adequately on, say, the *Johnny Vaughan Show* require similarly low levels of intellectual ability. There may be a requirement for a sort of well-practised glibness in each act, too. But this is pretty thin gruel from which to form a comparison, if we're honest. I suppose we could say that stumpy fat Engin has a certain penchant for occupations which afford immediate gratification and some public adoration. And there is something, perhaps, in the idea that nothing, in our society, can resist being appropriated for the purposes of entertainment.

But even here, we are stretching it a bit.

The chairman of the British Mosque Collective, Dr Zebedee Hassan (no relation), alleges that Engin has now twice betrayed his religion – firstly by the bombings, secondly by his imbecilic media career. Fair point, Zeb. But you might equally suggest that Allah saw Engin coming and delighted with the raw material at His disposal has used him as an example and a warning to others who might be similarly inclined. Just a thought.

Nor, incidentally, are you about to get an explanation of what drove Engin to try to murder people, apart from the catch-all reason, intense and consuming stupidity and an accommodating credo. It is true that Engin had an unstable and peripatetic child-hood, following his father from hotel to hotel – where he worked as a waiter – and from country to country. Lake Van, Ankara, Bodrum, Riyadh, Abu Dhabi, Yogyakarta – the Hassan family travelled many, many thousands of miles. Mr Hassan Snr ended his career in service in 1989 by taking an appointment at – and yes, perhaps there is some genetic Hassan trait on display here – the Hotel Intercontinental, Beiruit. But in fact nobody tried to blow him up.

No, now is not the time to psychoanalyse Mr Engin Hassan. I'm pretty sure it's not worth the effort.

And it's as well I warned you off the idea of some moral equivalence between killing and maiming people and appearing on TV programmes. There is no moral equivalence, of course. The world would be a much happier place if all the suicide bombers could be persuaded to give up their explosives and head, instead, for the make-up rooms. After all, we would be under no obligation to watch the bastards.

Anyway, according to his expensive team of lawyers, solicitors and barristers, there were only two possible defences available to Engin. The first was to the effect that Engin was so totally inept as to be virtually educationally subnormal, a retard, and an imbecile – and then to throw himself upon the mercy of the court. The second was to imply that Engin had, in fact, a visceral loathing of violence and, with astonishing chutzpah and intelligence, quite consciously sabotaged his own efforts at terrorism, time after time, thus saving the lives of a great many innocent people. Weighing up these two theses, Engin's lawyer, Mr Goldberg, decided upon the former approach as being the more credible – not least because Engin would at some point be forced to take the witness stand – something which would surely serve to support theory one and rebut theory two.

And, as a strategy, you have to say it worked, up to a point. Engin pleaded not guilty on grounds of diminished responsibility and was, it's true, nonetheless convicted by a jury of his (English, Christian, Infidel) peers. But his sentence was surprisingly light.

Summing up, the judge, Mr Justice Coriolanus Moorcock, spoke thus:

'It has been made abundantly clear to this court that you, Engin Hassan, are a witless idiot, a man capable – indeed, on a regular basis – of actions of the most unspeakable, staggering stupidity. Of the eleven attempts you have made, wilfully, to cause murder and mayhem in the spurious service of Allah, both here and abroad, the final death toll stands at one innocent civilian – an art gallery receptionist, Ms Tabitha Furniss – and (as a result of even by your standards, a particularly grotesque error of judgement,) forty-two members of your own so-called revolutionary Islamic cell. Had you been employed by, say, the CIA or our own, British, intelligence agencies, it is doubtful that you could have wreaked more havoc within the legions of those murderous, fundamentalist Mohammadons to whom you have mistakenly and tragically entrusted your loyalty and devotion. You are without question a singularly useless terrorist, devoid of even the most primitive vestiges of cunning, foresight or, it has to be said, good luck.

'This is not to deny for one moment your intent – which was undoubtedly, unequivocally wicked. But it does raise important questions about your ability to grasp even those most fundamental moral principles which underlie the apparently simple question of what is right and what is wrong. Ignorance is not, of course, a defence against conviction. But it *is* perhaps a mitigating circumstance.

'Engin Hassan: you will go to prison at Her Majesty's Pleasure for a total of four years on the count of the manslaughter of Ms Furniss and also trying to kill all those Jews. On the charge of violating London traffic regulations you will pay a fine of seventy pounds, or serve an extra twelve days in prison.

'It is to be hoped, Mr Hassan, that you will take this time to reflect upon your misdemeanours and surely conclude that you are startlingly ill-equipped for the occupation of international Islamic terrorist, regardless or not of whether you continue to support, in your heart, the repellent cause which, so far, you have served with such ineptitude.'

'Thank you, your Honour,' is all that Engin had to say. At which point they took him to Belmarsh.

Engin has this thing he does, when appearing on TV. He runs up to the front of the set and, facing the audience, unbuttons his jacket, pulls it wide open and shouts: 'BOOM!' And then, as the audience howls, he turns to the camera, winks and says quietly: 'Only kidding, folks.'

It's served him well, this little act. It was Mr Sternberg who suggested it and, you've got to say, it was a good call because it never fails to get a great big laugh. So, of course, he does it again when Parky introduces him and the audience fall about as usual and Parky is forced to grin along and say once more: 'Ladies and gentleman, *Mister* Engin Hassan.' Then Parky stands up and shakes his hand and motions for Engin to sit down, which he does with another of those self-deprecatory smiles, adjusting his suit as he wriggles into the leather chair, settling himself down comfortably.

'So,' begins Parky, with his clipboard on his knee, 'having attempted to blow us all to kingdom come –'

'Nothing personal, Michael!'

'– I'm glad to hear it. But having done all that – how are you enjoying your new life in the bosom of the beast, so to speak?'

Engin laughs. 'Ah, well, it is a very accommodating bosom, Michael . . .'

(Audience titters.)

'But seriously . . . I mean, Engin . . . these people who have just applauded you to your seat are people whom you would have cheerfully murdered three years ago. Do you still wish to murder them?' asks Parky.

Engin adopts a humble and repentant expression. 'Seriously . . . well, as you know, I am still a devout Moslem. And that requires of me a certain, um, philosophy and commitment. But since I've been out of prison I have to say that I've found a certain friendship and camaraderie with the British. A kinship, even. People have been extraordinarily kind, you know. And I have to say, I'm very grateful to each and every one of them.'

(Audience quietly applauds this generous benediction of itself.)

Parky smiles indulgently and says: 'So, no plans to kill us all for a bit, then?'

(Audience sniggers to itself.)

Engin suddenly feels a horrible, dead weight pressing in against his stomach, a tight band of condensed worry, and looks momentarily at a loss. But, mercifully, because he has become, as he averred earlier, a bit of a trouper, he quickly regains his composure. It is astonishing how rapidly one learns to become glib and fatuous.

'Ah well, who knows! If it is Allah's will . . .' he says, hamming it up, gazing at the heavens with widened eyes.

(Audience collectively chokes on lengthy fit of uproarious laughter.)

'Anyway, Engin,' says Parky, 'what I really want to

talk about is failure – because, let's face it, that's what you're famous for: failing. Failing, if I may say so, on a quite colossal scale, too. And yet, here you are, feted over, one could say . . . you've become almost a public hero!'

This is such familiar ground for Engin, a question he has asked himself every day. A question asked of him by his visitors too, for that matter. 'I think that it is something to do with common humanity, Michael,' he begins. 'Something shared by us all. We try so hard to succeed all the time, every day, and yet we are frail, terribly frail, and our minds and our bodies let us down. We fall short of the standards we set ourselves. We are weak! Failure is a constant in our lives for almost all of us and then, when we are confronted by someone like me who has failed hopelessly on every single occasion he has tried to achieve his goal, we feel, I think, reassured and we empathise . . .'

'You don't think we're all just laughing at you, then?' asks Parky, with a smile, 'because you're so utterly useless?'

Engin begins to feel the chair, and the ground beneath the chair, swaying, as if suspended by ropes from the branches of a tall tree. The tightness around his waist constricts still further. He cannot explain the sensation to his audience, or, indeed, to the nice Mr Parkinson. He smiles at the question, to buy himself time, and then he rather wonders why he is bothered about buying himself time.

They don't want a drink. And they don't seem very impressed by his cheerful offer of one, either, to tell you the truth.

Tariq instead leans back in the hotel chair and

appraises his subject. 'Engin,' he says, 'what do you think you're doing?'

Engin adopts a subdued and crestfallen expression. He is not always sure what he thinks he's doing, if the truth be told. 'How do you mean?' he asks Tariq, shifting uneasily on the bed.

'How do I mean, Engin? I mean playing the village idiot on these godless, vapid, mindless television programmes! Who exactly, by the way, is Graham Norton?'

Engin says: 'Oh, just another chat show host.' Sometimes it is better not to delve too deeply into the details. Tariq was never very big on sodomites and Engin rather doubts that Dr Abu Afshin al Anwar Mohammed is much more kindly disposed towards them, either.

Tariq nods sadly. 'Do you not see what you have become, Engin?' Tariq is leaning forward in his chair.

Engin has never seen him in such an imploring mode before. It is most disquieting. 'What's that, Tariq?'

'A house imbecile for the imperialist, infidel, western culture! You have committed fisq and are thus a major faasiq, outside of the fold of Islam. Remember the words, Engin, of Allah – peace be upon him: "And whoever does not judge by what Allah sent down, then they are faasiqun, rebellious sinners." Or perhaps you are a zaalim, which is just as bad.'

'A man's got to earn a living somehow,' Engin squirms. 'Especially after prison.'

'But not on *Changing Rooms*! What was that all about? Simpering around with that wide-mouthed, grinning, Scottish whore, Carol Smillie!' Tariq spits in disgust.

'She's very nice actually, Carol Smillie,' says Engin, a little weakly.

There is a sudden and rather disconcerting growl from the hitherto silent Dr Abu Afshin al Anwar Mohammed. 'Did you drink from the cup of sin which she carries between her legs?' he demands.

'What? No! No, no, no! I didn't,' he adds, a little ruefully.

'Engin,' reasons Tariq, 'can you not understand the damage you do to our cause – to Allah's cause, to the cause of the Palestinians and the Chechen brothers and the people in this very country fighting against all hope for what they believe in – by your brainless cavorting and conniving? Can you not see how every one of your stupid fucking television appearances diminishes all that we strive to achieve?'

Engin straightens himself on the bed. They're wrong, wrong! Tariq has been in the caves for far too long a time. 'No,' he says confidently, 'quite the reverse. Instead of seeing Islam as hostile, unaccommodating and, in a sense, alien and averse – they see fat, useless little me. And they recognise in me elements of themselves. I am, as you have kindly put it, Tariq, fucking useless. This much has become apparent to me in the last three years and it is apparent also that there's not much I can do about it. And therefore, when I appear before my public, what I have fought for is seen as eminently more attainable. And more attractive, too. It lets people know that even in our glorious and unbending faith there is room for those with fallibilities.'

This is quite a speech for Engin. He is almost exhausted by it. But does it make sense? He's not sure.

'What utter, self-serving shite,' says Dr Abu Afshin al Anwar Mohammed.

'Well, I don't know,' says Tariq, correcting his

colleague, 'it's a pleasant conceit. And it would be fine if they were laughing only at you, Engin. But they are not. Because those operations you carried out so spastically were not your operations, but operations demanded by Allah. And it was Allah working through your mortal body who drove your car to the art gallery, and sent off those parcel bombs and so on, and so forth. You see my point?'

'Yes,' adds Dr Abu Afshin al Anwar Mohammed, 'so when you make stupid jokes about it all on television, it is not just Engin Hassan at whom the Godless audience is sniggering. At the very same time, you are making Allah look like a bit of a cunt, too. And that's not on, frankly.'

This conversation, thinks Engin, is not going at all well.

'But the lucky thing is,' says Tariq, cheerfully helping himself to a Britvic from the mini-bar, 'Allah is munificent in his forgiveness! He understands! And, incredibly, he has forgiven you. He has forgiven you for the art gallery business and the mis-sent parcel bombs and he has even forgiven you for that hideous débâcle with the anthrax spores.' Tariq pauses for a moment.

'Why, by the way, did you store them in the jar clearly marked "Coffee-Mate" and then put the jar back in the kitchen cabinet?'

Engin, looking a bit sulky, lying on the bed, says: 'It was the only container to hand, I think, at the time . . .'

'Forty-two people, Engin!'

'Yes, I know. Dreadful business. I'm very, very sorry indeed. It was a mistake.'

Engin shudders. Those awful, dry, racking coughs.

The gruesome blood-flecked expectorant. It was this error of judgement which convinced his bosses – Tariq pre-eminent amongst them – that Engin was to be transferred to the suicide department as soon as humanly possible. Hence his immediate dispatching to London.

'A very bad mistake indeed, Engin. But Allah forgives you even for that.'

Allah seems in an unusually forgiving mood at present, thinks Engin. If he's so apt to forgive, just now, how come Tariq and Dr Abu Afshin al Anwar Mohammed are here in his room? They don't look very forgiving at all.

It is, in the end, something he'd rather not think about.

'We have been talking to your agent, Engin,' says Tariq quietly.

'That smug Jew, Sternberg – may Allah blind him and cause sores to erupt in his groin area,' Dr Abu Afshin al Anwar Mohammed elucidates helpfully.

'Tell me, Engin. Do you never tire of the banality of it all?' Tariq asks.

Sadly, it is more a case of the banality tiring of him, Engin thinks. The requests for television appearances have thinned somewhat, of late. But he says, with deep and abiding conviction: 'I'm banal, Tariq.'

'Yes,' agrees his old mentor, 'that's certainly true. You are indeed very, very banal. But Allah has time – and purpose – for even the most crushingly banal of us all. Do you think it is better to have their brief and contemptuous affection – or their eternal loathing, fear and respect?'

Engin doesn't reply. He doesn't know what to say. So he looks down at his feet and waggles his toes.

'Think about it for a bit,' says Tariq. 'Now, would you mind if I had another Britvic?'

'Quickly: let's have this done with . . .'

Engin is running as fast as his short, pudgy legs will carry him. Which isn't, as it happens, very fast at all. He is wheezing with the exertion of it all, dodging around irate shoppers and pedestrians, blundering across roads choked with traffic and which snarl abuse at him as he does so. Clumpity, clumpity, clump, he goes, stifled by the cruel imposition of earth's gravity.

He is on is way, of course, to the home of poor Mrs Aziz.

Oh dear! Is Allah capable of recognising a genuine mistake, made in good faith, he wonders? He does hope so.

But the road where Mrs Aziz lives – a row of rather magnificent, four-storey Regency houses interspersed with hideous, pre-war local authority apartments – is dressed in the paler shroud of normalcy. There are no policemen holding back the crowds, nor tongues of flame licking upwards at the grey sky, nor ambulances drawn up ready for the burned, the choking and the dead. Just the usual mundane dribble of local traffic and youths from the council blocks lounging against the wall of the Ishmaeli Community Centre.

Perhaps the stupid Czech detonator really didn't work! Or, maybe, the explosives are useless. He feels a rare and rather wonderful tingle of hope. These are straws worth clutching at!

He sees Mrs Aziz's block up ahead; and look – it's entirely intact! Or at least, it seems to be from here, he thinks. He runs up the grimy concrete stairs, panting, and turns left onto her landing.

There's the front door, still there! Thank God, thank God, Mrs Aziz!

He knocks frantically and hops from foot to foot in impatience. Come on, Mrs Aziz, come on! He resists, just about, the temptation to peer through the letter-box because – what's this – he can hear footsteps in hall! She hasn't had her legs blown off, then. Unless she's learned to use prosthetic limbs in a very short space of time indeed.

The door opens.

It is an entirely undamaged Mrs Aziz standing there – and she was clearly not expecting to be hugged, or, further, desirous of being so. Her crows' eyes tighten. 'Get off me,' she says, irritably disentangling herself, 'you fat imbecile.'

'I'm just glad you're alive, Mrs Aziz,' gasps Engin, unhanding her at last and peering past the little woman and down into the hallway of her flat.

'Of course I'm alive, you Turkish moron,' she spits.

'Well,' he blurts out, 'what did you do with the fish?'

'What fish?'

'The fish you asked me to bring you this morning, Mrs Aziz. The halibut,' he explains, as calmly as he can.

'Oh yes,' she says, brightening, 'the halibut. Sorry. I forgot, momentarily, that halibut was a kind of fish. I'm getting too old.'

'Yes, yes, but where is it?'

'Engin,' she says at last, 'I did not ask you to collect halibut or any other kind of fish for me. I can collect my own halibut, thank you. I didn't want any today, in any case.'

'But . . . but . . .' Engin splutters.

'No, Engin. And don't think for a minute that I'm paying you for it.'

Engin is quite beside himself with frustration. 'Well, where is it?'

'I gave it to someone to take back to the fish-monger's.'

'Who! Who!' Engin shrieks.

'That painted Hindu slut from the dry-cleaning shop. When she dropped off my burqua.'

'Nnnnoooo!!' howls Engin. 'Not Cassie!'

'I don't know her name. Nor do I want to. All I know is that she lacks modesty. That girl has, in my opinion, the depraved lips of a cocksucker.'

'Unnnngh,' says Engin and begins walking around in circles.

Mrs Aziz calls him back to her. She smiles at him and puts her hands firmly around his head and starts shaking it from side to side, as if she were sifting flour in a very heavy sieve.

'Now listen, fatboy,' she says. 'Stop worrying about fish and little Indian whores and go out and kill some Jews like you're meant to.'

In tears for the third time today, Engin breaks free and runs back down the passageway. The voice of Mrs Aziz, a sort of strangulated, crazed howl, pursues him with each step. 'Intifada! Intifada! Let the streets of every town and city run red with the blood of the filthy Jewish-dog usurpers and their Yankee paymasters. Kill them aaalllllllll!'

Mrs Aziz, you have to say, is a hardliner.

Oh, Engin is tired of running. It is not an act for which his body was constructed, if we're being honest. And he is, as you might well guess after this busy little day, emotionally as well as physically exhausted. He walks back down the road and regains the high street. In a sort of other-worldly way, because he does not entirely trust his senses – he thinks that he can smell smoke and hear sirens. But whatever it is, it's not coming from the dry cleaner's shop which is right there in front of him. He marches up to the counter prepared, now, for pretty much anything. But of course there is a symmetry and an inevitability to be respected in our story.

'Hello, Mr Shah.'

'Hello, Engin.'

'Do you know where Cassie might be?'

'Yes, she went out about half an hour ago to return some putrid fish to the fishmongers.'

'Oh, OK. Mr Shah . . . ?'

'Yes, Engin?'

'Can you smell smoke and hear sirens?'

Mr Shah leans forward over the counter and cocks his head to one side. 'Yes, I do believe I can, Engin.'

'Thank you, Mr Shah.'

'Goodbye, Engin.'

And he remains in this beaten, uncomprehending, catatonic state even when he bumps into Cassie Shah, a little way along the high street, scurrying back towards the dry cleaner's with all of her limbs intact.

'Where's the fish, Cassie?'

'I took it to the fishmonger's and . . .'

'Yes,' says Engin with unspeakable weariness.

'. . . and they said they wouldn't take it back. Wouldn't even look at it . . .'

'. . . So you . . .'

'So I left it . . .'

'Where?'

'Outside your front door. I know how much you like a nice piece of halibut.'

Aaaah, so that's where the smoke and the sirens were coming from. That's where the ambulances are pulled up ready for the maimed, the dying and the dead. The bomb went off at Engin's house! The religious of you might be wondering if there is a God, after all.

A little later, Engin stands at the edge of the police cordon, watching his apartment burn. What sort of terrorist blows up his own home, Engin? A shite terrorist, that's who. The big hoses spray plumes of silvery water up and down the walls, the smoke gets blacker and blacker. The small crowd of ghouls lucky enough to have chanced upon this small entertainment murmurs worriedly to itself and moves further back, away from the stench and the smoke and the heat. Engin stays where he is, though.

Charred fragments of Engin's things float up and away, borne on the hot thermals, rising and rising until they are specks of darkness which then become invisible. Engin gazes skywards. There's no epiphanous moment, however. Do not for a second presume that he feels regret at the act which he has committed; no, he feels regret only about *where* he has committed the act. That is, he fervently regrets blowing up his own home. He most certainly does not stand in awe-stricken contemplation and reconsider his descent into evil.

And then, mercifully, he passes out.

You would not believe the speed with which every terrorist group in the known universe issues statements denying, outright, any responsibility for this useless attack.

★

Something strange is happening to Parky's head. It is growing larger and somehow smoother, the lines and creases dissolving . . . Engin tries to look away and concentrate on the question. But he cannot remember what the question was. The audience, he can hear it, is growing restive and muttering to itself. You're a trouper, Engin, it is saying, and now you're letting us down, come on, say something!

But for Engin there is nothing but the swaying of the ground beneath his chair and, out of the corner of one eye, the sight of Parky's weirdly transmogrifying head, floating towards him like a madman's balloon.

Back in the dressing room earlier he thought he'd come to a decision; but in truth, Engin finds it very difficult to make decisions and even more difficult to stick to them. He threw the belt ('It's a special belt. You don't use it to keep up your expensive trousers, Engin,' said Tariq, 'you put it around your waist and underneath your shirt.') into the corner. And then he picked it up again. What to do! Hopelessly torn between the equally gratifying pleasures of making a group of people laugh and blowing them to smithereens.

'Your call, Engin,' said Tariq, back in the hotel before the nice limo arrived. 'You and Allah. Don't be a faasiq. Or a zaalim.'

But he does not think that Allah has helped him very much after all, in his quandary. A word of advice, he thinks, would have been very gratefully appreciated.

The floor beneath him tips a little further on its axis. He can feel Parky tapping his knee, asking him if he is all right.

No, he thinks. Not really, Parky, if I'm honest.

He looks up again, at the floating head. Except that

it is clearly not a head. It has no eyes, for a start, nor ears. But it does, he notices, have a strange, small, fragrant and delicate mouth. What is it, he wonders distractedly, this ethereal creature drifting across his line of vision?

Aaaaah. *That's* what it is. Now he realises. It should have been obvious all along. Thank you, Allah, thank you!

For the thing that is floating towards him, drawing him closer and closer, is the puckering, tawny, anus of a celestial virgin, the sphincter muscle contracting and expanding and all the time whispering, whispering to him: 'Engin! Engin! We are waiting, we are waiting. Just a little way over here, do you see? Come . . . come . . . come . . .'

Engin sighs, like he always sighs on occasions such as these. He feels a little sorrowful, to tell the truth; resolved but sorrowful. Oh, he thinks forlornly, I hope I'm doing the right thing.

Leaning back in his chair, he puts one hand in the pocket of his expensive black jacket and, for the very last time, screws shut his eyes.

(Religious guidance and inspiration for this story came from the work 'Allah's Governance on Earth: Ruling is Only for Allah', by Sheikh Abu Hamza al Masri, November 2001, available through Supporters of Shariah, Finsbury Park, London.)